ONCE
WE WERE
WITCHES

For magical Bryony

EGMONT
We bring stories to life

First published in Great Britain 2021 by Egmont Books

An imprint of HarperCollins*Publishers*
1 London Bridge Street, London SE1 9GF

egmontbooks.co.uk

HarperCollins*Publishers*
1st Floor, Watermarque Building,
Ringsend Road, Dublin 4, Ireland

Text copyright © 2021 Sarah Driver
Illustrations copyright © 2021 Fabi Santiago

The moral rights of the author and illustrator have been asserted

ISBN 978 1 4052 9554 3
Printed and bound in Great Britain by the CPI Group
1

A CIP catalogue record for this title is available
from the British Library

Stay safe online. Any website addresses listed in this book are
correct at the time of going to print. However, Egmont Books is
not responsible for content hosted by third parties. Please be
aware that online content can be subject to change and websites
can contain content that is unsuitable for children. We advise
that all children are supervised when using the internet.

MIX
Paper from
responsible sources
FSC™ C007454

This book is produced from independently certified FSC™ paper
to ensure responsible forest management.

For more information visit: www.harpercollins.co.uk/green

ONCE WE WERE WITCHES

SARAH DRIVER

Illustrated by Fabi Santiago

EGMONT

The Ring

The Old
Kingdom
of
SUSSEX

The Funeral
Parlour

Mouldheels School

London

Arundel

Knuckerhole
Village

PART ONE:

MOULDHEELS

Ingredients for a Spell

A black cat, who wears the moon

A lonely undertaker

Two sisters: different as day from night

A silver pocket watch

A portal, scabbing over

A telephone; its cry a portent of Death

Hot chocolate, swirled with nutmeg

An old book, passed down from witch to witch

A witch-hunt: the greatest of all time

A Wicked Girl to stop it dead.

1
Mistress Mouldheels' School for Wicked Girls

'All girls ooze sin.' Deputy Headmistress Wolsley's bonnet, high and round like a black moon, casts a shadow that trickles down her nose to pool in her lap. 'But Wicked Girls, unless corrected, wield it like a weapon.'

The taint of my Wickedness itches all over me. This is ceremony day, the most vital in our calendar. On this day, one Wicked Girl shall receive her soul. And my sister is not here. Panic turns into a hot sickness that threatens the back of my throat. I last saw her at lunch, before we went to afternoon duties. But she was missing from the register check before we filed into the assembly hall.

She'll be skinned alive. They'll have her guts for garters. How will Egg ever earn a soul of her own?

I sit on a bench in the hall with the rest of our dorm, dread coiled tight inside me. Mariam, Jameela and Isla all keep shooting me poisonous looks, as though it's my fault Egg's not here. Our whole dorm could be in trouble. Only Layla, Egg's best friend, offers me a small, reassuring smile.

Her warmth next to me is some comfort against the chill of the crowded hall.

But Isla leans forward, pretending to adjust her stocking. Fine strands of red hair have escaped her headscarf. 'Egg's for it now,' she whispers, with a sharp-toothed grin. 'And that means you are too, Spel.'

I stare at her.

'Shut up,' mutters Layla.

Mistress Wolsley's stony gaze flickers to the empty space on our bench, where Egg should be. Her lips are crinkled and the flesh of her cheeks struggles to cling to the bones. When her eyes graze mine and linger there, I shrink deeper inside my skin.

The Mistresses have always thought I'm trouble, just because trouble is Egg's speciality. So however much I work and however hard I pray, I'll never escape the Wrythe name. I was one when we came here. Egg was three. She's all the family I've ever known. What if she's done something really stupid this time? I feel sicker with every second that passes.

'Your parents were the worst sort of criminals, and our mission is to protect the Unwicked. As such, your sins must be cleansed.' Wolsley breathes into the hush, letting her familiar pre-ceremony lecture swell against the walls.

Watching from the wall, a clock ticks away the seconds, polished glass face unfazed by my problems. I feel the eyes of the girls behind me burning into my neck. Everyone here knows that Egg and I are the daughters of a murderer, so most of them have always hated us. High and mighty because their parents did awful things that weren't quite so awful as murder.

I fidget, biting the skin around my nail until blood bubbles up; lifting the edge of my coarse green headscarf to wipe the sweat that has dewed along where my hairline would be, if I weren't as bald as a fig. The Mistresses sit in high-backed wooden chairs on the raised platform at the front of the hall. But one chair is always empty – a grander one, with thick wooden arms and a velvet cushion. It belonged to Mistress Mouldheels herself.

Mistress Mouldheels is a figure of legend at this school, and the legends say her rule was comprised of a fiercer iron than the gates bearing her name. No one has ever seen her, and most of the girls think she must be dead by now.

But rumours drift along the cold corridors late at night, ragged as smoke. Rumours that she still stalks the hallways of this school, cursing the Wickedest of the Wicked Girls to a soulless eternity. One of the older girls swears she saw a shadow peel out of the walls to twist into her likeness. Egg says that girl is so hungry for attention that she fakes a different sighting every week. The girl fought Egg for saying it. Egg won.

'It is only hard work that might purge you of your Wickedness, and make you worthy to receive a soul of your own.'

But we will never be free, whispers a traitorous voice in my head, shocking heat into my skin. A wild little voice, which every day I do my best to iron flat.

'Three things will assist you in your work: discipline, obedience and atonement. Say it with me, girls.'

'*Discipline, obedience, atonement.*'

The words are like cold, hard stones sitting in my mouth, smoothed by years of use.

'*Discipline, obedience, atonement.*'

When I was younger, I didn't understand why it mattered, not having a soul. I couldn't feel the lacking in me. But now, at thirteen, I feel it every day, wriggling through my insides. I'll do anything and everything I can to cleanse it. I'll do whatever it takes to get my soul.

'*Discipline, obedience, atonement.*'

'Today we are gathered to bid farewell to Wicked Cecilia Norton.' Mistress Wolsley pauses for effect, hands folded neatly in her lap. 'Cecilia, step forward, please.'

I twist to watch as Cece steps down the aisle. Silent envy rises, filling the hall. Mine is sludgy: so thick it lodges in the throat and threatens to rot, like an infection of the lung.

She is dressed in a ceremonial gown of delicate white lace, which is long enough to trail gracefully behind her. Her face is draped with a veil. Her clogs have been exchanged for satin slippers, and on her head is perched a bonnet – a moon-shape identical to that of the Mistresses, but white as a pearl.

There are gasps, which go unscolded.

All eight of the Mistresses rise and flock to Cece. They propel her towards the basin near the front of the hall. Two of the Mistresses detach from the group and swoop to either side of the basin, lighting tall candles that show the rippling of the special water on the ceiling.

Mistress Wolsley and Mistress Baker stand just behind Cece, each placing a hand on her shoulders. 'Cecilia Norton,' one intones. 'You have proven yourself dutiful, obedient and modest. Your determination to scrub your sins clean has earned you a chance to become soulful, this day. So it is.'

'Let it be known,' responds Cece, in a small, tremulous voice that's nothing like the voice I've heard her use every other day of my life here.

'Cleanse,' calls one of the candle-lighting Mistresses.

The Mistresses fold Cece forward, until her head is swallowed by the dark and mysterious waters.

There are two types of girl in this school. Type one girls get really obsessed and determined to reach their soul-ceremony with as little trouble as possible. They are by far the commonest. But type twos self-destruct. Trends do the rounds, dares to do the stupidest things. Those girls always get caught. But we don't always find out what happened to them.

I'm a type one, and Egg is a type two. My sister is a daredevil who lashes out, but I hold myself still, hoping I won't be noticed. If I ever had a smidge of the wildness she has, I must've learned to keep it in.

Cece's head emerges from the basin, smooth as a seal. She gasps, and splutters a little. Ceremonial water drips off the ends of her hair. The Mistresses begin to move in a circle around her. 'Soul, instil this child with your purity,' they chant. 'Soul, find your home here, fill this child with your light. In exchange a sacred thread shall be woven, in the fabric of life. It is spoken.'

'It is known!' we Wicked ones murmur together, feverishly.

A Mistress takes Cece's arm and leads her towards the red curtain at the very back of the hall. Cece moves the curtain just an inch, before ducking through. Every girl in the room twitches to try to see something – anything – beyond that curtain. But what lies beyond is dark, murky and closed off to us.

My own ceremony can't come soon enough. I grind my teeth halfway into my jaw. I can't wait to get dunked into that sacred broth. Then I'll no longer be a Wicked Girl.

Beyond the window, storm clouds squat overhead, like tattered grey swans in a scowling sky. Rain lashes Mouldheels' School, while the wind worries the towers. A fresh wave of fear for my sister rips through my body. And as suddenly as I feel the fear, the double doors bang open behind us.

We all turn to stare.

'Wicked Meghan Wrythe has been found, Mistress!' cries a voice.

A shape glides out of the shadows: a mass of heavy robes and even heavier disapproval. Mistress Turner. My hand is covering my mouth before I know I've moved it. Turner is a short, thin, pale Mistress, whose steely blue eyes are the only things that tell the full truth about her cold sternness. Why did *she* have to be the one to find Egg?

A man follows her – a strange enough sight in itself – and he's dragging my sister by the arm.

'Where was she?' enquires Mistress Wolsley, almost sweetly.

Mistress Turner hesitates. 'Hiding in the butcher's cart, madam.'

'The *what?*'

'The meat is delivered on Wednesdays.'

Mistress Wolsley stares hard at my sister. 'Clever girl.'

Egg is streaked in blood. As she passes our bench, she leaves behind a cloying, coppery stink. She spins and spits and struggles in the butcher's grip like a cat with a caught claw.

Layla tenses and reaches instinctively for my hand. I meet her eyes for a second, searching for a sign that she knew something I didn't. But I find the same betrayal on her face that must be showing in mine. *Egg was trying to escape. What about us?*

My sister's teeth are bared and there's a pink triangle stuck between them. It's fleshy, and covered in bristly hairs. It takes me a second to realise she must have fought hard enough to bite the ear off a pig.

For one wild moment, laughter gurgles in my chest. My sister has a pig's ear in her mouth. My sister tried to escape. My sister is drawing all the attention in the world to her, and handing it down to me.

No! I want to scream at her. *Stop. They will punish us.* But my voice stays trapped down deep, where I locked it long ago.

Egg spits the pig's ear on to the floor. A girl shrieks.

'Silence!' roars Mistress Wolsley.

'For god's sake,' pants the butcher, shining with sweat. 'Will someone tell me what to do with it?' His eyes slip around the room, touching us all with his disgust. The Unwicked know what we are. By *it*, he means my sister.

Egg's breathing hard, with her hair stuck on end and her eyes shining like black jewels. 'Get off me!'

There's a cracking sound. A bolt of confusion ripples through the air. Then there's a shattering, as one of the windows high in the wall smashes to bits. The people nearest are forced to duck, covering their heads as slivers of glass rain down.

The butcher lets go of my sister. A stillness descends. But my chest tightens when I look at Mistress Wolsley's face. The butcher, the other Mistresses and the girls all wear the look of horrified fear usually reserved for large spiders. But Wolsley's face gleams with a ravenous, gulping hatred that makes my insides shrivel. The truth rings inside my head, as clear as a struck bell.

Nothing will be the same again.

2
Blood Tells All

When they take Egg away, I stare at my feet, imagining where they'll put her. The CLC – which stands for Confined Learning Centre – is a dark room in the crypt: the deepest of the seven floors of the school, where the tombs of long-passed Mistresses stand in judgement of the wickedest of the Wicked Girls. But my sympathy twists into a knife-edge of self pity.

How could she try to leave me here alone?

The rest of our dorm are sent to bed without supper. My stomach is already hollow and growling. We file past a group of cooks who are clustered near the foot of the back stairs, heads close together, gossip flurrying between them. They lean slightly away from us as one; a smooth, practised movement perfected by the Unwicked. We climb the huge spiral staircase curled at the heart of the school.

I can't believe she didn't even leave a note for me.

'Watch it!' whispers Jameela when I bump straight into her back, smacking my nose on her shoulder blade.

As soon as our door is closed, my dorm-mates swirl into a

panic. Their voices are all stretched and distorted. It feels as though time slows down, like I'm watching from underwater. Isla grabs me by the shoulders and starts to shake me. 'What did she tell you?' she demands. 'What do you know?'

Layla pushes Isla away. 'Don't be horrible,' she says. 'It's not Spel's fault.' There are tears in her eyes.

'I'm not saying it's her fault,' huffs Isla. 'I just want to know what she knows about it! They're going to grill all of us, you know.'

'Nothing,' I pipe up, my voice coming in tatters through the tears that pounce on me. 'She didn't tell me anything.' And that's the bit that hurts the worst, and the bit that fills me with shame.

'She didn't tell us because she thought it would protect us,' says Layla confidently, resting a hand on my shoulder. I feel the clawing of a familiar hunger. I wish Layla would care about me for *me*, instead of just out of loyalty to Egg.

'I can't believe she got inside a stinking meat wagon!' hisses Isla, shock splaying her eyes wide.

Layla snorts, cheeks dimpling. 'I can.'

'This isn't funny, Layla,' scolds Mariam.

'It is a bit, though.'

'Don't you realise what she's done?' Mariam squeals, thumping her mattress with both fists in a fit of temper she's never shown before.

'Yes,' says Layla. 'Obviously!'

Jameela backs Mariam up. 'I'm eighteen next month. I am *this close* to ceremony.' She holds her fingers an inch apart. 'If she's set me back, I swear I will find her and kill her if they don't do it first.' She's shaking with a frightened anger that looks like it's pulling at her skin from the inside.

'I don't understand why she'd want to leave,' says Mariam. 'There is nowhere else for us.'

'Haven't you ever wondered what might be out there?' asks Layla quietly.

Mariam stares.

'She'll get out of here soon enough,' scathes Isla, who got utterly sick of Egg a long time ago. 'But it'll be in her own personal meat cart – a wooden box!' She doesn't bother to say her good riddance. It's scrawled in the air.

'Why are you so vile at the moment, Isla Thomas?' demands Layla. But I can tell she's trying to cover the fear that has filled the room.

'Girls!' Mariam briskly claps her hands. 'Remember Henrietta.'

The name cuts like a knife, silencing everyone. Henri disappeared two years ago. She used to daydream so heavily the Mistresses had to shout to get her attention, and she was always late for everything. Then she walked out one summer evening to spend the night in a tree, hooting with the owls. We lay in our bunks, listening to those otherworldly utterances. The Mistresses let her stay out there all night. But the next morning, she was gone.

I close my eyes, Henri's soft brown ones flashing into my mind. She had a laugh as bright as a bird, but it disappeared with her when she broke the rules, and no one ever heard it again. She was the only person I ever dreamed might one day want to be my friend.

'And what's-her-name, from two dorms down,' says Layla. 'The one that somehow smuggled in that magazine.'

'Jenny?'

'Jenna?'

'Janey!'

'That was so much fun,' says Isla, wistful.

'It was not!' scolds Mariam, savagely.

The girl vanished, just like Henri. But not before the entire school had read the mag ragged. We all learned about lip balms and things called *video games* and pocket *money* – whatever that is.

'D'you remember reading about *besties* and what to do if your old bestie gets a new bestie?' asks Jameela.

'Yeah,' says Isla.

'That's like our word for *closest*,' says Layla, nodding. 'Like Jameela is closest with Maya and I'm closest with Egg.'

I can't stop myself from flinching a little. No one is closest with me. Not even my own sister.

'Maybe it's not as bad as smuggling in a magazine,' suggests Mariam, practical as ever. 'What Egg did can't affect other girls in the same way.'

'But if they don't punish her properly, others might try to escape,' Jameela points out. 'They'll have to make an example of her.'

I feel like they're discussing my sister's fate as they would a pile of dishes to be washed. I want to scream.

'She'll be just another disappeared girl,' whispers Isla. Her malice has evaporated like mist, leaving a cold, pure truth.

'What was with that window smashing?' asks Jameela.

Isla tips her head to one side, considering. 'It was a *Weird Thing*.'

Fear prickles all over me as I stare at her. My stomach bloats with painful fear. Everyone knows that a Weird Thing happening in front of the whole school is so bad that it's likely to unravel the very threads of Egg's life. If not all our lives.

'We have been overdue one,' admits Jameela.

Everyone knows about the Weird Things, but the unspoken rule is that no one mentions them in public. When a Weird Thing happens, the whole atmosphere of the school changes. Girls get punished, if the Mistresses find out. We all know how much they hate them.

We always know when something is a Weird Thing.

Layla sometimes predicts what will happen before it does. Same goes for Aisha and her little sister Mimi.

Leila from another dorm (whose name sounds the same but is written differently) says she left her body last Thursday night, and flew around the school.

Mariam fell down a big flight of stairs last week, but landed light as a feather, without a bruise or a scratch.

Maya ran outside in a thunderstorm, but stayed bone-dry.

Latisha plucks words from your head before you've spoken them aloud.

Olivia sees the future in dreams.

Lily says she hears voices on the wind, and a month ago, Isla made it gust more fiercely – until the building was swallowed in a hurricane. Amelia and Marli-Mae fix their eyes on the light they say glows around people's shoulders.

And when Egg gets angry, she can make stuff move. Last month, when a girl called Ruby threw a bar of soap at her head, Egg held up her hands, and the soap hurled itself back at Ruby, blackening her eye.

As for me? They say I'm my sister's shadow, living in my own world, somewhere apart from the world of the living. The most spiteful ones say I'm invisible. I'm not sure that's a Weird Thing, though.

There's a thump on the window. We flex towards the sound.

Outside in the early dark, a black thing beats against the glass. It thumps and struggles, as though trying to worm its way inside. Isla swears, scuttling backwards on her bunk.

'What's that?' asks Jameela.

Mariam climbs stiffly to her feet and approaches the window.

'No, don't!' gasps a collection of voices.

The windows in the dorms are high and barred, but we can open them a few inches by climbing on to the sill and propping open the iron handle. 'It must be a bird.' Mariam's hands are on her hips and her legs are planted firmly. But she steps no closer to the window.

Then the thing struggles again, thrashing against the glass. It turns and stretches in the air, wet wingtips pushing against the pane, which seems suddenly too thin a membrane between us and the awful, strange things of the world.

'Oh, for god's sake.' Layla stands, brushes past Mariam and pushes the window open, knocking whatever it is away into space. But as she's pulling the window closed, the thing – the bird? Though it's much too dark to say – shoots back towards our room again. The girls shriek, swear, beg. Layla slams the metal latch closed and jumps down from the sill, breathing hard.

The shadowy black scrap releases a sound that rings off the stone floor. An unearthly *screech*. Then it wheels around, gathering a clot of night in its wings, and disappears. But where its scream touched the glass, a circle appears, etched in the frost. It comes about as though an invisible finger is drawing it there.

The heels of a Mistress *tap-tap-tap* along the corridor and stop outside our dorm.

3
The CLC

The door opens. Mistress Turner steps into the room, face fixed in a cold grimace. We all stiffen. I feel the blood drain down into my toes. Her eyes fasten on me.

Oh no. My whole body turns hot and then cold. My hands start to sweat.

'Why'd you want her?' blurts Layla. 'She didn't have anything to do with it.'

Mistress Turner glances at Layla. A look I don't understand passes across her face – an almost *soft* look! But then her whole body grows taut with barely suppressed rage. 'I don't think you're really in a position to speak to me like that, Wicked Layla Dixon.'

And there's nothing else Layla can do. My stomach tightens. I find myself shaking and covering my mouth with my hand.

Mistress Turner grasps me by the shoulder and marches me into the corridor. I swiftly bend double and vomit all over her shoes.

She lifts one lace-up brown leather shoe, then the other, with delicate distaste. My weirdly yellow sick has splattered everywhere. 'Oh, Elspeth.' She snaps her fingers. 'Dorm, get this cleaned up, please. Then you can all get back to your duties.'

As we're led down the corridor, Isla's voice floats after us. '*Brilliant.*'

Turner's fingers dig hard into the fleshy part of my shoulder, making me wince. 'Blood will out, Miss Wrythe. Blood tells all.'

Blood will out. They really do think I'm just as bad as my sister.

'If either of you ever steps out of line again, I will personally see to it that you suffer enough to atone for a hundred girls' sins. Then, you will never have enough years in your life to make yourself clean, and you will *never* leave this institution. Do I make myself clear?'

I feel like I'm disappearing, through a crack in the floor. 'Yes, Mistress.'

She leads me all the way down to the ground floor, past girls polishing the banisters or carrying loads of laundry. 'This way,' she instructs, ushering me around the bend of the stairwell, to the stairs that lead down to the basement. At the bottom of the stairs, we round another curve – and Mistress Turner leads me down the final level of the school, into the crypt.

With each step down, the light is blotted out, until we're

standing at the bottom in darkness. Mistress Turner feels around for a light switch and the crypt is flooded with stark light. Ahead of us is a door marked with the sign that some girls – type two girls – know only too well.

Confined Learning Centre. Egg's been sent here plenty of times, but I've never been here in my life. I feel my breath shorten, coming in ragged gasps.

Inside, there are two rows of wooden desks. Under the clock is a great, gaping fireplace, like an ash-streaked mouth. To each side of the room there are ancient tombs, cold and silent, statues stretched along their tops – carved to look like the Mistresses whose bones they cradle.

Egg sits at one of the desks, left hand tied to her chair. She looks up at us casually, like, *what's the big deal?*

With an awful suddenness Mistress Turner pushes me into another chair and ties my left hand to my chair with rope.

Egg swears at her, and tells me to fight, but as soon as it's started it's done. I don't fight back at all.

Mistress Turner straightens her bonnet. 'I will return for you in the morning.' She places a glass of water on each of our desks.

Before she leaves, she tells us we're to write lines, even though we can't write with our right hands, however much they forbid us to use our left. Then she switches off the light, plunging us into darkness, and swings the door shut behind her.

21

'The morning?' splutters Egg, finally losing some of her cool.

Then the key crunches in the lock. The sound of Turner's clogs on the stairs, moving higher and further away, makes me feel terrible. We're being left down here in the dark with the dead, while life goes on upstairs.

Egg's eyes shine in the gloom. 'She can't seriously be talking about leaving us here all night!'

I pick up my pencil and start my lines, even though I can barely see the paper in front of me. *I am a Wicked Girl. Wickedness must be scrubbed clean. I must revoke my Wicked ways.*

'Why are you bothering with that?'

I shrug.

'Can't you just forget about ceremony for once in your life?'

'Of course not!' Tears come, plopping on to the paper. 'I'm grateful they're letting me write lines. You should be, too.'

She laughs at that. 'They'd be right. Why is there *sick* on you?'

'I don't know. I was scared!'

'How is being sick gonna help you?'

'I didn't plan it!'

Egg chuckles. 'Did you see the look on old Wolsley's face, in the hall? She looked like what would happen if a thundercloud gave birth to an old grey rock.' Her dark eyes almost burn into my skull. 'It was brilliant!'

'Why did you do it, Egg?' It's not my real question. My real question, the one that keeps pushing against the inside of my lips, is *why did you leave me?* But I'd feel too stupid and needy asking that.

She lifts her head, eyes puffy and underlined with dark circles. She's silent for the longest time, so when she answers I've almost forgotten I asked the question.

'It's like there's this whip curled tight, in the middle of my chest,' she says softly. 'It tightens up and around and burrows deep for a while. My breath gets so shallow it almost feels like it's being cut off. Then something – even a little thing – will happen and it sends the whip lashing and crashing out of me, and then I can't stop myself from doing something bad, or stupid. I felt the whip crashing out when that window broke.' She fixes me with her black-diamond eyes. 'Don't you ever feel like lashing out, Spcl?'

'Not really.' All I want is to stay as still as possible, and hope not to be seen.

'I did it.' Her eyes grow distant. 'It was only for a little while, but I slipped away, and they lost control over me.' She smiles.

'I'd never be brave enough to risk standing out like that.' The jealousy tastes raw in my mouth, and I hate the spite in my words.

'But you're the daydreamer,' says Egg, gently. 'There must

be so much going on in that head of yours.'

I suppose she's right. They scold me for letting pots boil over, for burning the milk, for pricking my fingers with my embroidery needle. Being distracted is the one thing I do to get in trouble. But I need to daydream, elsewise there's nothing to me. My life's all in my head.

I'm standing alone in one of the hallways of the school, shivering in my nightdress. A bonneted figure in a white gown is walking away from me, satin slippers shushing against the floorboards.

'Cece?' I try to follow but my legs are heavy and slow. The figure disappears around the next corner. I drag myself onwards, turning the corner, and see the figure in the distance, hurrying away from me.

'Cece?' My voice grows urgent, but she doesn't slow her step. I push myself on, willing my legs to move. Finally, I find myself growing nearer to the gowned figure. I reach out, fingers making contact with the delicate white lace. But something's wrong. The figure slows to a stop, and begins to turn round.

Suddenly, I don't want her to. Suddenly, I know she's not Cece at all. She's our mother. I try to turn away, but this time I'm fixed in place as a cloying horror begins to prickle along my spine. The moon-like bonnet topples from her head as she twists towards me, and her skin is sunken and her expression slack, and her eyes are hollow voids of darkness that begin to draw me in . . .

I struggle awake into the faint grey light of early morning, and all in a sickly wash remember where we are.

The worst thing is knowing that I deserve this. I deserve every nightmare, every punishment, every moment of fear and horror. Because our mother was a murderer, who killed an innocent woman. And my entire lifetime – and my sister's – will never be enough to pay for what she did. We don't even know her name. I'm glad we don't.

4
Forgotten

The 04:30 bell begins to toll. A smidgeon of thin light has trickled into the crypt. The crunching of the clock's second hand has started to scrape my nerves, like fingernails on a chalkboard. I stare at the outline of my sister, hunched over with her head on her desk. For a moment I allow my imagination to whisper that she's dead. What will become of us when the Mistress returns? Memories of Henri and Janey swirl in my head, making my skull throb. I remember all the whispered names over the years, belonging to the disappeared. The stories brewed up about what might have happened to them, and exchanged after lights out. Perfect recipes for nightmares.

Even now, they might be brewing stories about us.

Overhead, the school wakes up. The bell rings, but instead of stopping, it keeps ringing out its urgent call. 'Why don't they shut that bell up?' moans Egg.

We listen to the sound of hundreds of Wicked Girls traipsing down the central staircase above our heads, making their way to morning prayers and then breakfast.

'She must be coming to let us out soon,' says Egg, glancing over at the door. 'Whatever's going to happen, I just want it over and done with.' She's brazening it out, and I'm not completely sure I believe her.

The bell finally stops when the procession of feet – like a herd of elephants, according to Egg – reaches the ground floor, two floors above us. But instead of the usual quiet, a voice rings out, too muffled through the floors to hear properly.

Egg tuts. 'What are all those fools up to?'

A strange feeling washes over me, like whole worlds are pulling and splitting and being resewn, while we huddle underneath it all like earthworms. 'Something's wrong.'

'Well, yeah, I'd say so.'

'Why haven't they come back for us yet?'

'They're just taking their sweet time.'

But very soon, the whole school is hulking above us in a silence that I've never encountered before. There's not so much as the squeak of a floorboard.

My belly gurgles. 'How are we going to get food?'

'Someone will come,' insists Egg.

I give her a doubtful look but she turns away.

Later. No one has come for us. My belly feels swollen and sore. Both of us are trying not to pee. I've lost all sense of time. All I know is that we haven't heard a sound from upstairs for ages.

'Are they going to kill us?' I ask Egg. 'Can they do it, because of what our mother did?'

'What a weird thing to say! Weirdo.'

'You hit Isla for calling me a weirdo.'

'That was different. I'm allowed to say it – I'm your sister.'

'So will they? Kill us?'

She considers. 'No. They need us to do all the work around here.'

'Not *all* of us. What about Henri? And that other girl – Janey?'

She gets angry, then. 'No one will touch you while I draw breath, Spel! I will eat them alive if they try it.' The laugh she utters is tinged with wildness. 'Let them try, and let them see what I will do.'

I'm surprised she even cares what anyone does to me, given that she tried to leave me here.

Sometime in the night, Egg hobbles over to the right side of me and turns her back, ordering me to pick the ropes on her wrist. She can't reach the knot with her other hand. But it's tight, and I've only got one hand, and it's my clumsiest hand, too. I wince when the rope bends one of my fingernails back.

'Keep going!'

'I can't!' I suck my bent fingernail.

Egg jumps round to face me like some wrathful tortoise, all hump-backed. 'So what, then? We wait to starve?'

I start to weep, hating myself for it. 'I can't do it.'

The secret life of Spel Wrythe:
five things I wanted to do before I die

1. *Stand outside in the rain*
2. *Stroke a dog*
3. *Have a friend I'm closest with*
4. *Walk to the town, like the Mistresses do*
5. *Have my ceremony (and stop being Wicked)*

I think another morning has come, except this time, the bell doesn't ring. 'They're leaving us here to die.' Egg's voice is flat and parched. 'Maybe this is where they took Henri.'

I click my dry, sticky mouth open. 'And Janey.'

'And Janey.'

The thin stripe of light falling into the room brightens for half a second. But it's enough time for Egg to gasp, yell and lurch – chair and all – towards the back of the room, knocking into desks as she goes.

'What?'

'The stationery cupboard! They've left it open!' She opens the cupboard further with her foot and peers inside. 'Come here!'

I stand up and drag my chair towards her. The light is grey and hurting my eyes.

'Have a rummage in there, Spel!'

I do, knocking over pots of pens, a box of wooden rulers, and sending a huge block of paper thumping to the floor, loose sheets hissing across the boards. Egg rolls the toe of her shoe over the pens, sucking her teeth. 'There must be something, there must be!'

'I can't see.'

'I know you can't! Just feel.'

'My chair's too heavy.'

Egg starts to laugh, and the sound frightens me enough that I keep searching. I send a box smashing to the floor and something bounces out that rings against the floor like a bell. There's a flash of silver. When I squat down to pick it up, it's cool in my palm. 'No way!'

'What?' asks Egg, voice flat again.

'I've got scissors!'

A small, almost blunt pair of scissors, as it turns out. But they're probably our one and only hope.

Luckily, I'm not left-handed for everything. I can *only* cut with my right hand.

Egg hunches next to me again.

'I might cut you.'

Her shoulders sag. 'Anything is better than not getting out of these ropes. Even cutting me.'

I cut at her ropes until my hand throbs. The fibres snick away, one by two by one. After an age, I get them loose enough for Egg to wrench her left arm free. She roars as she does it, rolling her shoulder and sucking in her breath as the pain makes her wince. Then she grabs the scissors from me and slices determinedly at the knot on my wrist until the rope falls away.

We celebrate being untied like we've won a prize, even though we're still locked in this musty crypt room, two floors beneath the sun, with no food or water and not a friend on this earth.

5
Peaches and Beans

Egg has hold of the door handle, and she's pressing it up and down and rattling it and kicking the door and scrabbling with her fingernails at the gap between the door and the wall.

'It's locked,' I say, and the Look she gives me almost makes me swallow my tongue.

Then she grabs the door handle again and gets back to push-pulling, shaking and clawing.

Even though this situation is obviously Not Good, it still feels a bit weird not to be mending so many socks that my fingertips go numb or scrubbing so many sheets that my knuckles bleed.

It feels even weirder that we haven't heard a single sound from above since the morning after we were locked in here.

As soon as that thought has flown, there's a splutter behind us – a bit like a cough – and the sound of something falling. Egg shrieks. I gasp. We whirl around. A cloud of sooty ash has puffed out of the fireplace.

Egg hobbles over to look. 'Oh!' She turns to stare at me.

'What?'

She folds forward and snatches something up out of the grate. A small white envelope. 'It's a letter. It's addressed to us.' She sounds the least certain I've ever heard her, like she can't believe her own eyes.

'*What?*'

'Yes. It says *To Meghan Wrythe. Private and Confidential.*' She grins. 'How posh! We've never had a letter before, have we?'

I shake my head. But also *we* still haven't. Like with everything, the letter is just for her.

Egg fits her nail into a gap in the seal and breaks the paper apart. Then she slides the letter out and smooths it on her knee. 'Oh, for goodness' sake,' she mutters.

'What?'

'Ha. *Jokes!*' She thrusts the paper at me. The writing is bold and dark, done in proper looping ink. '*You must leave Mistress Mouldheels' School immediately. You have been appointed assistant to the undertaker, at the*

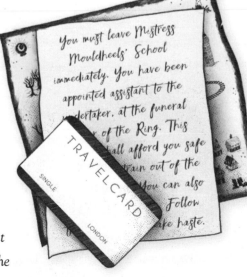

You must leave Mistress
Mouldheels' School
immediately. You have been
appointed assistant to the
undertaker, at the funeral
of the Ring. This
all afford you safe
ain out of the
you can also
Follow
ke haste.

funeral parlour of the Ring. This travelcard shall afford you safe passage on a train out of the city of London. You can also use it on the buses. Follow these directions. Make haste.' Another piece of paper peels away from the letter: a roughly sketched map, showing Mouldheels School in the north and the funeral parlour further south, near a tiny *x* drawn on a chunk of land marked '*The Old Kingdom of Sussex*'. There are instructions about taking buses and a train to get there.

'Must be that vicious little Isla,' says Egg, laughing appreciatively. Over the years, she and Isla have played pranks on each other on a regular basis, like a very twisted sort of friendship. 'Wait 'til I see that girl. Wring her scrawny neck, won't I. It's quite a decent prank, though, to be fair.'

'But what if this isn't a joke?' I ask. 'How would Isla have got up to the chimney?' I let my eyes drift to the ceiling. It's still silent up there.

'I suppose anything's possible, Spel.' She says it with an eye-roll in her throat.

'What's an undertaker, anyway?'

Egg shrugs awkwardly. She hates being reminded of all the things we don't know. 'Funerals are for when people die. Remember when that old Mistress keeled over a few years ago?'

I nod. 'So maybe it's something to do with dying.' I shiver.

'Who cares?' Egg folds the letter again and stuffs it back

into its envelope. 'This would be useless even if it wasn't a joke. What's the point of telling me – *us* – to leave if there's no way out?'

There's another splutter. Then a tiny metal chink, behind us. A shudder rolls along my spine.

'What was that?' whispers Egg.

'I don't know.'

Together, we turn back towards the fireplace. There, in the grate, is a long, slender key, lying innocently in the ancient ashes. Egg swoops down, grabs it and runs helter-skelter for the door, making freaked-out noises. 'Ugh, help, quick!'

The key works.

Egg stares at me. She grips my shoulders. She's crackling with full moon. I can see it pooling in her eyes and taking her to the edge, where she gets reckless.

We stumble out of the CLC, through silence thick as deep water, and haul ourselves up two flights of stairs, to the ground floor. The light burns my eyes. The stairs are empty, the corridor past the assembly hall is deserted, and the main entrance hall is silent as a grave. We crane our necks to look up at a clock. It's six o'clock in the morning. 'Breakfast,' murmurs Egg, through cracked lips.

We move like ghouls, turning right out of the entrance hall and along another passage, to the double doors that open into the dining hall. As we get closer, there's none of the usual noise – cutlery clanking on bowls, or trays being slotted into racks for washing. Egg pulls one of the doors open, and puts her eye to the crack. Then she flings both doors wide open, with a roar. 'What is *happening*?'

The dining hall is empty. As we step between the vacant tables, I feel as though I'm walking in a dream. You could hear a pin drop. There isn't a Mistress in sight. But I still feel as though they might be watching, that one of them might descend on us any moment.

Egg approaches the kitchen hatch and peers through. I flinch, certain that one of the cooks is going to yell at her for being late to breakfast. But nothing happens. She leans right over the hatch, staring left and right down the lengths of the kitchen. Then she darts to the side of the hatch and opens the door to the kitchen – the one that you're only allowed to go through if you're on kitchen duties.

Looking all around me first, I follow. The kitchen is as clean and neat as it would have been left the night before. It looks like breakfast never happened today.

After a few more moments of tentative glancing around, Egg rushes to the sink, twists the tap on and sticks her mouth underneath it, gulping and gulping. Then I take a turn, and she takes another, and we drink and drink until our throats aren't sandpaper.

Egg steps into the larder, coming back with an armful of tins – peaches, tomatoes and beans. She plonks them down on the table and peels the peaches open, shovelling the slices into her mouth with her fingers, dripping syrup everywhere.

'Don't!' I whisper.

'There's no one here!' Her words are peach-smooshed.

'Exactly! Doesn't that creep you out, even a little bit? Don't you think we should check?'

Begrudgingly, Egg abandons her peaches and we stagger back out into the hallway. We search the dorms, the exercise yard, the laundries, the bathrooms. We peer into classrooms, store cupboards, the gardeners' closet. We haul ourselves all the way up to the attic, exhausted muscles screaming, and poke and prod around in dusty corners, pulling open broom cupboards and stationery stores. From a window, we survey the grounds sprawled out beneath us: the long, snaking path that leads from the road, the vegetable garden, the isolated trees standing watch over the building.

'There's not a soul here, Spel.' Egg turns towards me, amazement making her eyes glitter.

Not a soul. She's right about that. All the life in Mistress Mouldheels' School for Wicked Girls has drained away, through the floorboards and the cracks in the walls. The only things left with ticking hearts are us and the clocks.

'Where are they all?' says Egg, voice too bare in the silence.

'Are they okay?' I whisper.

The emptiness feels like a ghost, all of a sudden. The back of my neck prickles as though a fingertip has brushed the skin there. Spooked, we race each other back to the kitchen, almost breaking our necks on the stairs in our haste.

We shut ourselves in the kitchen, tensing at the slightest sound. Egg finishes off her peaches. Despite the strangeness of it all, while she eats I find myself marvelling at the fact that it's just us two, alone. I have her to myself, for once. A ribbon of excitement begins to unfurl inside me.

'Why are you staring at me?' she demands, glaring. And just like that, the ribbon tightens back into a ball.

Egg opens a can of beans and dumps the contents into a pan.

'Shouldn't we find the bran flakes?' I ask, nerves slicing through me.

Egg pulls a face. 'I've had my life's fill of bran breakfasts! I'm having beans.'

'Well, can I have mine cold, then?' I like beans better cold.

Egg makes a retching sound, but she sets aside a bowlful of cold beans for me.

I find a loaf of bread in the bread bin and cut slices for toast. My hands are sweaty on the knife. Beans on toast is only for Saturday dinners.

'I can't believe Layla left without me,' says Egg softly, staring into the distance. Then her eyes harden, and she pummels the beans with a wooden spatula.

Images of their friendship flit through my mind, like how

since as far back as I can remember, they've been glued at the hip in a way that makes everyone joke that *they're* sisters. It stings so badly that my eyes water every time. When Egg's temper threatens to be the death of her, Layla's there to calm her down, endlessly patient. They hug with their foreheads pressed together in a way that makes me feel lost and lonely and stupid.

So I really can't believe Layla left without her, either. 'Why have they all gone? Has something bad happened? Maybe we should leave, too.'

'I don't know,' says Egg, grabbing two plates out of the cupboard. 'It's probably just something really boring, like maybe they're getting some kind of maintenance done and it's dangerous to be in here while it's going on.'

'Where are the workmen, then? And also, why didn't someone tell them we were still in the CLC?'

'Spel, you know as well as I do it's always every girl for herself round here.'

'But Layla –'

Egg throws down her spatula and whirls to face me. 'They all left us to rot, is that what you want me to say? Not one of them said anything, or they all completely forgot we were down there. Or how about this – *I don't know* what happened, so can we just drop it?'

We eat beans on toast – covered in grated cheese, like we've only ever seen the Mistresses do – while the sun gets up and throws beams of gold across the dining hall. The cheese makes the food taste really rich. Then we wash up, because I insist on it, and while I'm drying the dishes Egg screams from inside the larder, 'Spel, get in here!'

She's found the Mistresses' stash of special food. There's a little door in the larder that leads to another smaller pantry, with its own fridge. There are all kinds of meats, spices and jars. 'Plum com-pot,' reads Egg, grinning. 'Hon-ey? Honey! We've had that at Christmas, do you remember?'

There are boxes of cereal that are different from bran and whose names I don't recognise. There are tubs of something called cream, which is like solid milk, and there are bottles of juice and rolls of something called 'cookies', and boxes of another thing called 'chocolate'.

I run a finger across the shiny packages, staring at all the colours and pictures. A thrill begins to dance up and down my body. 'I've never seen food like this before,' I whisper.

Egg seizes a box of chocolate from the shelf and holds it tenderly against her chest. 'Chocolate was in that mag we read!'

'Put it back.'

'No way! Finders keepers.'

Seeing her clutching things belonging to the Mistresses makes me feel like the floor is tumbling out from under me. It's a confusing mix of excitement and horror that I have no idea how to handle.

We walk up to our dorm and sit on our bunks. As I gaze around me, I realise that the girls' things are still here. Clothes are still in the wardrobe, and wash things are still in the chest of drawers between the bunks. Egg opens the drawer belonging to the two top bunks that Layla shares with Jameela, and her eyes grow sad as she runs her fingers over the things inside. She lifts out a hairbrush with the letter 'L' pin-scratched into the handle.

'Egg?' I whisper. 'Don't be upset. I'm sure she'll be back soon.'

She blinks down at me, then shakes her head. 'Who's upset?' Then she stuffs Layla's hairbrush under her pillow, rips open the box of stolen chocolate and starts exclaiming at the contents.

When she offers me some, I refuse. 'I want to get my ceremony. When they find you doing that, you're going to be in so much trouble.'

She laughs at me.

'Do you think we should do some work?' I ask.

'Trust you to find a way to ruin a day like this.'

'When they get back they're going to find out we've been idle.'

'Spel, they left us for dead in that crypt!' Suddenly her head appears over the side of my bunk. 'You know what? We should do what that daft letter said. We should leave immediately. Otherwise we're just waiting for them to come back and shove us in the crypt again.'

'It's freezing,' I say, to get out of saying anything else. I don't want her to get serious about us leaving. I can't understand why she'd want to when we've always been told how evil the world outside is. But it is true that the place is freezing now that the stoves and the fireplaces aren't running.

Egg climbs down and squeezes into my bunk with me, then pulls the blankets over us and the envelope addressed to her out of her pocket. 'What if this isn't a joke?' she murmurs, eyes wistful. 'What if there's some other life out there, waiting for us?'

'I thought you said it was just a prank of Isla's?'

'But it's like you said – if it was Isla, how did she get it to fall down the chimney like that?'

I wish I'd kept my mouth shut. 'Maybe she tied it to the leg of a pigeon.'

Egg snorts. 'How would Isla get hold of a pigeon? And how would she get it to drop a letter down the chimney?' She takes the letter out. A small orange square falls from the folded paper. She picks it up, and then her faces changes, suddenly beaming with excitement. 'Hey, do you think this could be a real train ticket?' She studies the tiny writing. 'London Victoria . . . Arundel.'

'I don't care.' I cross my arms, digging my fingernails into my skin. 'We can't leave. They're going to come back. Everything is going to go back to normal.' And I'm going to get my soul.

'Spel.' She quirks her eyebrow. The ghost of a deep scratch, slowly becoming her latest scar, haunts the skin above it.

'I'm not going anywhere. They'll be back by tomorrow, if not tonight.'

'I hope we never see a single one of their stupid faces ever again,' spits Egg.

I know she's just covering her hurt and confusion with anger, because Layla's gone and we don't know why or where. But still a warm, contented feeling spreads through me, because we're alone together without anyone else to take her away from me.

'Maybe we can just live here, then,' I say. 'Just the two of us.'

If I carry on the Mouldheels' work, I'll still somehow earn my soul. Even if we're the only ones here.

Egg falls into a stormy sulk. We huddle in bed, hugging our knees. Egg picks holes in her stockings and I pick my lips. I know the contented feeling can't last, because we don't know what's happened to everyone or if they're ever coming back, but I let myself live in the bubble of the moment, where the whole world is just me and my sister. Between napping and going to the kitchen for snacks, the day passes. Beyond the dorm window, the daylight fails.

6

Once in a Lifetime

While Egg makes supper, I slip out of the gardeners' door into the vegetable patch. I stand in the rain, tip back my head and open my mouth wide, letting the heavy raindrops hit my tongue. My dress welds tight to my legs. Thunder grumbles. Storms are one of my favourite things.

The secret life of Spel Wrythe: favourite things

1. *When birds have frosty breath – it's like seeing the song*

2. *Cold baked beans*

3. *Purple trainers (saw them in that smuggled magazine)*

4. *Runny eggs (only had them at Christmas)*

5. *Rainbow hairbands (also in the magazine)*

'Elspeth!' yells Egg. 'Stop daydreaming, supper's ready!'

Lightning makes the white sky flicker. I wipe the rain from my eyes and hurry inside. She's made a mass of scrambled eggs and laced them with butter and cream from the Mistresses' pantry. The taste is so big that I feel my eyes grow wider than the plates.

After supper, we become night creatures, drifting around the dark, silent school. We don't talk about it before we do it. We're just driven by a nightmarish sense of compulsion and restlessness. There are so many parts of this place – our home, really – we've never seen. I feel like my feet are moving of their own accord.

The corridors are wide and dark, gulping us whole. Every time we pass a door, I tense each muscle and dart past it, terrorised by the thought of a Mistress sliding out of the dark and gripping me with bony hands. Our stockings squeak on the polished floors. Once, I slip, falling on to my elbow and summoning a smear of blood that dries so fast it's like the school has sucked it down.

The silence is thick and still so odd. There's the gentle thudding of our heels, the tide of our breathing, and . . . nothing, but for the ticking of the clocks on the walls.

Except that, with each one we pass, the sound of the ticking dies. When I look up at the wall, the clock I've just passed has stopped, its second hand twitching slightly back and forth, but never moving forward a full step. Egg joins me and stares up at it, then back along the way we've come. 'They're all stopping,' she breathes. 'Maybe I'm doing it, somehow. Maybe it's another Weird Thing!'

'I don't like it.'

But she's already dancing on down the corridor. The thrill of Egg's excitement – the electricity of it – buzzes in the air. It's so strong that, inevitably, a few sparks of it catch hold of me, and I find myself scuttling after her. 'Wait for me!'

Egg glances over her shoulder, a laugh dancing out through her wide smile. 'Isn't this amazing, Spel?'

I test out a smile. 'Um, maybe?' But I can't quite forget about the clocks. What's wrong with them?

Egg leans into every doorway, pirouettes through every room, and laughs blindly into the darkness as though it isn't such a thick web of horror and oddness that is trying to swallow us whole. I'm just trying to force myself to relax and enjoy the feeling of having the place to ourselves, when – 'Egg?'

She's gone into Mistress Wolsley's office. 'What are you doing?' I whisper. Panic frays off my voice and flaps around the room like a bat, carrying any smidge of excitement I felt off with it.

On the wall above the window, the clock shudders to a halt.

Egg stands behind Wolsley's desk and stares at me. 'I don't know why I didn't think of it straight away!'

'Think of what?'

'We can look for our personal files.' Egg snaps on the desk lamp. 'And we might be able to find out more about our parents' crimes!'

Her words smack me in the stomach, winding me. '*What?*'

47

'I should have thought of it sooner,' she mutters feverishly, pulling open a drawer and rootling around inside, like some kind of snaffling hog.

'Stop it,' I beg. Tears prick my eyes. 'They could come back at any moment!'

She ignores me.

'Isn't it enough to know our mother was a murderer? I don't need to know more.'

'Don't be daft!'

'I *don't*.'

She sighs, heavily. 'You don't want to leave, you supposedly don't *need* to find out the truth, you don't want to eat the chocolate . . . Things don't stay the same forever, Spel! You've got to grow up.' She turns to one of the grey filing cabinets standing by the back wall and rattles the drawers, but they don't open. 'Aaagh, it's locked!' She wheels around, eyes raking the room. She looks right through me. 'There must be a key somewhere, Spel. Help me look!'

'No way.'

She runs over and catches hold of my hands, shaking them up and down. 'Don't you know what a *once in a lifetime* chance this is?'

Inevitably, her franticness catches on to me, and because I know she's never going to drop it, I start searching with her, scanning the windowsill and behind the curtains, the top of the desk and the drawers underneath it. I pause by the back wall and look up at a lot of black and white photos showing groups of people standing in front of the school.

Each one shows five long rows of Wicked Girls, arranged on benches, in the grounds at the back of the school. In the foreground the Mistresses are seated on chairs, hands folded neatly in their laps. They're the photos taken every year of the whole school.

'What're you doing?' asks Egg, coming over to see.

'Looking at these –'

'Never mind photos, we need to keep searching!' hisses Egg, still frenzied by her determination.

Then my eye is caught by the way the Mistresses wear their belts, in the photos – hung with a heavy circle of keys. 'The Mistresses carry the keys on their belts!'

Egg beams, showing the chip in her front tooth that she got in a fight three years ago. 'Of course!' Before I can say anything else, she races from the room and back along the corridor of dead clocks. I rush after her, hating the thought of being left alone. 'Where are we going?' I gasp, as we plunge up the stairs.

We arrive on the third floor completely out of breath. She opens one of the doors. A Mistress's bedroom. I've never seen inside one of their rooms before. There's a sofa and a writing desk, and the windows are draped with heavy purple curtains. There are two small beds to the room. Egg crosses over to them and pulls open a cupboard in between the beds. Inside, there's a ring of keys. She clutches them up triumphantly.

Back in the office, Egg tries every key in the filing cabinet, until the top drawer comes hissing open. She flicks through file after file. 'Come on, come on . . . aha! Wrythe. Here we go!'

She pulls out two brown folders and drops them on to the desk. We both stare down at them as though they have teeth and claws. 'Now what?' she whispers.

'Well, you wanted to know the truth,' I tell her, folding my arms.

She glares at me, before opening the first file and pulling out a sheaf of papers.

But we both wince when, not far from the open office door, something creaks. It sounded like a floorboard. 'What was that?' I ask breathlessly.

Egg laughs in that big-sister way that I hate, which is full of unspoken patronising meaning. Her eyes lighten as suddenly as a cloud uncovering the sun. 'Don't worry so much! It's a big old place. It was probably just the pipes.' But still she crosses the room and sticks her head through the door, scanning up and down the corridor. Then she pulls the door closed.

Crossing back to the desk, she picks up the files, holding them close to the lamp. 'Meghan Wrythe. Elspeth Wrythe.'

Egg selects her file and starts riffling through it with a feverish look on her face. She reads out her own name, and date of birth, and the date she came to the school, aged three. 'Ha! It's got a list of all the times I've been trouble and – *ooh*!

– a whole page of my Weird Things. I'd forgotten about some of these!'

Huh. *I* hadn't. 'What else does it say?' I ask, aware that my breath is coming in short gasps. 'Does it mention me?'

'You have your own file, Spel.'

When I pick up my file, I'm barely allowing myself to breathe. *Elspeth Wrythe. Date of birth: unknown. Parentage: unknown. Date brought to school: 18th September, 2009. The child was estimated to be approximately one year old at this time, and accompanied by an older child; Meghan Wrythe.*

'Oh!' Egg's shoulders sag. 'Mine says parentage: unknown.' Her voice is bitter.

'It's all right. That's what mine says, too. We've come this far without knowing, haven't we?'

Then something slithers out from between Egg's papers, as though out of a gap in the air. It thuds on to the desk; a round lump of silver, shiny and smooth. A chain is attached to a loop on the top of it. Egg snatches it up, eyes flashing. We both peer at it.

There's a button underneath the chain loop. Egg presses it, and the front falls open, showing a small clock face. 'It's a watch!' gushes Egg. 'And there's something hidden inside it!' She pulls a tiny photograph out of the front casing.

We both do a small gasp.

The photograph shows a smiling woman with long dark hair and huge, laughing eyes. A black cat sits on her lap, green eyes bright. The cat wears a moon-shaped charm on its collar, the slim silver crescent a slice of light against dark fur.

The woman in the picture has Egg's eyes and silky black hair, and my long, thin nose and small mouth.

I reach over to take the photograph, but Egg pulls it back. As she moves, small black writing flashes underneath the photo. 'Something's written there!'

She flips it over. *Amara Penhaligon, with Artemis.*

Egg stares from the photo, then back to me. 'Who is she? Why was this watch in my file?'

'What if she's –' I swallow, my mouth horribly dry.

Egg turns back to the filing cabinet. While she's riffling around I pick up the watch. The second hand begins to shiver back and forth. Must be broken.

Egg wrenches another file free. 'Yes! She's here. Amara Penhaligon.'

I put the watch down and stare over her shoulder at the papers. 'So, whoever she was, she went to Mouldheels' as well?'

'I guess so!' She leafs through the pages. 'There are a few different documents here. This first one has her details. Born 13th January, 1974, London. Brought to Mistress Mouldheels' School for Wicked Girls in 1984. Did not achieve ceremony!' Egg pauses and looks up at me. 'Pupil declared missing in 1990. Eventually discovered in 2007, after committing an attack that led to the deaths of seven people and injured several others.'

'Seven people!'

'There's more.' Egg's voice has taken on a strange urgency, like she has a fever. 'Trial by jury arranged in the name of the anti-witchcraft laws, conducted by the Official Witch Hunt of Great Britain and Northern Ireland. Died in advance of execution.'

Silence falls over us. Outside, wind shivers the windowpane. I shake my head. 'I knew this was a bad idea.'

Egg clears her throat, blinking down at the paper in her hands. 'There's some newspaper clipped here.'

I press closer to her and stare down at the ageing scrap of paper. The headline is bold and harrowing.

ANOTHER WITCH DISCOVERED IN OUR MIDST: WHEN WILL THEY ALL BURN?

Notorious leader of the witch rebellion, Amara Penhaligon, found guilty of using witchcraft to maim and kill in lifelong campaign of unrelenting hate against the Unwicked.

My sister and I gaze at each other in mute terror. What if Amara was our mother? We knew she was a murderer . . . but a *witch*?

Eventually, Egg breaks the silence. 'Let's see what this next piece says.'

She turns the page. It looks like details of what happened as a consequence of the murder. '*In the case of Amara Penhaligon; all property seized: House. Vehicle. Furniture. Jewellery. Collection of valuable books. Silver pocket watch. Animals: one cat and one dog, euthanised. Dependents: x1 female witch child, b.2006, unaccounted for.*'

The next page Egg turns reads *Witch Trial #255, May 2006. The case of Amara Penhaligon.* I put out a hand to cover the page, but not quickly enough. We both see it, stamped with horrifying clarity at the bottom of the page. *Verdict: GUILTY. Sentence: DEATH. Deceased before sentence passed: December 2008.*

Thou shalt not suffer a witch to live.

The rain tips down, while my mind tips out a boxful of all the things I've ever been taught about witches. Wicked. Ugly. Have animal familiars. Hate children. Cause sickness and death.

Without a word, we start pulling out other files, and flinging open their covers. The first one I look at belongs to Henrietta Baklava. Henri. My eyes scan the writing, settling on the details of her parents. *Margot Goldbaum and Charles Baklava. Deceased: executed in Witch Trials #487 and #529, during the Hunt of 2006. Dependents: x1 female witch child, b.2008, despatched to London witchcraft reformatory Mistress*

Mouldheels' School for Wicked Girls.

It all fits so well with lacking a soul. Is this school really a witchcraft reformatory? A thing like a worm begins to swish around the deep, dark waters of my belly. A worm called terror.

'Everyone else is the same,' whispers Egg, gesturing at the files she's scattered across the desk. 'They're all the daughters of witches, too.'

I hardly even know where to start. Because even this doesn't seem to include me. 'Amara's file says she had *one* child, born in 2006?' The tears are running down my face, surprising me more than my sister.

'What's wrong?' asks Egg.

'There's nothing anywhere about me!' I wipe my cheeks with the back of my hand. 'How come I don't even have a date of birth? How come that watch was in your file, and it led us to finding out about Amara who had *one* child born the same year you were born?'

'Why would you want the Mistresses to have a load of details about you anyway?' Egg puts her arm around me. 'It's just stuff they don't know. If Amara was my mother then obviously she was yours, and there's just a mistake in her file. Or maybe it was even written before you were born!'

I scrub at my eyes. 'Maybe.' I push her away, even though I feel like I'm falling, disappearing through the cracks in the floor. Everyone's always teased me for being nothing but my sister's shadow. Now I feel like I don't exist at all.

'It said she had one *witch child*,' says Egg suddenly, a strange look of delight smearing across her face.

'Stop it!' My shout comes like a slap, shocking us both. I just don't want her making light of anything right now. No jokes, no enjoyment of any of this horror.

'It's okay,' she says, turning serious when she sees how upset I am.

My dry tears have left my face stiff as a mask. Egg retrieves the tiny photo of the woman and the cat from under the pile of papers, and tucks it safely back inside the silver watch.

The worst of it all is beginning to dawn on me. Our mother was called Amara and she made a real life for herself somewhere out there. I never knew the Wicked could do that. But what she was found guilty of . . . I can't even wrap my mind around how awful it is.

I move away from my sister, and find my attention caught by the photos again. I'm standing underneath one labelled *1989. Mouldheels' School.*

In the middle row of the group, a pair of girls lean their heads towards each other, as though they're sharing a secret. Something about the half-smile they both wear makes me think they must have been closest with each other. One girl has dimples set in smooth brown cheeks, and sparkling dark eyes. It's Amara! The other has the kind of pale skin that looks as though sunlight can fall right through it, and a wide, clever-looking mouth. Her features are more streaky, as though she moved when the photo was taken.

Egg joins me beneath the photos. 'It's her,' she whispers.

'I wish we'd never come.'

'Spel –'

'This is so much worse than I thought it would be!' She touches my arm, but I pull away.

'Don't be ridiculous, Spel! How is it worse?'

'She was a witch!' I shout. 'Witches are meant to do *all sorts* of bad things, aren't they?'

Egg cocks her head. 'Do you think *we* do all sorts of bad things?'

I shake my head, misery sinking deep into my bones.

She smiles. 'What if we're not really Wicked at all?'

7

Behind the Red Curtain

The next evening, after dinner, we wind down the main staircase to the ground floor, and wander through the corridor until the assembly-hall doors loom in front of us. Egg eats cherry jam from a jar while she walks, dripping blobs of bright red juice all over the stairs and floorboards. 'Do you have to make such a mess?' I hiss, through gritted teeth. All through supper she kept going on about the Weird Things. She thinks that the Weird Things are proof that we Wicked Girls have powers. That we are *all* witches.

Maybe I don't have powers – and therefore am not a witch – given that Weird Things never happen to me. Plus, Amara's file didn't say anything about there being more than one witch child. My heart lifts as I consider the possibility that the file didn't mention me because I am just a normal person. I tuck this treasure of a thought into my heart, and it loosens the knot in my stomach slightly, allowing me to take a deep breath.

The only thing we've been able to agree on all day is that

we're both feeling sad about Amara, even though we never knew her and she did terrible things. It feels like we've gained and lost a mother, all at once. Or at least the hazy outline of a mother.

The hall is the one place we haven't been into since the others vanished, and since it's so important in the life of the school, Egg's decided she wants a look around, in case there are any clues about the witchcraft thing we discovered. My breath catches in my throat, but Egg just shoves the doors open as though she owns the place.

I follow her inside and we both freeze in the aisle.

The hall is full. Wicked Girls sit on the benches, leaning against one another, their breathing thick.

Without speaking, me and Egg join hands. 'What is happening?' I whisper.

Egg's fingers tighten on mine. 'Hello?' she calls out, her voice horribly loud.

No one moves.

Egg takes a step forward. I try to hold her back, but she pulls me with her. 'Come on,' she says grimly. 'We have to.'

We pass row after row, and each bench is the same – Wicked Girls, breathing softly, some with eyes closed, others staring into space. 'They were here all along,' murmurs Egg.

'I thought they were dead,' I whisper, blood rushing in my ears.

'Me, too. But they're – asleep?'

We find our dorm and Egg shakes Layla by the shoulders, calling her name over and over. But Layla won't wake up.

I turn to the bench in front of our dorm and shake another girl whose name I don't remember. She blinks open her eyes and looks around the hall, but her expression is blank.

'What's happened here?' I ask her. 'Are you okay?'

She looks at me mildly. But she doesn't reply.

'Don't you want to get up?' I whisper.

Egg comes over to join me. 'Come on, get up!' she snaps.

The girl stands up. But she just stands there, looking at us. My sister and I draw closer together. We're both trembling. 'We have to go get help,' I say.

'I want to see what's behind the red curtain first.'

My stomach knots itself even tighter, which I didn't think was possible.

'Meghan Wrythe, don't you *dare*!' I hiss.

But she isn't even hearing me. She's gone feral.

She stalks up to the curtain, rips it aside and walks into the place all Wicked Girls go after ceremony. I freeze in the aisle, chest tight, fighting a gale of tears. This is all wrong.

'Egg!' I stamp my foot. 'Come out. Now!' I flinch, staring back at all the blank faces.

'You have to see this!' comes her muffled voice.

'Of course I do,' I mutter between gritted teeth. 'I always have to see everything, because everything is always so amazing. You know what's more amazing than anything, though? *Safety*. That's what.'

A creaking sound makes me jump, twisting to look behind me. No one has moved. Probably just another water pipe, after all, big old places like this are full of noises . . . but before I know it, I'm hurrying towards the red curtain. The sooner I go and look, the sooner she'll come out of there, anyway.

The curtain brushes my arm as I follow Egg into a small room, empty except for a vivid tapestry that covers the whole back wall, showing a forest in winter.

It must be old – I can tell, somehow – but the threads are gleaming and as colourful as if someone wove the tapestry yesterday. The whole thing is shining – almost glowing.

I know it sounds completely mad to say it looks as though it has skin, but it *does* look like that. The surface is waxen, and somehow fleshy.

The scene shows a clearing in a deep green forest, with a thick fall of snow on the ground, and the branches of the trees all dusted with white. The shadows between the trees are a velvety black that makes me feel drawn to step closer. In the distance looms a building behind a set of wrought-iron gates. It's Mouldheels' School, but in some other place. In the middle of the clearing is a woman wearing a long red cloak, with a fur-lined hood pulled up over her head. Her eyes are closed, and her hair is a long golden-red tumble, spilling over the neckline of her cloak. Her arms are held out at her sides, with her palms open. And – 'Oh, *urgh*, look!' I whisper. 'Behind the trees.'

61

When Egg sees what I've seen, she swears, and steps back. 'That is too creepy.'

Peering around each tree in the tapestry is a tiny, staring face. They're the faces of girls, and on their heads are green scarves, just like the ones *we* wear. Every inch of my skin begins to prickle.

There's a silence rolling off the tapestry that's as thick as snowfall. In fact, the snow in the scene is so real-looking, that I feel like if I just stretched out my hand . . . My fingertips have almost grazed the tapestry when, behind us, there's a thump. We jump back, clutching each other. My head is spinning.

Footsteps enter the hall. I can feel the heavy presence of the tapestry, almost tugging at my back. When I twist to look at it, the woman in the middle is staring at me, her eyes two bright knots of blue. But I'm certain her eyes were closed, before.

Egg whispers in my ear, startling me. 'We have to hide!'

'But what if it's them, coming back? Wouldn't it be better to go and face them – own up?'

Egg smirks. 'Um, no!'

'Well there isn't anywhere to hide, anyway,' I say.

'Meghan?' calls a voice, curdling my blood. 'Elspeth?' I know that voice. It's Mistress Turner. Goosebumps flare all along my spine.

I try to pull away from Egg, but she holds on to me and clamps her hand over my mouth.

Mistress Turner's footsteps move closer and closer towards the red curtain.

Egg lets me go, but presses her finger to her lips. 'Stay close.'

We creep towards the curtain and peer down the gap in the side of it. Mistress Turner pauses at the stone basin, staring straight towards us. Then she walks on, heading for our hiding place. I feel Egg's muscles tense. Just before the Mistress pulls back the curtain, Egg springs out at her, knocking her off balance.

Then we run for it.

'Wait!' bellows Mistress Turner.

'Not on your life!' shouts Egg. When I hesitate, she grabs my hand and hauls me along. She pauses next to our dormmates, shouting Layla's name, but she still won't wake up, and then it's me hurrying Egg along, because Mistress Turner is coming towards us again, and so we plunge down the rest of the aisle, out of the hall and into the corridor.

'The letter – it's still in our dorm,' pants Egg, as we tear up the stairs. 'We're going to have to go and get it.'

In our dorm, Egg rips the letter from under her pillow and grabs two green waxed jackets out of the wardrobe, shoving one at me. 'Put that on!' she orders.

'I don't want to go,' I tell her.

Below, Mistress Turner's feet creak on the stairs.

'Well, we're going!'

I shrug the coat on even though it's miles too big, and zip it up to my chin. Egg pulls a bag of food out of the bottom of the wardrobe, too. Turns out, she's been hoarding things ready for when we leave. It stings that she didn't tell me.

Then she opens the door of our dorm, peering out into the second-floor hallway. 'Let's take the back stairs,' she whispers. We tiptoe out of the room, turn left and rush along the hallway towards the door that leads to the damp old stairwell that's hardly ever used.

At the bottom of the stairs, we crouch in the shadows in the hollow of the stairwell, catching our breath. 'Back door,' whispers Egg, urgently.

But when we reach it, the back door is locked, and there's no sign of a key.

We rush back the way we've come, rattling the side doors in their frames. But they're all locked, too. So we turn and run in the other direction, clogs slamming horribly against the wooden floor.

Eventually we reach the front door, hideously exposed, with our backs to the main artery of the ground floor of the school. I keep glancing over my shoulder, while Egg fumbles with all the locks and bolts, swearing and sweating.

A shape drifts out of the shadows. Long robes shush against the floor. 'Egg!' I hiss.

'I'm trying!'

'Meghan,' calls the robed figure. 'Elspeth. Please, stop. You don't have to run from me.'

We whirl around and press our backs to the door.

A shadowy figure topped by a round black moon advances towards us.

'What's happened to everyone?' calls Egg hoarsely.

I wish I had even a pinch of my sister's rage, instead of all this fear. Perhaps it would lend me courage.

'I cannot tell you,' replies Mistress Turner. She stares up at Egg. My sister is almost five foot eleven, and Turner is barely five foot nothing.

Egg snorts. 'What's happened to them? Why won't they wake up?'

Mistress Turner casts a quick glance over her shoulder. 'You must both listen carefully.'

'Must we?' says Egg, through tight teeth. 'You left us down there to die.'

'It was not intentional, but I'm very sorry.'

Egg laughs bitterly, while I stare in amazement. I've never heard a Mistress apologise to any of us before. It sounds exactly like the world turning on its head.

Then Egg says, 'You've been lying to us about who we are!'

And I want to hit her, because we're trying to survive and as usual she's pushed too far.

'Meghan, we have always done what was best for you.'

'Yeah,' Egg mutters. 'By locking us in crypts and not letting us out when you said you would.'

Mistress Turner ignores her. 'You must come with me, girls.'

This time, Egg's laugh is startled. 'Tempting as it is, I'll say no. We're going somewhere else.' She grips the letter.

'Where?' The Mistress looks frightened, and the fear ages her. Suddenly, I see her as she really is: tired and old and slight, with wisps of greying hair escaping her bonnet.

Egg draws herself up to her full height. 'That's our business.'

Mistress Turner sighs a weary sigh. 'I cannot permit you to leave here unattended. It is thanks to this institution that you have been so sheltered from the world, and know so little of it. If you tried to make your way through the city, you might, despite your abilities, fall into the wrong hands.'

'Yours are the wrong hands,' I mumble, surprising myself and evidently both of them, from the way they look at me.

Mistress Turner gives a small smile. 'Let me make it up to you, Elspeth. Let me help you. You are . . . extremely valuable, to certain people.'

I think her kindness might be scarier than her cruelty.

A shadow blots the light in the hallway, sudden as an eclipse. Even though it's a darkening, I lift my arm to shield my eyes.

Mistress Turner twists away from it, like a creature on a hook. 'No, oh no!'

'What?' asks Egg, wrinkling her nose. Then she pulls me very quickly towards her.

The shadow has become a draining – a being that pulls the light and air inside of it, growing as it does so. Sticky, furtive eyes emerge in the shadow, as it pops a head out from its bulk, and then two gaping nostrils become apparent. They stretch wider as the thing sniffs the air, ravenous. The probing of its eyes and nose scrapes a sickly hole in the pit of my stomach.

When it screams, once, in our direction, I know it is akin to the thing that came to our dorm window. Egg's fingers cut painfully into my upper arm.

They're coming for us, because they think we're witches.

Mistress Turner moves to stand in front of us, and I watch as her edges begin to fray like old cloth. 'Run!' she gasps, pushing us away from the creature that is most certainly not any kind of bird.

'What about the others?' yells Egg. 'We can't leave them!'

'You have no choice. It is hunting for you, not them!' Mistress Turner hisses. 'I will try to hold it off. Now go!'

Egg throws back the last bolt on the door and the hinges squeal when she wrenches it open. She shoves me through and slams it closed behind us. We tear down the driveway and dash through the tall, wrought-iron gates, which Mistress Turner must have left open. A black car sits on the drive, gleaming with rain, twin headlamps painting the night with stripes of black and gold.

I gaze up at the sky. It seems bare-boned when looked at out in the open, instead of through a film of glass. We're standing in a quiet lane. To our right is a sprawling heath, scrubby and exposed. 'Which way?' I whisper.

Behind us, someone – or something – bangs against the front door of the school.

Egg grabs my hand and leads me in a half run along a dirt path to our left. I steal a quick glance behind us, as the hulking black outline of the school fades from view. Just like that, it's gone. *Discipline, obedience, atonement.* I shake my head to unstick the chant. But how will I ever grow a soul of my own, away from that place?

We pass hollowed trees and the driveways of grand houses, and when we have to pass a lamppost, we rush through its light as though it's spilling fire.

A chalky moon rises. It rolls on the rooftops like a giant egg. The lane slopes downhill and the heath gives way to rows and rows of skinny townhouses. Little lights glow in their windows.

Thin, frozen, biting rain begins to drive down. A fox knocks over a bin and stares at us with shining eyes.

8
You're From Up at That School

The rain turns the street oily. The night seems to be rising, rather than falling; patches of darkness sneaking up from between dustbins and out of the mouths of alleyways. Every sleeping house we pass feels like a trick. Like eyes are watching from the walls. 'Is it coming?' I ask, twitching to look behind us every few seconds.

Egg shakes her head, doing the same as we stumble along. For once she must be too shocked to speak.

'Should we go back for them?' I whisper, an ache growing in my throat.

My sister shakes her head again. 'How can we? We're being *hunted*.'

The word is no stranger than anything else that's happened. But still it drives a cold spike through my heart. Eventually we come to a busier street full of brightly coloured lights, hurrying people and cars gliding through the rain. I keep scrubbing water from my face, staring round at everything while trying not to *look* like I'm staring. Egg stuffs her hands in her pockets and keeps her head down. 'Act normal,' she whispers. So I copy her, staying close by her side.

A bit further up the street is a big metal shelter with people huddled under it. Egg grabs my arm and yanks me inside, so we're standing uncomfortably close to the other people, who eye us disdainfully.

Within a few minutes, a huge red bus hisses to a stop next to us. I flinch, covering my ears with my hands, but Egg yanks me upright.

We queue to get on. People take small plastic cards out of their pockets or bags and tap them on a yellow square. When it's our turn, I step inside the bus and stare all around me. I can't believe so many people can get into a machine like this and be carried along, and so fast. Egg flashes her travelcard and tries to bump me along with her, but the bus driver yells out at us.

'Hey! Where's her pass?'

We slump back a few steps and stare up at him. 'What?' says Egg.

He sighs. 'Zip photocard? Travelcard? Otherwise you'll have to pay a child fare.' He points at me.

I watch Egg squint at him. 'Um. Forgotten her photocard.' She tries to usher me on again, but the bus driver swings open his little window that he's sitting behind, and starts climbing out of his seat. Someone sitting on the bus starts complaining about us loudly.

We squeeze past the driver while he's still manoeuvring himself out of his glass cubicle, jump down the bus steps and run away, up the busy street.

We stop at the top of the street, at another bus shelter. 'Right,' says Egg, setting her teeth. 'It looks like this isn't as easy as I'd thought.' A bus slides towards us. This time I notice how there are letters printed along its front, all lit up. *C1. Victoria.*

Egg brightens. 'That's where we want to go!'

'Victoria? I thought that was a girl's name.'

'It's the place we need to take the train from, Spel.' Another crowd has massed at the shelter, and she eyes the people with the closest thing to nervousness I've ever seen her wear.

'How do we get on a train?' I remember trains from the books they used to teach us to read.

'Shhh,' hisses Egg defensively, chewing her lip. 'Be ready.'

This time, when the bus door opens Egg pushes me into a gap between two ladies, and I'm jostled aboard. While the one in front is fishing around in her bag, I slip out sideways into the aisle between seats.

When I look back, Egg steps towards me, grinning. I think we might have done it.

'Oi!'

A man gets hold of Egg's hood, pulling her backwards.

'She pushed past me and didn't pay,' declares an old lady, pointing at me.

The grin drains from my sister's face. Her hood hangs around her shoulders, leaving her green headscarf visible.

'Let her go!' I rush towards her.

The man stares us up and down while people grumble and tut. 'You're from up at that school, ain't ya?'

'Get off me.' Egg's voice shimmers with danger.

A murmuring arises among the other passengers, who watch us fearfully, eyes glazing with hate. A word buzzes into the air, swarming the bus. *Wicked.*

Egg looks at me with helpless, panicked eyes.

Then an extremely elegant man steps aboard. He's wearing a long green coat and shiny brown shoes, and a pair of gold wire glasses frame his long-lashed blue eyes. He meets my gaze and gives me a quick nod, before gently tapping the man on the shoulder. 'Sir? I believe you dropped something?' He holds out a piece of paper.

As the man drops Egg's hood and turns around, the atmosphere in the bus loosens from wire to wool. People start chatting again, and the old lady's expression softens as she turns away from me, towards her friend.

Egg stumbles forward. 'Go and find a seat,' says the man in the long coat, running his hand through wavy golden hair. 'There's nothing to worry about, is there, friend?' He claps the other man on the back, who stares at us with a vacant look in his eyes.

'Nope. Nothing to worry about at all.'

Egg grabs my hand and we hurtle through the passengers to the back of the bus. As it pulls away, I rub my sleeve on the misted window and look down at the street – only to find that the elegantly dressed man is staring right at me. His expression is as smooth and blank as a polished stone. Then he turns and walks away.

Even though he helped us, a nameless unease stirs in my stomach. 'What just happened?'

Egg pulls her hood back up, concealing the Mouldheels' headscarf. 'I have *no* idea. But at least now we're on our way.' She reaches underneath her hood and unties the scarf, rolls it into a ball and stuffs it into a pocket in the seat in front. Then she shakes out her thick black hair.

But when I start to take mine off, I hesitate. 'My head's going to get really cold.' Honestly, no one with hair can ever understand how freezing cold it is being bald.

'Yeah, but the priority is to look as normal as possible, right?' she whispers. 'We'll find you a hat somewhere, but for now maybe just wear your hood?'

I reach up to untie the scarf. The material has been worn thin by all the washing and wearing of it that I've done, and I've hidden under it for so long that it feels like a friend. So instead of throwing it away, I wrap the cloth around my wrist, over and over, and then get Egg to tie the ends.

She looks disgusted. 'Mad one, you are.'

Twisting in my seat, I look out through the back window of

the bus, wishing there were already hundreds of miles between us and that gulping shadow.

'You look shocking,' Egg says suddenly.

I glance at my reflection in the glass. My eyes are sunken hollows and my expression is one of only half-restrained terror. 'You don't look much better,' I whisper, jabbing my elbow into her ribs.

She croaks out a weak laugh.

'Egg –'

'Don't. I can't.'

I drop my voice to a tiny whisper. 'But . . . what was that thing?'

She wraps her arms around herself. 'Spel! I said *don't*. I feel like we shouldn't talk about it here.'

I know what she means. Even the thought of it makes my bones feel tainted, and sends a chill through my blood. So instead of thinking about what's behind us, I focus on what might be ahead. Why did someone send a letter to Egg? *Who* sent it? When I close my eyes, I can still see the sweeping loops of ink. *You have been appointed assistant to the undertaker, at the funeral parlour of the Ring.*

Neither of us has ever had a letter before, but honestly – what kind of letter is *that*?

'What if we shouldn't be going to . . .' I lower my voice, 'the funeral parlour of the Ring?'

Egg shrugs. 'What choice have we got?'

About forty minutes later, the funny disembodied voice that announces the stops calls out 'the next stop will be London Victoria.'

Egg whooshes to her feet and beams down at me. We push through the passengers and step out into another street thrumming with chaotic life.

We follow the signs and squeeze inside a big building, past people shaking the rain off umbrellas. Not a single one of the women are wearing bonnets or long dresses. There are more people here than I have ever seen in my life, all wearing different coloured coats and scarves, with different types of hair and boots and some walking dogs on leads. My heart leaps, and when I reach out to stroke one, he nuzzles his wet brown nose into my palm. The human with him smiles down at me. That's already two things done from my 'before I die' list!

Then someone bumps into me, tutting and scowling. Everyone is walking so fast that it's hard to know how to not crash into them. There are also so many brightly lit signs and shops that my eyes hurt, and Egg has to keep dragging me back when I drift towards them. 'Concentrate, Spel!'

We battle our way forward, and stand in front of a sign full of writing lit up like the writing on the buses was – all bright yellow lettering. I don't understand how any of it works at all. But Egg spots a sign which lists Arundel, the place we need to go, and says the train is leaving from platform 19, so we walk deeper into the station until we come to a barrier between the people and the trains. It's made of lots of grey gates that whisk open and shut, letting people through and blocking everyone else.

Egg makes us hang back and watch how other people get through the gates. They do it fast, but we quickly learn how – by putting the orange tickets into little slots.

'But we only have one travelcard,' I mutter hopelessly.

'Save your sad eyes,' says Egg, mouth hardening. 'We're *going* to get on that train.'

She pulls the travelcard out of her pocket. 'Stay *right* next to me,' she orders. I feel a lurch of panic when the gate sucks the ticket in, but then everything happens in a flash – Egg swiftly pulls the ticket out of a different slot, and as the gates swish open, she bundles me through with her, and then leads me away so fast it feels like my legs have detached from the rest of my body.

But it worked. No one stops us. Everyone looks too grumpy or busy to even notice us at all.

Getting on to the actual train is scarier than I expected. It's not like a train in the first reading books at all. Those were all red and shiny and puffing steam, with a friendly driver waving his hat. This one is a great, long metal tube and there are lots of tired-looking men and women inside, reading or tapping on shiny squares in their hands.

We shuffle all the way through the train, almost to the very front, and find two seats together. When the train starts moving, then gathers speed, I try hard not to scream. It makes such a terrible noise. I clutch the seat and try not to watch the window, because everything is rushing by so fast it makes me feel sick.

Egg grits her teeth, glaring round at everyone. 'Let's have a look in here, shall we?' The bag of food has apples and a loaf of stale bread and a jar of honey. I take an apple and crunch it, watching as more people get on the train every time it stops.

When Egg starts to unzip her coat, I jab her in the arm. 'Don't. Someone might be following.'

She scowls, ripping a bite from an apple. But she zips her coat back up.

'Can I see the map?' I ask.

She glances over her shoulder down the train carriage, before pulling the roughly sketched map out of her inside pocket and smoothing it out on the little table that folds down from the seat in front. 'We're supposed to get here.' She points at the little x drawn at the place called the Ring. 'The instructions say that we have to travel to Arundel, and then take a bus.'

'So many buses!' I take another bite of my apple. 'It's actually really far away.'

She nods. 'It kind of is, yeah.' Then she tips her head to one side, a playful look crossing her features. She puts her mouth by my ear. 'Do you think we'll find out more about being witches, at the place we're going to?'

My heart thumps. '*I'm* not a witch,' I hiss angrily, angling myself away from her. The apple sours in my stomach. I think of those files about us, and how no one even knows when I was born. It feels like I barely exist at all.

Egg laughs. 'Cheer up, little Spel! We're well on our way now.'

But her words ring in my ears, as hollow as I feel. Because what are we on our way to, exactly? I'm not at all sure I like the sound of being assistant to an undertaker. And the undertaker might not even have space for me.

9

The Shadow of the Ring

We reach the place called Arundel when the moon is rising. There is a castle – we see it from the window, all lit up. 'Maybe we could go and live there?' suggests Egg, winking at me.

We tramp into the town and then consult the instructions again to find out the next bus we need to take. But it turns out that the travelcard only works for London buses, and also because it's quiet out here, there's no way of slipping on unseen. Back at Mouldheels', girls would sometimes learn bad words from the delivery boys. Egg spits out a very bad word now, and the driver threatens to throw us off. But then she looks us over, and a sad, curious expression settles over her features. She lets us on, but only after we've promised that someone is coming to meet us when we get off.

The bus sets off, trundling through narrow lanes. I keep falling asleep, knocking my head on the window and feeling embarrassed, even though no one else seems to have noticed.

Then Egg's poking me awake. My cheek is slick with drool. I rub it dry as we clamber from the bus and across a strip of wet, muddy grass, plonking ourselves down on a bench in the bus shelter.

On one side of us is a deserted road, lined with grass verges and, further up, a few quiet houses. On the other side is a steep grassy hill. The shelter is just a squat, stone building full of cobwebs and no information whatsoever.

We wait a while, as the darkness thickens around us. Then Egg starts to pace up and down outside the shelter.

'We've been abandoned, haven't we,' I say. There's nothing I can do to make my voice less flat. I swallow down a noseful of sudden tears.

Egg glares at me. 'Do you always have to be *so* negative?'

I shrug. 'It's just that someone should have been here to meet us, shouldn't they? Maybe it *was* all just a joke.'

'Don't start, Spel. I am really not in the mood.'

'How am I "starting"?' I could honestly just kick this girl, sometimes.

But she ignores me. 'They'll be here.' She hugs herself around the middle, inhaling a big breath of the damp, slightly rotten-smelling air. 'Don't you just love this fresh country air? It's so invigorating. Something about being here just feels so right, doesn't it? It feels familiar, somehow.'

I swish my feet in the dirt, letting her babble on to herself. Then I notice it – a scrap of shiny cardboard, wedged into the grooves of the bench. I pull it free, unfold it and goggle at the writing inside. The message is scrawled in red ink on the back of a bit of card.

Artemis will lead you to the house.

I've seen that name before . . . I scurry outside into the damp air, and almost tug Egg's shoulder out of its socket.

'What?' She rounds on me. But when I show her, she takes the card and stares at it.

'So what?' she fumes. 'Must be a common name or something.'

But she is so wrong.

A small, fluffy black cat appears on the grass verge in front of the bus shelter, with her tail curled neatly around her front paws. I bend down to look at the tag hanging from her collar. It's a slender silver moon, with her name etched delicately along the curve of the moon's back. Exactly the same as in the photograph inside the pocket watch that Egg's kept with her ever since it fell out of her file. Artemis blinks up at me with thoughtful-looking green eyes. As soon as Egg joins me, the cat turns tail and trots away across the road, towards the ups and downs of the open fields.

I hurry after her.

'Spel!' shouts my sister. 'What are you doing?'

I twist round to stare at her. 'I don't think we should lose sight of that cat!'

'That cat hasn't been sent to meet us, you fool!'

'Well, no one else has!' I yell, over my shoulder.

The evening turns crooked; filled with gaping and

shrinking shadows, and echoing with strange moans. Mist hangs over the hills and snags in the claws of the trees. If I'd had any hair, it would've snagged in that, too.

'Why the hell have we been summoned to this nowhere?' Egg gargles, overflowing with rage. Her big dark eyes flash in the gloom and her hair billows around her head like a smoky cloud.

'Nowhere is nowhere,' I husk. 'Everywhere is *somewhere*.'

'This place is nowhere. It's just a filthy muddy swamp!' Egg kicks out at the gleaming wet grass, sending a clump of mud flying. 'And *you. Are. So. Annoying*.' She huffs and sniffs, wiping her nose on the sleeve of her coat.

'I thought you said that you loved the invigorating country air.'

'Never mind what I said!' she spits. 'That was before we ended up following a wretched cat halfway back to London!' Then she proceeds to curse the very needles on the trees and the roots in the earth and the bats flickering in the sky.

Despite all Egg's fussing, we stumble onwards, heading for a circle of trees on the hill in the distance. 'Where are we even going?' Egg stops, staring ahead.

She lifts her hands high, gesturing towards the moon. 'Where on earth has that cat vanished to? I can hardly see!' She rips her hands back down from the sky, and as she does so, her fingers pull *a ribbon of moonlight* with them.

'Urgh!' she stutters, trying to unstick the light. She throws

it away from her, and the light scatters into the trees, making coloured orbs of light pop into life like lanterns.

Now *that* was a Weird Thing. 'What did you do?' I whisper.

Egg stares at her hands, then at me, and then she points, mouth gaping.

The little lights show a crooked wooden house as wrinkled as tree trunks, or old skin. The house huddles near the edge of the trees on the hill ahead.

We swap a startled glance. Then a tiny miaow calls from up ahead and we press on.

But we only move another few feet before jerking to a stop again. Ahead of us stretches an enormous bridge, made from the carved open roots of a giant tree. I put a hand on the twisted brown rail. Beneath the bridge lies a valley, full of steely rocks blading up through tufts of grass silvered by the moonlight.

'Come on,' urges Egg, grim-faced, hefting her bag of food. My clogs slip on the wet tree roots. I try not to look down.

The ring of trees looms closer. The trees are twisted and bent into strangely human shapes. Our shoes sink into thick, dark mud that sucks at my boots as though hungry for the flesh and bones inside.

We skirt the right-hand side of the trees and the cat leads us along an overgrown front path, past a sign saying 'S. *Putch, undertaker*', to a wooden door. Egg pauses underneath the sign. A long gleaming black car lies like a snake under a tree, on a little patch of driveway. First sight of it sets my heart thrashing, until I realise it isn't the same as the one we saw outside the school.

The cat starts to scratch and whine at the door. It cracks open. A whip of grey hair, spangled with cobwebs like snagged ghouls, sticks out. Underneath the mad hair lurks a creature like a man, peering at us through tarnished silver eyes buried under folds of skin. A sallow, thicketed man, with no trace of welcome about him whatsoever.

'Who are you?' he rasps, in a voice as ancient as tree roots. 'How did you find me?'

PART TWO:

THE RING

10
Shranken Putch

'Are you the undertaker?' demands Egg, offering her hand. The rest of her tenses for a fight, like usual.

He eyes her. 'Might be,' he whispers, like he isn't quite certain himself. He keeps his fingers spidered around the door.

Egg lets her hand drop. In the back of my mind, a murky thought twists and tumbles. *Egg was wrong. This place is not nowhere. This place is Elsewhere.*

The cat shoots through the door, briefly tangling around the undertaker's ankles, before disappearing into the gloom.

'Don't usually do dealings with live ones, do I?' His eyes narrow so thin that the eyebrows take complete control of his face. 'Must be a couple of skin-soaked ditchlings, sent to haunt me!'

A couple of what?

Egg is not fazed. 'Did you send us this letter?' She rummages in her pocket and produces the crinkled rectangle, the weight of its broken red seal making the envelope flap like a mouth.

'Two?' he mutters under his breath. 'Council didn't say

anything about two.' His eyebrows lift, and his unburdened eyes continue to assess us with an expression I find hard to name.

'We're your new assistants!' declares Egg, brightly.

'Witch?'

My stomach clenches.

Egg blinks at him. '*What?*'

'*Which* of you is?'

Oh.

'I'm Egg Wrythe, and that's my sister, Spel. *We* are your assistants.'

The undertaker's fingers tighten on the door. Egg steps forward a few inches, as though afraid he's going to shut it in our faces. He closes his eyes for a few moments, shaking his head.

I sneak a look at Egg and she sneaks one at me.

When I turn back, the undertaker is giving me the longest, strangest look. A tinge of sadness has touched his eyes. Then he releases his eyebrows, allowing all the heavy skin to sag down on to his eyes again, forcing them to strain open against the weight. 'You're late!' he snaps, in a tone rich with disapproval. Then he turns and scuttles away, leaving the door ajar.

'It wasn't our fault,' Egg retorts. 'No one came to meet us!'

We shove through the heavy door into a dark passage, past an old telephone sucking the wall like a huge black beetle.

'Artemis came to to meet you!' quails the undertaker's faint voice from the back of the house.

I peer around through the fog. The house has the heavy weight of a graveyard. There's something solid and comforting about it. I immediately like the quiet.

'Watch out, Spel!' Egg stumbles into my back. 'Is there any chance of a bit more light around here, Mr . . .?' She trails off awkwardly.

There's a mess of tutting and scratching. A rattling of drawers. Then the hiss of a match being lit. The man shuffles back down the corridor with a lantern swinging from his wax-scabbed fingers. He wears thick green velvet trousers that look like they've been sewn from a pile of old curtains. 'Shranken Putch,' he croaks.

Egg looks at me sideways. 'Pardon?'

He clears his throat, then repeats the same noise, but louder. '*Shranken Putch.*'

'What's that?' squeaks Egg.

'Name. No mister. Just Putch.'

That sign outside. *S. Putch, undertaker.* 'Oh!' says Egg.

He twitches his neck to look at me. 'That one – speaks, does she?'

Egg sighs. 'Of course. She just mostly doesn't like to, especially in front of strangers.'

The usual painful heat creeps into my face.

The secret life of Spel Wrythe: the quiet list & what I wish people knew

1. *Quiet people can be strong*
2. *There isn't always something wrong*
3. *But sometimes, there is*
4. *It's just the same as for everyone else*
5. *Except we don't keep going on about it*

'Cancer?' he asks, when I pull down my hood and he sees my shining baldness.

Egg's mouth twitches like it does when she's exceptionally annoyed. 'No,' she says coldly. 'My sister has alopecia.'

'Oh.' He nods. He looks kind of disgusted and sorry for me, which I hate. I started going bald when I was five, and I've learned that *everyone* is spooked by a quiet kid with no hair. To me, hair is just about looks, and a bit about warmth. But scarves and hats can do warmth. Why are adults so vain?

'Listen, Mr – ah, Putch,' says Egg, snapping me back into the moment we're actually in. 'We've had a long journey. Could you show us our room?'

'I was promised one helpful worker,' he grumbles. 'Not two lay-abeds!'

Egg puffs herself up, glaring. 'It's night-time, and we need to rest.'

He squints. 'A lot of our work is done at night, matter

of fact.' From somewhere in the gloom, the cat yowls. The undertaker rolls his eyes. 'Right, come on, then! Better at least show you round first, hadn't we?' He leads the way to the end of the hall, and starts climbing a break-neck set of rickety wooden stairs. At the top there's a knot of darker wood in the banister that looks like an eye. I shrink away from it as we pass.

Our room is a narrow little attic at the top of the house, sparsely furnished, with peeling floral wallpaper. There are two unmade iron beds with a scuffed chest of drawers huddling between them. 'Linen's in there,' says Shranken Putch, grudgingly.

A mean fire snuffles in a badly swept fireplace. The wind rattles down the chimney to shiver the flames. Raindrops clatter against the tiles of the roof, inches from our heads.

'That roof's going to leak, isn't it?' whispers Egg, fatally.

I nod.

The undertaker points out a set of black clothing, hanging on the back of the door. It consists of a black shirt, a blazer with long tails, black trousers and a black satin top hat.

'Uniform. To be kept clean and neat. I'll have to order another one, now.' His face squeezes into a pained expression. 'You'll wear them for collecting bodies and helping at funerals.'

A shiver wriggles through me. Egg's jaw hangs like a broken hinge.

'Come on, come on,' says Shranken Putch, ushering us from the room. 'No time for dither-dallying!'

He shows us the bathroom, which is on the floor below, along with the room where he sleeps. On the ground floor there's a sitting room with a couple of faded old flowery armchairs and a shelf crammed with books. A clock ticks on the mantelpiece. Across the hallway is the door to what the undertaker calls the 'laying-out room', which he says will 'make sense soon enough'.

The kitchen is at the back of the house, with a dining table in the middle, and shelves of pots and pans and copper-coloured jelly moulds, and a smell of baking.

Just outside the kitchen door is another staircase, dropping away to a lower level. 'What's down there?' asks Egg, peering into the gloom.

He points at both of us in turn, his finger barely an inch from our faces. 'That down there is the basement. And that is a forbidden place. Stay away from there and we can all be happy working together.'

Even without looking at her, I sense the electric gleam that enters my sister's eye. I want to bury my face in my hands. Why *oh why* did he have to use the word 'forbidden'?

'Mr Putch?' says Egg, tugging on the ends of her hair.

'No mister,' he says firmly. 'Just Putch.'

'Do you know what happened at our school? Why have we been given this job?'

His face darkens like a thunder cloud. Then a scream sweeps into the air, punching me in the head.

I'm felled to the floor, like a sack of potatoes. Shranken Putch hauls me to my feet with one hand and snatches up the bleating phone with the other. 'Shranken Putch, undertaker,' he squawks into the black mouthpiece.

It was the phone. It was just *the phone*. Sharp, bitter embarrassment floods my whole body. Egg wraps her arms around herself and bends double, shaking with helpless laughter. The undertaker listens to the person on the phone while still clutching my arm. I peer up at him, a list taking shape in my head.

The secret life of Spel Wrythe: Shranken Putch

1. *There's the bony jut of his chest and how*
2. *Wide his eyes are (they're frantic) and how*
3. *Wild his hair is (electric) and how*
4. *Gritted his teeth are (yellow) and how*
5. *Tensed his shoulders are (he's wearing them up round his ears, like a pair of arm-earrings)*

He unpeels his fingers from my skin, one by one, and turns briskly away from me. There's a scratching sound as he starts scrawling on a notepad by the phone.

'Stop the clocks, cover the mirrors, turn down the photographs,' he tells the phone, before slamming it back into its cradle, spinning on his heel and scampering down the corridor like a spider down a dark hole. 'To bed,' he barks at us, over his shoulder. 'There will be work soon. Get some rest.'

I watch him go, a strange feeling pooling in my stomach. Then I stare up at the big black box of an old phone. *The death phone*, whispers a tiny voice in my head. That must be the death phone, telling him when someone's *passed*.

'You heard the man,' says Egg, wrapping an arm around

me. 'It must be getting late! I hope you didn't hurt yourself falling over like that.' She starts laughing again, and I punch her on the arm.

We head upstairs and take turns washing in the grubby bathroom. Having such privacy, and hot running water, without having insults barked out by a watching Mistress, is beyond startling. It's beyond luxurious.

When I walk back to our room, Egg is in hysterical raptures over a few bags of stale-smelling clothes. 'Spel, are you seeing this?' she stutters.

'Yeah. It's some sacks of rotten old undies?'

'Spel.' She glares daggers at me and starts pulling out moth-eaten dresses and thick woollen skirts and a sweater with the word 'Chicago' emblazoned across the front and musty berets and some kind of shawl encrusted with gold sparkles, which Egg immediately wraps around her shoulders. 'I thought this was the worst day ever.' She beams. 'But it's actually the best!'

I roll my eyes.

'You don't understand,' she yells. 'This stuff can change our identity! We can finally choose how to define ourselves, *for ourselves!*'

'But – do you not think those are probably *dead people's clothes?*'

She hesitates, clutching a jewel-red jumper to her chest. Then her look hardens. 'So what? They don't need them now, do they?'

Why don't you get how weird that is?

Soon enough, Egg has swathed herself in the gold sparkly wrap with a long stretchy black dress, battered black boots and a string of clacking pearls. I choose a sweatshirt with a picture of a mouse with giant round ears, a pair of blue trousers and a grey beanie hat, plus a pair of yellow rubber boots.

Egg gets bored as soon as she's finished examining every item, and throws herself down on one of the beds, burying her face in the pillow. 'We look ridiculous,' comes her muffled voice. Then she turns on to her cheek and whispers to me with her lips all smooshed, 'Spel, don't say anything to him about us being witches.'

'We're *not*!' I snap, with more venom than I knew I had in me. 'What do you even mean, anyway? You don't know anything about witches, or being a witch!'

'Calm down,' she says, pushing herself upright and giving me a lofty look.

'I *am* calm.'

'I might not know anything about witches, but I do know about the Weird Things, and now I *know* there's more to it all than we thought. I know that the Mistresses always hated us, but more than that – they were afraid of us, too. I want to see if we can find anything out about it while we're here, but don't say anything to the undertaker. I want to find out what he knows, and we can't risk him getting rid of us if he hates us too.'

'Can you just leave it? I don't want to think about it any more.'

She blows out her cheeks, defeated. 'Fine.'

We spend a few quiet minutes listening to the puttering of the dying fire and the pattering of the rain – heavy drops that hit the window and slide off, forming miniature rivers on the glass. I settle on the other bed, enjoying the feeling of it being just the two of us. Egg turns her head and I meet her gaze, and we grin at each other as a tiny glimmering crackle of something unfamiliar – *adventure?* – swims in my belly.

The quiet here is very different to what I'm used to, which is *quiet-ish*-ness, crammed with the noisy breathing of hundreds of girls. What happened to them? How can they all have been weirdly asleep like that, and why was that girl acting so strangely when we woke her up? The not knowing has given me a lingering sick feeling, low down in my stomach. *Layla, Mariam, Jameela, Isla,* and so many other names, whispering through my head like fallen leaves. *Chloe, Emily, Leah. Charlotte, Annabel, Bethany. Harri, Lorna, Soraya. Billie. Mary. Aisha.*

'Egg?'

'Hm?'

'What do you think happened to the other girls?'

Her face fills with sadness. 'I have no idea. It's just so weird. Like some kind of huge collective Weird Thing?'

My mind races so fast it makes my head ache. 'Also, don't

you think it's a bit odd that it happened while we were in the crypt, and just before we – *you* – got the letter to come here?'

Her face grows thoughtful. 'Like, you mean, did someone want to make sure –'

'It didn't happen to us?' I whisper.

Egg frowns. 'The problem with that theory is that "someone" would be Mistress Turner. And obviously Mistress Turner was a vicious old sow, and she didn't want us to follow the letter to come here anyway.' She burrows under the blankets and peeps out at me. 'There's only one thing I do know, Spel – I want to find out what happened to them and make sure they're safe.' She blinks suddenly, and I know she's thinking of Layla.

'How're we going to do that, now we're all the way out here?'

She shrugs again. 'I don't know yet. But this witch thing definitely means we've got powers – look at what happened on the way here, with the moon and those lights. I bet we could do some more Weird Things, but on purpose.' She sits up, brightly alert. 'The other times Weird Things have happened, I've been really angry. What if I could work out how to channel my feelings on demand, without waiting for something to upset me?'

Her words make horror rise, lashing, up my throat. 'That is a wicked thing to suggest, Wicked Meghan Wrythe!' As soon as the name is out of my mouth, I desperately wish I hadn't said it.

She gives me a wounded look and flumps over in her bed, sweeping the blankets around herself.

'All that stuff about "powers" just makes me feel so sick,' I whisper. *It makes me feel years and years further away from receiving my soul.*

Silence.

'Sorry,' I say, misery hollowing me out.

But she doesn't reply.

Soon Egg falls asleep, breathing softly. The cat hurtles up the stairs and scratches at the door, so I let her in. I curl up on my bed under a torn old patchwork blanket that smells like damp. Artemis jumps on to my lap, making my breath stick in my chest, until she turns around three times and settles, purring heartily. Her tail has a little kink in the end of it.

Eventually the moon travels into the bit of night outside the window. The fire is sleepy, and so is the cat. I glance down at the little bundle of black velvet fur snoozing in my lap. But I'm wide awake. Why are we in this place? And who is Shranken Putch? Why did he look at me so strangely? Artemis cracks open one green eye, then closes it again. I pull off my boots and settle down in bed, my chest curled around the little cat. Eventually my fears and questions blur into one tangle and I lose all the threads. I'm so tired that I fall asleep like a rock hitting the bottom of a pond.

*

It feels like only a few seconds later when we're woken by a frantic hammering at the door, except that the fire's gone out and the cat's gone, and the room's even colder than before.

'Lay-abeds! Lazy flittermice!' comes the undertaker's impatient rasp. 'Get your skins dressed and downstairs. Work must be done!'

The curtains are tinged grey around the edges and there's a fresh coldness sitting on the very tip of my nose.

'Urghhh,' groans Egg, stirring in her bed. 'What is he talking about?'

I'm out of bed without another thought. Maybe if I work hard enough here, there's still a chance I can get my soul, somehow. 'He's talking about work. Get up, quick!' I flick on the light.

Putch thumps on the door again, making me flinch. 'Smaller Wrythe – I've cobbled a uniform for you. Some of it might be too big.' He inches the door open and his skinny hand thrusts a set of undertaker's clothes at me.

I reach out and take them, and the door bangs shut again.

I'm expecting Egg to growl and grumble, but instead she vaults out of bed like a thing possessed. 'Brilliant! We can start trying to find out what he knows.' Her hair is stuck to one side of her face and her cheeks are sleep-flushed.

The chill is tinged with smoke from the dead fire. I take two steps and almost trip over Artemis, who rushes out from under my bed. She yawns, showing off a set of teeth like little chips of moon.

'Cats creep me out,' says Egg. 'All that staring, their eyes following invisible moving things in the air.' She gives a dramatic shudder. 'What does it want?'

'She's not an *it*.' I already do like cats, lots. Though I haven't a clue how to know whether they want to be stroked.

We climb into our stiff uniforms. My shirt and coat are miles too big, and the top hat keeps slumping down over my face. On the landing, I force myself not to look at the eye in the wood of the banister, but I can sense it watching. By the time we get downstairs, we're met by an open door and the sound of the car engine purring. Dawn is barely a scratch at the edge of the sky.

Shranken Putch sits behind the wheel, wearing a similar outfit to ours. The hat is so tall that it's wedged in against the ceiling, and I wonder how he's going to move his head.

As soon as we slam the passenger doors, the long car slides out from under the trees. Egg drums her hands on her thighs. 'Our first time in a car!' she squeals.

'It's a hearse,' corrects the undertaker, wearily. He drives it along a narrow path to the left of the house, downhill until we reach the road. Then we're zooming past the bus shelter, and soon we're passing through a sleepy little village, where all the shops and houses are still dark. There's a sign hanging from one of the shop fronts. Apparently, the village has quite an odd name.

WELCOME TO
KNUCKERHOLE VILLAGE

*Home of the 1645
Sussex witch trials*

Egg pinches me swiftly under my ribs, making me hiss. 'Did you see that?' she whispers excitedly. 'This is a witchy place!'

But seeing the word 'trials' sends my mind flickering back to Mistress Wolsley's office, where we read about the fate of Amara. What would someone have to do, to be tried as a witch? A sickly shiver skitters along my spine.

Underneath the sign, a cut-out shape of a witch swings in the breath of wind that's begun to stir. She's riding a broomstick with a cat sitting on the handle. There are signs in the window of a bakery about things like 'covenstead bread' and 'cauldron cakes'.

When I look back, the Ring is a blot of deeper night, watching the village from the hill above. I can just about distinguish the lines of the house where it huddles beneath the trees.

Egg doesn't waste any time. 'Mr Putch?'

His startled eyes find her in the mirror. 'No mister. Just Putch.'

'Okay. That sign, about the village. The witch trials . . .'

'A dark time in our history,' mutters Putch, eyes twitching between her face and the road ahead.

'Only in history?' presses Egg, leaning forward in her seat.

He harrumphs. 'Of course in history! Whenever did you hear of a witch, scurrying about in this day and age?' His body hunches over the steering wheel, face grown determined.

Egg bunches handfuls of her trousers in her fists. 'Mister –'

'No mister!'

'Um, we received a letter inviting us here, with a map and a travelcard. Did you send them?'

When he shakes his head, it moves independently of his wedged hat. 'All arranged for me.'

'Do you know who did send it? You see, we're not quite sure why we've been invited here.'

He shrugs. 'A letter came from the council, telling me to expect an assistant. I wouldn't worry about it too much. You'll have enough on your plate in a minute.'

'What if we *are* worried about it, though?' Egg persists.

I jab her, and she slaps my arm.

'Shall I write to the council asking for new assistants? Turf you out on the street?' he snaps.

'No.' Egg sniffs. 'Maybe – don't.'

'There we are, then.' Shranken Putch falls into a stormy silence, occasionally glaring at us in the mirror.

'I think that went really well,' I whisper, close to my sister's ear.

She pinches me.

By now, we've left the village behind us, and we're on a bigger road, with a few other cars and the occasional big lorry. Shranken Putch mutters insults about other drivers out of the corner of his mouth. As the sky begins to lighten, the road grows busier. I feel an unexpected pang of longing for the parlour, already. The place might be weird, but it's quiet and Artemis is there, and I prefer both of those things to busyness and noise.

After about half an hour, we turn off the road and pull up at a towering block of flats. Lights are on in lots of the windows. Shranken Putch climbs out of the car and pops open the boot, removing a bag and a folded metal contraption on wheels. We stumble after him, holding on to our hats in the strong wind that's kicked up. Putch presses a buzzer. The front door clangs open.

We squeeze into a lift and go up fifteen floors. Egg leans against the wall, snoozing, until the undertaker claps his hands in her face. She startles, then seethes like a boiling kettle.

Next we walk down a long, mildewed hallway and stand in front of a door. 'Be respectful,' the undertaker instructs. 'Do what I tell you. This is your first test.'

I wince, and Egg rolls her eyes.

He knocks on the door.

A man in a shirt and tie opens it. He's wearing a badge

around his neck that says *Ian Brunswick, Arundel District Council*. 'Ah, Mr Putch.' He says the name like it tastes bad in his mouth.

'No mister,' I say quietly, and both Ian Brunswick and my sister shoot startled looks at me.

The undertaker's lips quiver with the spectre of a smile. 'Coroner? Police? Family?' he demands.

'See for yourself,' retorts Ian Brunswick, thrusting a sheaf of papers at him. 'Bedroom.' He steps out of our way.

Putch tucks the paperwork into his bag and we move through a narrow, cluttered space. Egg bangs her knee on a table, and bites off a swear halfway through. The air is close, and tainted with stale smoke. A sense of dread begins to swill around in my stomach. When Shranken Putch opens the bedroom door, Egg stifles a yelp. A man is lying in bed, staring up at the ceiling. And, even though I'm no expert, he looks really quite a bit dead.

The next minutes pass in a sort of dream-like blur. Shranken Putch bows before the man, removing his hat. Then he takes a tape measure from his bag and measures him lengthways and crossways. As he does it, I become aware of a shimmering, flickering shape, that's a bit like when you've stared at a light for too long, and then it follows everywhere you look. The shimmer drifts after the undertaker's hands, and then pings into the air above the dead man's head, where it quivers almost expectantly. I shake my head, trying to clear my eyes, but the shimmering stays put. Every now and then, it darkens like a cloud. A smell seems to cling to it. A smell like damp, or drains.

Then Putch snaps the tape measure back and pockets it, before unfolding a cloth zip-up bag and laying it on the bed, next to the man. He pulls on a pair of blue plastic gloves, and throws some to us. 'Come on, then. Help me get him into the bag.'

'What?' bleats Egg.

I pull my gloves on. 'He said we have to help him get the body in the bag,' I tell her.

'I heard what he *said*, Elspeth,' she hisses, through tight teeth.

I don't know if it's because I'm not scared for once, and she needs to compete, or if it's because she wants to look tough, but Egg puts her gloves on and steps closer.

The man is unbelievably heavy.

'Put. Your. Backs into it!' instructs the undertaker, red-faced. He's astoundingly strong for such an old and thin-looking man.

We heave and lift and roll and push.

Once we've shifted the man into the bag, Putch turns to the metal thing on wheels, fiddling about until it makes a clicking sound and lengthens into a trolley. We realise both at the same time that we're going to be expected to help lift the body on to it.

Egg and I each take a leg and Putch takes the shoulders, and with an almighty effort we transplant the body on to the trolley. My arms are shaking and Egg is panting, sweat making little glistening rivers down her face. 'This is not on,' she mutters. As we leave the bedroom, Putch pushing the trolley and Egg pulling, the same pearly, shimmering shape as before flickers in the corner of my eye. But when I turn my head, it disappears.

Ian Brunswick opens the door for us and Putch gives him the barest nod before we leave.

We manage to cram the trolley into the lift at a diagonal angle, but only one of us can fit in with it, so Putch has me and Egg take the stairs all the way back down to the ground floor.

Outside, he's tapping his foot impatiently as we straggle through the double doors and into the waiting cold. Loading the bag into the back of the hearse is another sweaty challenge which makes Egg spit curses through her teeth like arrows. Finally, we slump into the passenger seats with exhaustion.

'I am not doing this again,' Egg whispers in my ear, while the undertaker's feet thud towards the driver's door.

'Work earns ceremony,' I remind her.

'This work is too hard,' she insists, eyes stormy. 'And it's disgusting. And I *told* you. I never would have got my ceremony, anyway.'

'Please don't say that.' I feel my stomach work itself into

a knot. 'How will you earn your soul?'

She shakes her head bitterly, and stares out of the window the rest of the way back to the funeral parlour.

12
Secrets

Artemis greets us in the driveway with a cheerful trill, fur sparkling with dew. Golden morning has cracked open across the Ring.

Putch has us lift the body out of the car and back on to the trolley. We wheel it through the hallway and into the laying-out room. He shows us where the coffins are kept, and how to match up the measurements with the correct-sized coffin. The whole time, I keep wondering about who the man was, and why the only person at his flat was someone from the council. I don't know what comes after death, but I assume that it's peace, for the Unwicked.

Horror nudges along every bone in my spine. What if we die Wicked?

Then I have to focus because Putch is opening the bag, and together we heave the body into the coffin, and Putch pushes the table forward – turns out it's on wheels – into a cupboard that is actually a freezer, and even though I'm not scared, that's when I start to feel a little bit shocked and sick about it all. It's also when I notice the pearly, shimmery haze again, concentrated in a patch in the air near the freezer. Watching it makes me feel dizzy.

In the middle of the room is a twisted brass dip in the floor, a spiral like the shape inside a person's ear. I stand and peer down into it. 'What's this?'

'Drainage,' barks the undertaker, and something about the way he says it makes me step away from the spiral quickly.

We all wash our hands, and then Putch leads us into the kitchen, and puts the kettle on for tea. 'I mostly do pauper funerals.' He fixes us in turn with his steely eye. 'We lay the bodies out here, because they've either got no homes, or not a soul to watch o'er them. Undertakers have always watched over the dead, between the death and the funeral. The cat shares the task.' A well-fed fire crackles in the grate. I watch the flames reflected in his eyes. 'We sing the wake-dirge, the old words to help prepare the soul for the great journey ahead.'

My mind snags on the word *soul*. I feel myself leaning closer to listen, my chair tipping on to its front feet. Could this place be the closest I've ever come to the thing I've always wanted most in the world?

'I don't understand,' squawks Egg, incredulously. 'What will we actually have to *do*?'

He stands up to make the tea, turning his back on us. 'I'll need you to help with funerals – organising, transferring the bodies, standing with me at the graveside for the funeral service. You can type death notices and we'll send them to the local paper. You'll need to answer the phone and take messages. There is a catalogue you can study, to learn all the coffins and shrouds.'

Egg kicks me under the table. She mouths, '*Bo-ring*,' eyes rolling around in her head like marbles. I can tell she thinks he's giving us a school lesson, but I'm not finding it boring at all.

He clears his throat. 'I can teach you to bathe, dress and do make-up for the dead, before the funerals. Then there are the funeral customs.'

Immediately, my sister's back straightens, and her eyes shine, clear and curious.

Shranken Putch plonks three scummy mugs of tea on to the table, and continues. 'We tell people to stop the clocks in the room the person died in to prevent bad luck, to cover the mirrors so the souls don't get trapped in the glass, and to turn family photographs face down so that the people in them won't be possessed by the spirit of the dead. And when a beekeeper dies, we tell the notifier of death to cover the hives in black crepe, to keep the bees alive.'

'Ooh!' interrupts Egg, grimacing with excitement.

The undertaker thins his lips at her. 'If you want to keep this job, you must learn all you can these coming weeks.'

I watch the undertaker's creased, gloomy face, and I smile. I'm certain the dead will be easier to deal with than the living.

'Thank you, Mister Putch,' I say quietly.

He looks at me and nods. 'No mister. Just Putch.'

Artemis hops up on to a chair and blinks at me slowly.

'That is a cat kiss,' says Shranken Putch, sullenly. Then he scrapes back his chair and strides from the kitchen. The cat leaps on to the stove top, where she starts washing a paw, splaying out her toes for thoroughness. The little moon on her collar gleams.

By the end of our first day, we're both exhausted. Shranken Putch set us about a hundred tasks each, including studying coffin catalogues, learning his dead people's make-up collection, doing general housework and reading the first three chapters of a book called *Hurstpier's Primary Funereal Tome* which, as it turns out, is not exactly light reading material. Lucky Mouldheels' got us used to hard work.

When we finally have permission to return to our little attic, Egg collapses into bed as though she was already asleep on her feet. I'm too tired to bother undressing for bed, so I just curl up on my side.

'Throw something at my head,' demands Egg, leaning up on to one elbow and staring at me.

'What?' I reply, through a yawn.

'Get that hairbrush and chuck it at me.' Her expression is deadly serious.

'*What?* No. Why?'

'I want to practise making Weird Things happen. Remember Ruby Thompson, when she threw that block of soap at my head and – I swear – it swerved round and thumped her instead?'

'I think you were exaggerating,' I grumble, pulling my blankets tighter. 'And I'm tired.'

I'm almost sure she won't be able to make anything happen. But I also don't want her to, because I don't want having some kind of special *power* to be another thing that makes us different from each other.

'Spel! How will I learn if I don't practise?'

With a groan of despair, I lurch out of bed, grab the brush from the table between our beds and hurl it straight at her excited face.

There's a crack, and Egg screams and buries her face in her hands. 'Spel!' Blood nudges out between her fingers. 'I think you've broken my nose!'

'I'm sorry!'

'You were supposed to warn me!'

'Should powers need warning?'

The Look she gives me could sour milk.

I pass her some tissues and she tips her head back and presses them against her nose.

'Is it stopping?' I ask. 'Are you getting any of those horrible big clots that slide down your throat?'

'Another word and I will be trying out the Weird Things on *you*!'

The bleeding stops pretty quickly. To make up for what I did, I agree to help her practise properly tomorrow. Then we settle down.

For a little while, the room is quiet. I feel my mind begin to drift.

I'm almost asleep when Egg pushes her whisper through the night's middle. 'I can't believe we're sleeping in the same house as a dead body!'

'Go to sleep,' I beg her. Honestly, sometimes what *I* can't believe is that I'm the younger one.

The blankets rustle as she turns over. Then, 'Spel!'

'*What?*'

'I knew I could smell a secret.'

'What do you mean?' I ask thickly, my mouth like cotton.

'Come and look at this!' says my sister, flapping a corner of her blanket around and jabbing her finger at the wall.

When I get out of bed I'm swaying on my feet with weariness, but I lean forward to look where she's pointing. Faint handwriting is etched into the wall just below the line of her mattress.

'It can't be,' I whisper.

'It is!' insists Egg.

I climb into her bed and lie flat so that my eyes are level with the writing. In the faintest pencil marking, someone has written a single word.

Amara.

'She was here.' Egg's voice seeps wonder.

'You don't know that. Loads of people must have that name.'

'Really, Spel? Don't you think it's a bit of a coincidence that we find out our mother's name after all these years, and then find the same name scratched into the wall at the place we've been summoned to? Plus, she's in that photo with the cat, inside the watch. It has to be her.' She pulls the watch from her pocket, cradling it between her hands.

You mean your *mother.*

The thought is too horrible to speak aloud, but it's not quite a new one. I still feel grim that there was almost no paperwork for me in those files. It's all very well for Egg to say it's because they've been lost. I bet she wouldn't be saying that if things were the other way around.

'Are you ignoring me now?' she sulks.

A sickly wave of fear and sadness rolls up through me. 'No,' I snap, skulking back to my own bed and clicking off the bedside lamp. 'It's just time to sleep.' I turn my back to her.

She's right that there's some kind of secret here – it feels like there could be many. Because what about the strange shimmers I saw at the dead man's flat, and again when we got back to the parlour?

Instead of Egg's inevitable retort, a scuffling starts – it's faint, somewhere outside the room. Then a snarling, a yipping and a rustling.

A high-pitched stuttering. A croaking, a jabbering.

I slip out of my bed again, stumbling towards hers, and she's already holding her blankets open for me, tucking us both in as soon as I've whisked my feet inside. She puts her chin on my shoulder as we listen. 'Foxes,' she murmurs, her breath warming my neck.

I shake my head in the heavy dark.

'Mmm,' she says. 'There must be cubs.'

But it can't be foxes, making that sound. We both know it. For one thing, it's not coming from outside. It's coming from underneath the floor, far below our beds. The metal frames are rattling slightly with it – mine more so, without my weight to hold it down. It goes on and on. Egg thumps her pillow, groaning. 'I wish it would stop!'

Then the noises stop abruptly. Egg rolls over in bed, loosening her held breath.

But a long, low growling starts, vibrating up through the floorboards. Egg shoots upright, clutching the blankets to her chest. Every muscle in my body tenses.

Then wailing – *human* wailing, and fragments of shouting that are oddly disconnected.

An image of the man we went to collect flashes into my mind. The cold, lonely room he was lying in, and the shimmery haze of half-light that floated around the room.

'What the hell is happening?' cries Egg.

'It's for your own good!' yells another voice – the voice of the undertaker, Shranken Putch.

Next to me, Egg's body tenses in a foreshadowing of movement.

'Don't,' I whisper.

'Come on,' she says, determined. She gives me a little push in my back.

So we slip out of bed, into the cold air. Our hands meet and we lace our fingers together, crossing the room and ghosting through the door. We tiptoe downstairs, feeling out for walls and handrails.

The noises grow louder. The space around us feels taut, like that feeling before a thunderstorm. I tighten my fingers around Egg's, and she squeezes back.

When we reach the landing outside the kitchen door, I sense the gulping void where the staircase to the basement drops away beside us.

Egg untwines her fingers from mine, and I hiss at her, but she's only gone for a second while she flips on the kitchen light, providing a pool for us to stand and shiver in.

The wailing and growling fill up the spaces in between the tattered words. It's definitely coming from down there.

'I don't want to stay here,' I murmur, and I don't even know if I mean here on the landing or here in this house, full stop. Either way, Egg lets me pull her away from the landing. We stumble back up the stairs to our room. Without a word, we climb back into her bed and pull the blankets tightly around us. But we can't shut out the chill.

13
A Pauper Funeral

The next day is the funeral of the man whose body we went to collect.

I can't stop thinking about those noises we heard, coming from downstairs. Morning has never come as such a relief. 'What do you think was going on last night?' I ask, while I'm buttoning up my black shirt.

Egg whirls towards me, splendid in her long coat and shining top hat. 'I don't know. But consider it another thing I intend to find out!'

We head downstairs. Egg grumbles her way down every step, saying she has more important work to do than 'lug dead bodies around with that old weirdo'.

'Like what?' I ask, shoving my top hat on to my head.

'Um, like finding out about what happened in the witch trials and what happened to our mother? And how we're going to help the other girls?'

It's the first time I've known her to be so interested in anything in our whole lives. She's been full of romance for herself; wearing a red faux-fur jacket stolen from the dead, lighting smudgy sticks of incense and surrounding herself in circles of candles stolen from Putch's funeral supplies. Trying to 'find myself in this Witch Thing'. It's really irritating.

'You can't exactly leave me to do it all alone. You're expected at the funeral. Putch needs our help.' The cat makes a silent yowl and bumps against my ankles.

Egg storms away into the kitchen, but I pause in the hallway outside. To my right, the floor drops away into the staircase that leads to the basement. I stare down into the gloom, wondering. What is down there, and why can't we see it? What was making all that noise last night?

Shranken Putch is in the kitchen, standing at the sink and furiously scrubbing his nails with a brush, his elbow jabbing out sideways like he's sawing at a violin. The whole kitchen looks like a baking bomb has exploded – all the surfaces are covered in puddles of egg and milk, and splodges of flour. There are dirty pans and moulds and rolling pins everywhere. We watch the undertaker for a minute or two. He gasps when the brush bristles jab at the skin under his nails and blood sprinkles the bowl of water he's leaning over. 'Great dirty stinking thing,' he mutters. 'Terrible beast. Should have known better, should Putch.'

'Maybe the noises were him baking,' mutters Egg to me, out of the corner of her mouth. 'Good morning, Shranken Putch!' she sings, cheerily.

121

I wrinkle my nose at her. I know she's only trying to charm him into answering her wretched questions. And probably so she can get out of helping, at some point.

Putch almost hits the ceiling with his head when he startles. 'Girls! Tall one and bald one. Why are they always pressing eyeballs on Putch? Girls always cluttering the place up.' He continues grumbling, more and more incoherently. Wow. He is in a seriously bad mood. 'I suppose you'll be wanting tea? Guzzling me out of house and home, aren't you!' He strides across to a cupboard and begins rattling the things inside. 'There! There! There! And there!' he snaps, banging two mugs, a teapot and a grubby-looking old tin on to the counter.

Egg isn't bothered by his mood. She sets about making the tea, and he drops the scrubbing brush in the bowl of water.

'Be ready by quarter to eight,' he says. He darts into the pantry, and comes back carrying a tray covered with a tea towel under his arm. Then he storms off.

'What was that?'

Egg shrugs. 'Something for the funeral, probably.'

While the tea brews, I stand by the sink and press on to the balls of my feet to peer through the filmy glass at the trees outside, their branches waving this way and that as though in warning.

My eyes drop to the bowl of water in the sink. I watch the brush floating there, and a frown catches my brows and draws them together.

The surface of the water is cluttered with thin, clear shapes that look like leaves, or wings, or petals. Each one is about an inch long and half an inch wide. The water is choked with them. I dip my fingers into the water and lift one out, placing it gently on my palm.

It's a filmy membrane, with jagged edges like rows of little teeth. Flecks of gold glitter in the thin flesh.

I don't think it's a wing, or a petal. And it's definitely not a leaf. No, it's more like . . . a *scale*.

'Tea's ready!' Egg calls, pulling my focus. 'I've just put some toast on, too.'

I turn towards my sister. There's a thump. Water splashes me. I twist back to the sink. The bowl of water has overturned and the things that were choking the surface are slithering and slipping down the plughole, making it throb and gurgle. I screw up my nose. I never even touched it.

The funeral happens outdoors, in a graveyard. We drive there under a leaden sky heavy with the promise of rain. We pass the village again. Egg and I stare out at the shops and houses, and the people bustling around. People who grow still and watchful as the hearse sweeps by.

Putch mutters that it hasn't taken long to arrange this funeral, because the man had no family, no possessions and no will. His funeral is council-funded, so now I know what

Putch was talking about before. Pauper funerals are for people with no family, no close friends and no money. Which is the saddest thing I've ever heard, even though Egg doesn't seem bothered by any of it in the slightest.

The only mourner is a thin rain that begins to slant down out of the ashen sky. The three of us stand around the coffin. Across the graveyard, four suited pallbearers – men Putch hires to carry the coffin at funerals – lean against their car, smoking and wearing sunglasses even though there's no sun. Someone from the council sits watching from her car, waiting for it to be over.

At the last moment, a woman turns up clutching a bunch of roses. She sidles across to me, and when I give her a questioning look, she whispers that she goes to as many of the funerals of strangers as she can.

'There's always one,' mutters Putch, eyeing her with distaste.

But I think it's kind of her, so I smile. 'We're glad to have you here,' I tell her. Especially since no one else has come. Again, I find myself wondering why this man was so alone.

Rain runs down the side of my top hat, over the brim and down my neck, making me squirm. Shranken Putch gives a short reading about the man. Turns out his name was Oliver Todd, and he'd been an ambulance driver before he retired, which was quite a long time ago.

Thunder cracks in the sky, and the rain suddenly

strengthens, hissing down on to the trees and gravestones. Shranken Putch pockets his speech and makes us throw handfuls of dirt on to the coffin. I'm enjoying the fact that when someone dies, being quiet is what's needed. It's one of the only times when the whole world doesn't want you to be loud.

The coffin is cranked down into the ground. The woman from the council hurries over, ticking something on her clipboard. The pallbearers drive off, tyres squealing on the wet ground. It's up to me and Egg to shovel the wet earth on top of the coffin, while Shranken Putch slopes off with the council woman to sign some papers.

Soon our uniforms are welded to our skins, and my teeth are rattling in my head. I lean on my shovel, wiping the rain out of my eyes.

'Hold this,' says Egg, passing me her shovel. Then she begins to back away, glancing around.

'What are you doing?' I snap, stepping towards her.

'No, Spel, you stay here. I won't be long.' She sets off at a run, feet slipping in the mud, taking a wide arc around the edge of the graveyard and disappearing down the driveway we drove up.

I dig the tips of both shovels into the sticky earth and yell after her, but my voice is swallowed by the nerves sitting in my throat, and the watching gravestones.

I'm pacing miserably when I notice the shape – a hazy

outline of a man, drifting between nearby gravestones. It's a clear shimmering, a bit like the heat that rises from a candle flame, but tinged with flashes of blue and green. I rub my eyes, but when I open them again it's still there. My mind flickers back to that shimmery shape I saw in the corner of my eye, at the dead man's flat, and then later at the funeral parlour. As I watch, the outline alternately throbs clearer and then more faint, but when it's clear, it's like there's a real man there, floating just off the ground. The more I look, the stronger his presence grows. He turns his head, and stares straight at me.

While he stares, his outline darkens like thunder, and the smell of drains drifts into my nose again.

'What are you?' I whisper. I feel like the greyness of the day is squeezing into my brain, turning everything too vivid and too improbable.

Shranken Putch is by my side, though I never noticed his approach. He shields his eyes. 'I can't see anything.'

A cold feeling sweeps through my body and across my skin, as though someone invisible has brushed a hand along my arm.

'Come on,' he says, hoisting the shovels out of my grip. 'Let's go. Where's the bigger one?'

I swallow. 'I don't know. She ran off. She said she wouldn't be long.'

A grievous frown settles over him. 'Did she, now? Liberties taken, left and centre.'

The rain thickens and the cold nips harder then, so we hurry over to the hearse. When I glance back, the shape has dwindled to the barest of shimmers. But I still want to get away from here.

We climb into the car and Putch switches on the car headlamps as we glide away.

'Wait!' I squeal.

'We'll find her,' he mutters darkly. 'Hopefully before anyone else does.'

'Before who does?'

His silvery eyes flicker to my face, once, in the mirror. Then he stares straight ahead again.

We find her tramping back towards the graveyard, a few minutes' drive away, sodden but grinning.

Putch swoops in with the car and pulls up beside her, clearly before she's noticed us because she jumps backwards, glaring. She clicks the passenger door open and makes me scoot over. The car moves off again and they both maintain a sullen silence.

'I – needed to find something in town,' Egg offers, finally. She digs her fingertips into the seat in front.

'Valuable place you have, as my assistant. Nowhere else for you to go, is there?'

Egg opens her mouth to reply, but he cuts her off.

'Not sure what you think a job is, but it involves staying until the work is done. Not abandoning your co-workers. Not running off in the rain when who knows what might be looking for you.'

'Who?'

'Who what?'

They're duelling with words that might as well be knives.

'Who might be looking for us?'

He clamps his jaws shut. They glare at each other in the mirror.

'Where did you go?' I whisper to her. 'What were you doing?'

But Egg keeps her jaws clamped shut, too.

I clench my toes in frustration, stabbing patterns into the steamed window with a fingertip.

Back at the parlour, we stamp off the mud on the door mat. 'Into the kitchen with you,' instructs Putch. 'Time to warm up and dry out.'

Egg hangs back, chewing her lips moodily.

But it turns out that Shranken Putch is a master baker, and while we were out the house has filled with delicious smells. We peel off our hats and coats and slump into kitchen chairs. Putch brings out a cake that is deep, chocolatey and layered with thick wedges of cream. I imagine how scandalised the Mistresses would be. *Chocolate cake for lunch!* Hot chocolate bubbles away in a cast-iron pan. Egg kicks out at the table legs and rolls her eyes everywhere. But a word I had no idea I knew bubbles up into my brain, like one of the bubbles in the chocolate. Cosy. Is this *cosy?*

I give the old man a small smile.

Which he flinches at. 'What you doing?'

Um. 'Smiling?'

'Oh.' He coughs. 'It just looked a bit . . . odd, is all. If you don't mind my saying.'

'Well, I don't do it much!' I squeak.

Egg lets out a clatter of laughter so loud that Shranken Putch starts violently. He puts a hand on his chest and gapes at Egg. 'You'll wake the dead,' he accuses.

There's a beat of silence, and then we're *all* falling about laughing, clutching our sides, chairs, each other, anything. I laugh helplessly, painfully, my face pulled apart by the laughter.

Egg ruins the fun by asking more questions. 'What're you keeping in the basement, Shranken Putch?'

He places his fork down, hands shaking. 'Look here, girlie. You've no business asking things like that. Especially after your disappearing act today.'

'Haven't I? We know you're keeping something in there. We've heard noises.'

'Knew you two would bring trouble to my door.' Putch harrumphs. 'You need to forget about what's down those stairs, and worry about your work. You'll have plenty to keep you occupied.'

'If you want us to forget about it, then you have to tell us the truth. About why we're here, and what's really going on.'

I can almost see steam beginning to seep from his ears. 'I didn't want to tell you anything, because there. Is. Nothing. To tell!'

Egg leans forward, speaking urgently. 'We know about our mother – Amara Penhaligon. She was a witch, and there's a photo of her with Artemis, and her name is written on the wall upstairs, and we know we're witches, too.' She fishes in her pocket and brings out a thin booklet, folded in half. She spreads it smooth on the table. 'There were witches here, once. Looks like they were as hated as we've always been. Now there are witches here again.'

The booklet says *History of the Knuckerhole Witch Trials*. 'Where did you get that?' I ask, turning to goggle at her.

She flashes me a small, satisfied smile. 'Tourist Information Centre. Amazing what you can find when you show some initiative.'

She doesn't even look abashed when Putch and I both glare at her. An icy calm settles over the kitchen.

I look at Putch and shake my head to make it clear that I do not agree with a thing she's said. 'I'm not one,' I whisper.

Out of nowhere, Artemis vaults on to the table, sending Egg's cutlery crashing to the floor. 'Oh, god!' snaps Egg, clutching the ends of her hair. 'Where did you spring from?'

The cat stands close to the undertaker, staring straight into his eyes. A long, low growl begins to emit from her sleek black throat.

'I wasn't going to get angry with them,' he says, letting out a tight puff of breath. 'And I *was* going to tell them!'

The cat leaps from the table to the kitchen counter and perches contentedly on top of the bread bin, where she washes a paw as though it is the most important thing to be doing in the world.

The undertaker speaks from between clenched teeth. 'I know who you are,' he replies. 'Blood never forgets. Not completely. Once a witch, always a witch, or so the saying goes.'

Blood will out, Miss Wrythe. Blood tells all.

'So we *are* witches.' Egg's face is rapt.

He nods. 'You were, once. You are, yes. The magic in your blood cannot be undone. That so-called school of yours may have tried to tame it, but magic knows how to grow deep roots into bone, and survive in the harshest of conditions.'

Despite myself, I feel my bones responding to the word *witch*. A picture flashes in my mind, of people with starlight in their eyes and mud under their nails. But at the same time, terror grips me tightly around the throat, squeezing the vulnerable flesh there. All I want is my ceremony. All I want is for someone who matters to tell me I'm good.

'I'm not,' I say again. 'The papers we found said Amara only had one child.'

He gives me a long, grave look. 'Certain as the moon, Amara had two children.'

So we were part of a family, once. What an unfamiliar thought. My heart lifts a little, though it's a confusing feeling. Because I definitely want to share any mother Egg has, so nothing divides us, but we know that mother was a murderer, and a witch.

'So you knew her!' Egg beams.

He nods. 'She was apprenticed here.'

'Did she want to become an undertaker?'

'She showed promise as my assistant.' Mysterious conflicts shift underneath the surface of his skin. 'She would have been a great undertaker, had she completed her training.'

Sounds like she enjoyed the work here, like me!

'What happened?' asks Egg.

He stares from one of us to the other, and draws a deep breath. 'Once, there were many Others. Creatures that took different shapes. Rare animals that thrived, before they were hunted out of existence. People with ways of sensing the mysteries of this world, and ways of communing with them. These isles were steeped in magic.' Putch stares down at his hands. 'Thirteen years ago, the final battle in a great, longstanding war was fought, and won by the wrong side. They took full control. The last magical places were destroyed. Magic became a crime, and the Others were hunted – some to extinction.' Putch falls into a deep silence, eyes glazed, until Artemis mews from the bread bin and the undertaker startles.

Thirteen years ago? It's strange to think of all that going on while I was a blissfully unaware baby. Gooseflesh spreads across my body. The idea of being hated is nothing new to me. But being hunted – that feels like something all together worse. Like hate in motion. A memory of the shadow creature at Mouldheels' School slithers in the back of my mind.

'The witches helped defend trees and plants and creatures. Moon-attuned folk, they were, celebrating the cycles of the earth and sky.' His eyes flick to my face. 'They never deserved such a fate.'

'But what does it *mean*, to be witches?' demands Egg, greedily.

Putch speaks gently. 'There were witches strongly connected with the element of earth, others with air, some with fire, or water, and more rarely, witches of the spirit realms. But what it really means to be witches is to be plugged in to nature's ways. It's to *be* nature's voice, keeper of the old ways, of the *wise* ways. That wily otherworldliness gave the witches keen senses and, often, strange powers.'

I can feel myself goggling at him.

'So they don't do curses and strike people down with the evil eye?' asks Egg. 'Or ride broomsticks and have warty noses?'

'It couldn't be anyone's fault if they had a warty nose!' he splutters. 'Those are lies. Centuries-old, but still alive, I see!'

'How do you know all this?' says Egg, leaning back in her chair.

Muscles flicker in his jaw. 'Witches often came to the Ring to meet. Hedgerow Allies, too.' He speaks again before Egg can ask. 'Country people, like myself, living close with the land, who respected the witches' kinship with nature. The last time the witches met here, you were a toddling thing of two, and *you* were a swollen belly.' He points at each of us in turn.

Fascination ripples through me. I glance around the room. We were here before, all that time ago. We were here with our mother. At a *witch* meet.

'What were they doing here?'

'They came to celebrate the full moon esbat. They also came for a war council. Your mother was in deep trouble. She had endured trial as a witch and with the help of her friends, had managed to escape while awaiting her execution.'

I nibble my fingernail. 'Was this before or after she killed seven people?'

Egg tuts at me. 'Spel!'

Shranken Putch rubs his face wearily, every muscle of his body seeming to sag earthwards. 'That is a lie.'

'How can it be?' I mutter. 'We saw it in print.'

The undertaker offers a strained smile. 'Do not believe everything you read, child! It was a terrifying time. The lies spread about witches were the most vicious they'd been for centuries. Everything was blamed on them: fires, floods, sickness, drought, accidents. Then new laws were passed. Laws that, once and for all, made being a witch and practising magic a crime.'

'Who spread the lies?' I ask. 'Who made the laws?'

'The Hunt.' He says it gravely, and as though he already wishes he hadn't.

'The Hunt?' repeats Egg, hugging herself against the chill of his words.

'The witches were followed to their moon-meet. Their plans were incomplete. An enemy blended into their midst

135

– a corrupt witch, who had been suspected of working with the Hunt. Your mother lost her life, that night. The exact events were not witnessed by anyone. The truth died with them both.'

'This all happened the same night I was born?' I ask, mind wheeling. If she'd been pregnant with me when she arrived at the Ring, she can't have been when she died.

Putch narrows his eyes at me, and gives a barely perceptible nod. 'The loss of Amara struck the witches like a hammer blow. The rest of us fought hard to craft new identities for her children. So the main thing you need to know is that if any unusual abilities start to show in you, you *must* keep them hidden, as I will do my best to keep you. Heads down, weather-eyes open. That's the plan.'

Unusual abilities. Weird Things. The question floods my mind with an urgency that spills my words without hesitation. 'What happened to everyone at our school?'

Sadness traces a gentle fingertip across the undertaker's face.

But before he can speak, the death phone rings.

14
Stop the Clocks, Cover the Mirrors

The phone shrills along the hallway and into the kitchen. 'You can get that.' The undertaker gestures at us, looking exhausted as anything. 'I think I've earned a rest.'

'You can't open up a conversation as major as that and then snap it shut again!' Egg protests.

'I've already told you that you're beastly witches!' The undertaker clutches his head as though to stop it falling off. 'Is nothing ever enough?'

'No, because we already knew that,' says Egg, a little unfairly. 'I asked why we're here, and what's really going on.'

I reach over and touch Egg's arm. 'Maybe we should be patient,' I whisper. 'Putch has told us lots of things.' Lots of things that I need time to untangle, instead of adding more mess to it all.

But she shrugs me off. Patience is not a creature she entertains. The phone cries again, filling the hallway with urgency.

'Tell them to stop the clocks, cover the mirrors, turn down

the photographs and get off my back!' hisses the undertaker, hurrying to his feet and out of the kitchen.

Egg bangs her fist on the table. Then she stares at me. 'It's your turn to answer it, you know.'

'Don't take your impatience out on me.' Dread plops into my stomach. 'I can't do it.'

She makes a big 'L' with her fingers. *Loser.* 'Spel, I can't do everything for you. You have to face your fears sometime.'

The phone stops ringing, and I can't stop myself sagging in relief. But then it starts again, after only a few seconds. Terror reclaims its grip on my throat. 'Can't you just –'

'No!' My sister sips her tea, thinking she's so splendid and grown up. 'You're like my own little shadow. If I always do things for you, then how will you ever get over being frightened of them?'

Her words swirl together with other hurtful times, like when our dorm-mates said I never had my own opinions, or asked me if I'd forgotten how to talk. Maybe I'm not a real person at all – I'm not a witch, we're not even really sisters, and the real Spel Wrythe is lurking somewhere, waiting to step in and replace me.

I will never matter. I will never be good. I will never have a soul. The pain turns to rage. I wait one more second before rushing from the kitchen.

I step closer to the screaming black box and wrench the handset from its cradle, pressing it to my ear. 'What do you want?' *Oops*. 'Um, I mean, you've reached the funeral parlour of Shranken Putch, undertaker of the Ring. How may we help you today?'

I jot down the details of the death on the little notepad. 'Stop the clocks,' I tell them. 'Cover the mirrors. Turn down the photographs. The undertaker will come.'

I hang up the phone as Egg thuds past me, hair in a messy bun and another mug of tea snug in her hand. She wrenches open the cupboard under the stairs and pulls out the heavy black drapes for covering the mirrors. We carry out the customs at the parlour, too, ready for bringing the bodies here. Putch says we also do it out of respect and solidarity with the dead.

I run into the sitting room and rip open the glass covering of the clock on the mantelpiece, wrapping my fingers around its little brass heart, until it stops dead against my skin. I've already half turned away when I notice. The clock hasn't quite stopped. The long, slim needle of a second hand is quivering, like what happened at school. Then the second hand crunches, very slowly and deliberately, *backwards*.

'Egg?' I whisper.

'What?' she snaps, face half obscured behind the drapes.

'The clock . . .'

'Didn't you hear me, like the *thousand* times I said it before? I will not do everything for you, Elspeth.' She heads across the sitting room to the nearest mirror, throwing a drape over it like she's netting a prize.

I can't believe her sometimes! 'No, I've done it, you idiot!'

'Good for you.'

The second hand crunches back another second. My stomach twists. An icy feeling trickles over me.

When Shranken Putch slouches through the sitting room, he stops abruptly next to me and stares at the clock. He stares from the clock, to me, and back again, his jaw slack and his eyebrows quirked up almost into his hair.

'Shranken Putch, you were about to tell us –'

'The Other Way,' he croaks, interrupting me.

I press my lips together, nerves jumping straight to attention and making my palms wet. 'Um?'

'It's turning the Other Way.' He reaches out and places a gentle palm over the clock's hands. Under his influence, the clock sighs to a stop. 'You did that.'

I step back, fear sparking. Shranken Putch is looking at me as though I'm a ghost.

15
The Golden-Haired Man

The secret life of Spel Wrythe: star-fishing

1. *Egg says if she had a bigger bed she'd stretch out her arms and legs like a starfish*

2. *She'd call it star-fishing*

3. *But I'd use that name for something else*

4. *For looking out of the window and hauling a star down to earth from the sky*

5. *With nothing but the power of my Wicked eyes*

'Elspeth Wrythe,' crows the Mistress. 'You have proven beyond all doubt that girls are without souls, and the wickedest of earthly creatures. You have failed to qualify for ceremony. You shall remain soulless for this life's duration, and onwards into the next.' She smiles, and her face looms closer, and closer, and closer . . . and then her skin grows scales, and her eyes begin to blaze, as bright as a torch . . . and I'm falling into the stone basin, full of bubbling ceremonial water . . .

I wake up panting and sweating, the booming voice still

echoing inside my skull. As my heartbeat slows, I look over at Egg, sitting up in bed and practising her powers. As I watch, she strokes her fingers through the air, as though pulling at something. And the little pile of paperclips in her lap flurries up into a whirlwind before her face, glinting silver as a shoal. The sight sends tingles of shock and excitement through my body. But I also wonder, as I have so many times before, how she can be content to remain Wicked and soulless. Where does she think we'll go when we die, if we have no souls?

Shranken Putch told us to keep our abilities hidden. He said I made the clock turn the Other Way. Does that count as something that needs to be kept secret? But also – the thought thumps behind my eyes – secret from who? There's just me, my sister, the cat and the undertaker here, and they know everything that happens. So who does he want us to keep it hidden *from*?

The day is bright and clear, with the trees' arms black and velvety against the sky. How can the world let itself be bright when my blood is dark with fear? I keep thinking about the noises we heard coming from the basement, and how Shranken Putch says we're witches, and how our mother was hunted. We might have escaped the school, but are we safe here? Can we be safe anywhere? The only thing that makes me feel better is knowing that Amara didn't really hurt all those people.

Shranken Putch stands by the window, slurping a cup of tea. He's wearing an old orange jumper the colour of the leaves outside, with holes at the elbows. The house is full of a smell of burnt bread. There's a long, angry-looking scratch on his face. Like a claw mark.

Nothing ever feels the same twice, in this parlour. It seems to change size and shape, so that I might trip on a stair I should have learned the depth of by now, or take a wrong turn where there should be no other option. The place has moods as wild as the wind. The strange noises in the basement keep happening, whenever we collect a body. Every time Egg tries to ask Putch about it, he turns quiet as stone.

But this place already feels a lot more like home than the school where I spent my whole life up until this point.

The undertaker scrutinises my face for a moment, as though trying to see the thoughts squirming beneath the bones. 'Eggs want collecting.'

I stare back at him, unable to understand what on earth he could mean. 'I think she's gone off walking somewhere,' I say, finally.

'No, no – *eggs*.' With a great wheezing sigh, he stoops to rummage in a cupboard, producing a small wicker basket which he pushes into my hands. 'Go on with you to the henhouse, then!'

'Oh.' I take the basket from him, familiar embarrassment flooding my body.

Outside, there's a fresh crispness to the air that smells faintly smoky. I walk down the path through Putch's little vegetable garden, take a left at the shed, and walk towards the wooden henhouse. The edge of the ring of trees brushes the left of my view, and the hill slopes downwards from here, towards the town in the distance. The grass sparkles with frost.

The air is close and warm inside the henhouse, and full of morning clucking. I greet the hens, running my fingers across their smooth red-brown feathers. We had hens at Mouldheels', but they were packed tight in cages, and never let out to roam. I never knew what their feathers felt like until we came here.

When I feel underneath the hens, inside their nests, my fingers close over the smooth, oval shapes of their eggs. Gently, I lift them into my basket. 'Thank you,' I whisper.

When I creak the henhouse door back open, voices are carried to me on the wind. They're coming from the front of the house.

Staying low, I scurry around the edge of the house, squeezing between the wall and the overgrown branches of an old pear tree. A car is parked in the driveway, next to Putch's black hearse. A clinging mist has crept up the hill to tangle in the branches of the Ring.

When I peer around the corner of the house, I can just see the front door, and Putch's big feet sticking out over the threshold. His hands are gesturing wildly. A man and a woman stand under the eaves of the house, wearing faces as serious as a storm cloud.

As they stand there, the bright morning darkens with clouds scudding across the sun. They're too far away for me to make out their words. But when they turn and walk back towards their car, a shock runs through my body, as sharp as the edge of a knife. The man wears a long green coat, and shiny brown shoes. A pair of gold wire glasses are perched on his nose, and his golden hair catches the light as he moves.

It's the man who helped us get on to the bus, on our way to Victoria station.

'No mister,' calls out the undertaker. 'Just Putch!' Then the door thumps shut.

I wrack my brain, trying to remember the day we ran away from Mouldheels'. My memory holds mostly rain and mud and fear. But I remember that man like a bolt of lightning, etched on to the backs of my eyes.

Back inside the kitchen, I stamp on the doormat and breathe into my hands to bring my frozen toes and fingers back to life. Shranken Putch peers into the basket and makes a pleased face at the sight of the six eggs nestled there.

'Who were you talking to before?' I ask him.

His face tightens. 'No one. Just . . . people. Wanting a funeral.' He busies himself with pots and pans and plates.

'Why didn't they phone?' Egg's suspicious tones float in from the hallway.

'I'm sure I've seen the man once before,' I tell him.

Putch concentrates hard on poaching the eggs I collected.

'*Really?*' says Egg, to his turned back. 'You're just going to blank us?' She flounces to her usual seat, grabs a spoon and lays it flat on the table in front of her. Then she starts staring at it, really hard, with this fierce focus. At first, nothing happens. Then there's a faint smell of burning that creeps into my nose, and a restless feeling. Like before a storm. The spoon wiggles on the table. It's just the tiniest movement, but it's enough to send Egg into eye-gleaming triumph. 'I did that,' she breathes. The tension dissolves. Maybe a spoon is heavier than a lapful of paperclips, even when you're using your mind to move it.

My mind travels backwards again as I remember all the Weird Things that happened at Mouldheels'. I haven't felt even the slightest stirring of anything magical inside me, which makes me both relieved and jealous, all at once.

Egg focuses on her spoon again.

Artemis yowls at her.

Putch finally turns away from the stove to look at us. 'What're you up to?'

With a concentration that makes a bead of sweat roll down the side of her head, Egg lifts the spoon up, where it hovers and twitches, and moves towards Putch.

Shranken Putch yelps, and snatches the spoon out of the air. 'What did I tell you about keeping your abilities hidden?'

Egg glares up at him. 'From who? You're the only one here!'

'Anyone could appear,' he retorts, flinging the spoon back into the cutlery drawer. 'Your dabblings could draw the wrong kind of attention to my parlour.'

'If magic is a crime,' I say, with more poison than I expected, 'then we should just have her arrested right now.'

'Oh, that's very nic–' Egg starts to say, but Artemis growls and lashes out at me, swatting at my face. She keeps her claws retracted, but her fur is raised into spikes, and her shoulders are hunched.

Egg shoos her away. 'What's the matter with that ridiculous creature?'

Artemis hunches stonily on the floor underneath the heater, watching us from narrowed eyes.

Putch grumbles and glooms like a drain. 'What a jagged thorn-patch that wretched beast is.'

Artemis responds with a distinct, prolonged hiss.

'Girl didn't know what she was saying,' he says, in a more soothing tone.

Artemis turns her back.

Me and Egg exchange a weary, confused look.

After breakfast, I decide I need some time alone, before we have to get ready for a funeral in the afternoon. On my way upstairs, I notice Egg poking around on the mantelpiece in the sitting room, peering behind the clock and then sidling over to the bookshelves. 'What are you up to?' I ask, pausing on the stairs. But she doesn't even hear me. She looks totally lost in thought.

At the top of the attic stairs, I hurry past the dark eye in the wood of the banister. I hate how it always feels like it's watching me.

Up in our room, I sit on my bed, huddled among the blankets. Artemis comes to make friends again, wedging herself between my hip and the wall, paddling her paws against my thigh and blinking up at me. 'Apology accepted,' I tell her. She nudges my hand with her head, so I give her a good scratch between the ears.

The witch trials booklet is sticking out from under Egg's pillow. I reach across the space between our beds and ease it free. Artemis chirps, pressing her nose against the cover.

I peel the booklet open, and the map of the Ring, the one that was sent to us at school, flutters out. Egg must have stuffed it in here. Inside the booklet, the image of a gruesome-looking witch stares up at me, mouth twisted into a cackle. That's what I'd always thought of as a witch. But now, my own sister's face is conjured by the word. So it doesn't seem fair, or accurate.

Don't let our quaint surroundings and gentle country lifestyle deceive you, assures the text. *Knuckerhole village – named for the legendary water dragon lairs dotted throughout this ancient county – was once the setting for some of the most infamous witch trials witnessed by this country, most taking place in the seventeenth century.*

Water dragons? My mind flits back to Putch telling us about the Others once living here. Goodness knows how many beings might have dwelled around here, once.

The well at Knuckerhole is thought to date back to the 11th century, and in old country farming records there are accounts of witches and dragons alike, rampaging through the land, causing sickness and blight. Fortunately, rescuers in the form of organised Huntsmen and women aligned themselves to defend the people against this malevolence.

'Bleh.' I stroke Artemis. 'Some of these words are so difficult.'

She winks at me.

Trials by water are known to have taken place in the village square in the 1600s, and continued into more modern times, for as long as the witch scourge weighed upon us. These trials resulted in many an execution, usually by burning at the stake. This also took place in the village square, not far from where the village sign hangs today. If you visit the museum, you will find a range of mementos from this time, including real locks of witch hair, scraps of burnt clothing, and even a bottle of teeth!

The cold creeps close to my bones. I fling the booklet away from me, sickened by the thought that anyone would display things like a dead person's teeth.

Egg's voice drifts up the stairs towards me. 'Spel?'

I sigh. At least I got half an hour to myself. She barges the door open and sticks her head into the room. Artemis raises startled green eyes towards her. 'There you are! What are you doing skulking around up here?'

'Trying to get five minutes' peace.'

She blows a raspberry. 'Whatever. I need you to help me with something important.' She drops her voice to a whisper. 'There must be a key to that secret room in the basement. The door's always locked, but I've never seen any keys anywhere. I've started searching every room in the parlour. I need you to search in here.'

So that's what she was doing in the sitting room. Before I can say a word, she thumps out of the room again. 'Look in all the nooks and crannies,' she calls back through the wood. 'Not the first place someone would think to look!'

I scowl after her. 'Of course, *Your Majesty*.'

Artemis yawns and stretches. I wrap a blanket around me as I begrudgingly shuffle around, letting my eyes scan the room. Which takes all of five seconds. I open the drawers and look on the windowsill, and then stand back, baffled. Why would she ever think something important would be hidden in here?

Just then, a shuffling sound starts in the chimney. I step towards the fireplace and squat in front of it, lifting my gaze to stare up into the blackness. The shuffling quickly turns into a thrashing, like flailing wings. What if a bird's stuck up there?

Lucky I didn't light a fire! I kneel on the cold hearth stones and wriggle forward, until my head is engulfed by the long black throat of the chimney. I look up. The walls are blistered and gritted with ash. I scan them, up and down, side to side.

There – a shape, heavy and black, stuck fast in the chimney's gullet. I lean on to my knees and reach up, brushing the thing with my fingertips. Is it dead? Suddenly, while I'm touching its shadowy edge, it shifts under my fingers, slips, scrapes the wall, and then starts falling. I shriek, pulling out of the way, as a great splutter of dust and bits of ash cascade down. When my eyes have stopped streaming from the dust, I see it: lying amid the embers, a wink of old gold.

My first thought is that I have actually found the key Egg's looking for. I glance around me, waiting, barely breathing, but no one comes. The house is still, and only Artemis peeps at me from her spot on my bed, tucked neatly between the wall and my pillows, purring like a train.

I shuffle forward and dip my fingers into the ashes, picking out the gold thing lying there. But it's not a key. It's a ring. There's nothing else, even though the creature that fell was big and struggling. Where did it go? A creeping sensation edges up my spine. Whatever it was, it reminded me a lot of the creature that flew at the window of our dorm.

Artemis stops purring, carving the room open into the loudest silence.

I turn the ring in the fading light. It's a smooth band, with a tiny green gemstone set in the middle. There are symbols etched around the inside. The letters aren't from the alphabet – they don't look like anything I've seen before. I slip the ring on to my middle finger, guilt nudging my insides. Who did this belong to? Why was it in the chimney?

When I twist the ring on my finger, I can feel the symbols rubbing against my skin.

I slowly become aware of a low whining noise, like a drill.

Artemis is standing up on my bed, with her head hunched low between her shoulders, fur spiked on end. Her tail is puffed up big and bristling. Her eyes are fixed on the ring. She utters a jagged hiss.

'Artemis?' Suddenly, I'm scared she's going to scratch me.

She continues to yowl until I've taken the ring off. Then she races for the door, paws it open and shoots away down the stairs.

I sit on my bed, staring numbly at the ring in my palm. Egg's footsteps bang the bare steps up to the attic. I stuff the ring under my pillow and keep my face blank as I turn towards her.

Her hand dives into her pocket and she pulls out a long key, dangling it and grinning at me triumphantly. 'I'm going to find out what's in that basement.'

'Why?'

'Aren't you sick of being told what to do and what not to do?'

I shake my head. 'Not really. I don't *know* what to do, otherwise. And *why* do you need to know what's in the basement?'

She sighs dramatically. 'Because it's a mystery. Because the old toad won't answer our questions properly. Because we've found out a few things but all it's done is made me hungry to know more! Because what else is there to do?'

'Lots.'

'I'm not going to work for some old man in a tumbledown cottage in the middle of nowhere for the rest of my life,' she huffs. 'And I'm not interested in coffin silk and shrouds, either. We've got to make sure the other girls are safe! We need to find out where he keeps his money if we're going to be able to go and find them. I bet that room in the basement is where he keeps his stacks of gold.'

A sickly feeling swoops through my middle, like I'm falling. I haven't thought of them for a while. How could I have started to forget already? 'Well, we've got no idea where to start looking, have we? And anyway, you can't steal from him!'

'Why not?' she asks, blunt as a toe.

'Because! He's given us a job, and a place to stay.'

'Only because he wants us to do all the work.' She flops down on her bed. 'There are far more interesting things to do than work, Spel. There's magic in me. I can feel it. Isn't it amazing that we're witches? It means we can make things happen for *ourselves*.'

'I'm not sure it really means that,' I say moodily. 'Shranken Putch was talking about stuff like kinship with nature.'

She laughs. 'Sure. But one thing doesn't cancel out the other, you know.'

Truth is, I'm so obviously jealous it's painful. While I've been reading casket catalogues, she's been coaxing the pages to turn themselves.

'Let's run through everything we know so far,' demands my sister. She grabs the map from my bed and turns it over, then snaps her fingers, and a pencil flies across the room from the pocket of her uniform, straight into her hand.

'Now you're just showing off,' I accuse, my insides curling in on themselves.

She beams. 'It was good though, wasn't it?'

I shrug.

'So.' Egg plumps up her pillows and settles herself cross-legged on her bed. 'We know that the witch hunt has been going on for centuries, and that this village was the centre of the trials and executions. Our mother was called Amara Penhaligon, and she was tried as a witch, and sentenced to death.' She scribbles a list on the back of the map. 'We know there was a big hunt thirteen years ago, and kids like us were sent to Mouldheels' School, which turned out to be a witchcraft reformatory – maybe there are others, too! And basically we all thought we were the daughters of criminals, but actually we're the daughters of *witches*.'

I give a resentful, one-shouldered shrug. 'Seems like it.'

'Then Mistress Turner locked us away, just when everyone else was put into the hall and – what? They were put into some kind of trance? And after that the letter came summoning us

155

here – to a place where witches once lived.'

I nod. 'And also Mistress Turner came back to find us.'

Egg curls her lip. 'Yeah.'

'No, but . . . hang on.' I jab my finger into my bed. 'What if she did try to hide us? What if she was actually helping us?' Guilt stabs my stomach at the thought that we left her to face whatever that shadow thing was.

Egg raises her eyebrows. 'Well, we'd never have thought it possible, would we? But I suppose we'll never know, now. Anyway, have I missed anything?'

I think for a moment. 'Amara's name, written on the wall.'

'Ooh yes, of course!' Then her eyes dart to my pillow, and her face grows suddenly more keenly alert. 'By the way, what were you hiding under your pillow before?'

How is it that sisters always *know*? 'Nothing.'

She rolls me over as easily as a plum, and pins down my arms with one hand while fishing under my pillow with the other. Then she pulls the ring free, even as I bite and kick. 'Spel! Where did you get this?'

'Why do you always assume my business is your business?' I say, sullenly.

'Less of your cheek, girlie.'

'Can you give that back, please?'

'I'm only keeping it for a little while. You'll get your turn.' She turns the ring in the light, making the gemstone wink. Then she pops it on her finger and fans out her hand, smiling.

16
Getting to the Root of Things

Egg stands up and stretches, leaning on to her tiptoes. The paper she was writing on, with the map on the other side, flutters to the floor. She's so tall her fingertips brush the low attic ceiling. Outside, the light darkens. A low grumble of thunder begins to ripple through the air. 'Right, then,' she says through a yawn, before turning and wrenching open the bedroom door.

'Where are you going?' I ask, miserably.

'To the root of what is going on here.'

'Now?' Fright scratches the inside of my stomach.

'Of course, now.'

Tears threaten again, sharp and sudden. I feel like the world is tilting and falling away underneath me. 'Fine,' I tell her, trying to keep my voice strong. 'Go on your own. Have fun. Let the rest of us get ready for the funeral later.'

She scowls, hesitating between our beds. For a moment, my heart lifts. Then she laughs carelessly, turns on her heel and slams out of the room.

'Egg?' I call. '*Egg?*'

But I know my sister better than I know myself, and I know when she's pretending not to hear me.

'Urgh!' I burrow into my blankets, sunk in a gloom that won't shift. Then a gleam catches at the corner of my eye. It's Egg's pocket watch, stashed among a pile of hair ties and lipsticks she's stolen from Putch's make-up collection. In a moment of spite, I lean across and grab it, enjoying the smooth weight of it in my palm.

Why didn't Amara leave something for me, as well? I suppose maybe she didn't have time, if she died the same day as I was born. Anyway. Now this is mine. Two can play at the stealing game.

As the day ages, the shadows of the bare trees outside our window scratch against the ceiling. I roll over on to my front, praying for the door to open and Egg to come back in. But it doesn't. She doesn't.

Eventually, I feel myself drifting into a thick, oblivious fog of sleep.

When I wake up, I have no idea where I am. The attic is fully freezing, since I never made a fire. The pocket watch is still in my fist.

'Egg?' I call, groggily. 'Oh no,' I whisper into my pillow. Why didn't she wake me up? I must be late to work!

I try to distract myself so I can calm my panicky breathing.

The secret life of Spel Wrythe:
favourite things since we got to the Ring

1. *The smell of the grass after rain*

2. *Artemis sitting on me and kneading my belly with her paws*

3. *When Putch dusts the hot chocolate with nutmeg*

4. *Listening to the trees whispering*

5. *The way quietness feels useful around death*

Urgh. It's not helping. I slip out of bed and skid for a second on the map that Egg dropped on the floor. Stifling my curses, I stuff it into my pocket along with the watch, and poke my head through the door. The hallway and the staircase are deserted. There's no sign of Egg making her way back upstairs. Maybe she got into the basement and found Putch's money? I wait a moment, imagining her bounding up the stairs with a big excited grin slopped all over her face. But it doesn't happen.

I creep down the stairs, flinching as I pass the eye in the wood, which I could swear is in a slightly different place from where it used to be. The sitting room is empty, but the second hand of the clock on the mantelpiece is crunching doggedly *backwards*. It must be broken. It says 04:00. How could it possibly have got that late?

'Shranken Putch?' I call. 'Egg?' No one answers me. There's no sign of Artemis, either. I go down the hallway, towards the kitchen. As I walk, I feel my socks slipping like the floor's trying to tip me up. There's a dizzy feeling in my head and belly. It feels like the house is twisting, which makes exactly zero sense.

I find the back staircase that leads to the basement. It's darker down there. I pause on the stairs, swallowing, hating the thought of stepping into that murkiness.

Keeping one hand on the wall, I feel for each stair with my toes, inching into the basement. My heart spasms in my chest, like it's trying to worm up into my throat. I can't speak. I want to call out for her but I can't bring myself to do it.

Something bumps against the backs of my legs. Fear grips me, but when I turn to look, it's just Artemis, twirling her tail in the air. 'Oh, cat!' I scold.

The forbidden door is closed, but the key's there, nestled deep in the rusty old lock.

I put my ear to the door, but I can't hear anything. 'Egg?' I call, and the voice is horrible – all torn and desperate. Lonely.

Has she done it again? Has she left me?

Maybe she never came down here. Maybe she just said that, but really she was leaving the house.

Slowly, as though I'm sleepwalking, I put out a hand and push the door. It groans inwards. A wall of damp, stale air pushes against me, its fingers crawling into my nose and ears. The room is dark, except for a single candle flame, fizzing and quivering far across the room. Huge shadows loom on the walls, which are bare stone fitted with a few shelves crammed with old books and glass bottles full of different coloured liquids.

On the low ceiling there's another one of those brass whorls that the undertaker said was for *drainage*. It must be the underside of the one in the laying-out room, where the freezers are.

A big round lump of stone bulks in the middle of the floor.

I move deeper into the room and spot the outline of my sister, sitting up high on the edge of the stone, twisting the gold ring on her finger. The darkness had almost swallowed her whole. Relief rushes through me. 'Egg! What are you doing? What is that?'

The stale smell worsens the closer I get to the middle of the room. Now there's a slightly sweet smell mixed in, like something's rotting.

'I think it's a well.' Egg waves me over urgently.

I reach the lump of stone, and my feet bump into a lip at the bottom – a step.

'Careful,' warns Egg. 'You have to climb up. Come on.' She holds out her hand and I cling on, letting her help me up. The lump of stone is an old grey circle with thick walls covered in black slime. She's staring down at the surface of the water with such fierce admiration that it almost hurts my eyes to look.

'We're not meant to be down here,' I whisper, glancing nervously back towards the door. 'What if he finds out?' My heart jumps so hard that electric shocks race up and down my body. I don't know why she's excited about any of this, when the whole idea of it fills me with dread. I mean, it turns out that the house is sitting on top of a deep, dark well full of stinking, murky water. Personally, I don't feel very comfortable about that.

'What is he keeping down here?' breathes Egg, eyes sparkling.

'What do you mean? We've seen it, haven't we? Let's go.'

She laughs at me. 'No, I mean there's something *in* the water.'

That's when I notice the things floating like scum in the well, pale gold in the candlelight. They're those little membranes I saw in the sink. Like wings, or . . . scales. For a moment I'm entranced by the sight of them, and I let myself stand by my sister and watch them scud around on top of the foul liquid.

Then a shudder rolls through me, and I get scared. 'This is wrong. I don't like it.'

'But there's something moving down there,' insists Egg, squinting into the depths of the water. Her voice is thick with excitement.

'Like what?'

'I don't know – maybe eels? Or a fish?' Sheer enjoyment of the strangeness licks into her voice.

Bubbles begin to pop at the surface. 'Let's get out of here,' I beg.

'I *knew* there was a secret here, and I want to see it!' She leans low, her chin inches from the water. 'There's a silver circle down there, right at the bottom.' She laughs, and the sound echoes off the stone.

There were only one or two bubbles at first. But now there's a whole seethe of them, like the well is a pot bubbling on a stove. We watch for a moment, and then something in the atmosphere changes. It grows tense, like a sharpened knife.

'Um,' says a voice. I think it might be mine.

A mass of faintly gleaming muscle, like a long, tattered blob of ink dropped into a glass, whirls suddenly below us, close to the surface. Egg gasps.

Then the surface is cut apart by the dark angle of a scaled jaw. Sharp spines pierce the open air. Yellowed teeth like ancient bones catch the candlelight. A lungful of rank breath blasts right into our faces. It's hot and it stinks so badly that my eyes sting.

I'm frozen in place. Distantly I realise I'm gripping the stone so hard that my fingers have turned numb.

The reeking bulk in the water rolls and swirls beneath us. Then, just underneath the surface, a leathery fold of skin cracks open.

It must be an eyelid.

Because directly beneath my ghoulish reflection is a great amber eye, blazing like a torch.

163

Egg screams. A wrinkled, webbed wing flaps into the air as the thing darts down, back into the depths of the well. The bubbles dissolve into a stinking foam.

Who knew secrets could take the shape of scaled, wild-eyed things, with a haunted look and a long neck covered in flesh sores?

'Is it some kind of bird?' I whisper. 'Or a fish?'

'A *bird or a fish*? More like an absolute *dragon*, you fool!' Her voice is plated with gold, and her black eyes are glittering.

Knuckerhole village. Lairs of the legendary water dragons. But . . . 'What is a dragon?'

'Don't you remember? We saw it in one of those learning to read books. A creature with a long snout and scales and spines.'

'Whatever it is, it's the wickedest thing that ever breathed. He must have been feeding the souls of the dead to it. Don't you think that must be what we've been hearing at night? It's always after a body's been collected.' She doesn't reply. I jump down from the well. 'Egg – get away from the edge.'

But she keeps twisting the ring, staring deep into the water.

'What's the matter with you?' I jump up and grab her hand, trying to pull her away. But she's too strong, and her hand just flops back down by her side.

'Egg!'

I almost don't see it. The movement is so quick, like the

flash of a slip of midnight, tearing at the edge of the world. Slimy flesh breaks the surface again. Something – a fin, the edge of a tail? – lashes into the side of my sister's head. She teeters on the edge of the stone, and topples, with an awful plunk.

Then she disappears.

My hands are in the water, splashing and scrabbling around. 'Egg!' The stagnant water soaks up my voice. There's no sign of her. Not even a bubble.

The door thunders on its hinges. 'What you doing?'

My skin as good as twitches off my bones.

Rough hands grab me around the waist and pull me away from the well. I twist and struggle until I'm put down. The undertaker looms over me, lamppost-tall and utterly agog.

The tears leap up my throat. 'Oh, Mr Putch! My sister – she's gone.'

'Did she get in there?' he asks urgently. 'Into the water?'

I shrink back. 'Yes.'

Then all the tension floats off the undertaker, into the stale air. 'Stop the clocks,' he tells me, gently. 'Cover the mirrors.'

At first, I don't understand him. But then his meaning causes something to break inside me, and a storm of wailing crashes over my head, bending me double. 'No!'

17
A Binding Curse

'Egg's in there.' I point at the well, now just a quiet circle of stone, pretending innocence. 'You have to help her.'

Shranken Putch shakes his head.

'*Yes*.' I pull on his hand, trying to drag him across the room.

The undertaker crouches down to my height, taking my hands in his. I can feel the heaviness of his heart through his skin. 'Child. If your sister got in there, she won't be coming back.' His voice snags in his throat, but his eyes hold mine, steady.

'That can't be true,' I beg. 'It's just a well. We need to get in there and pull her out!' I'm dimly aware that my voice is flooding out more strongly than it ever has in my life. But it feels like I'm the one falling underwater.

'It is not just a well. And it's too late.' Stubbornness mixed with something sharp – fear? – makes his voice flat. He disentangles his hands from mine as he stands.

I grab his wrist. 'We have to get her out!'

'Stubborn little bug-bear!' he squawks.

'Help my sister!' I let go of him and scramble towards the well, hoisting myself up and peering into the water. '*Egg!*' The surface is black and blank and motionless, as though I only ever dreamed a dragon, or a sister. When I lean over far enough, my own face stares back at me.

The undertaker's reflection joins mine. 'She's gone,' he says, a hint of bitterness bleeding into the sadness in his voice. 'She was wearing the ring, was she?'

'How do you know about that?'

He turns away from me, folds his arms around himself and sags slightly, as though bearing an enormous weight. I realise with a start that Artemis is close by, a little patch of shadow studded with bright eyes. She hisses at Putch.

A cold suspicion settles in my stomach like a weight. I turn away from the well. 'What's going on?'

He sets his jaw as though he's thinking he might not tell me. But when I open my mouth again, he speaks quickly, in a low, urgent voice. 'It was to guide you to the right place.'

'Guide us? Where?'

'No.' He shakes his head impatiently. 'Guide *you*. It was supposed to be you who found it. It was supposed to be you who went through.'

'You wanted me to find it? Why would you do that? What did that ring do to my sister?' I'm shouting but my own words sound like they're coming from a very long way away.

'Believe me,' he begs, 'I did not want any part in this. But they threatened to destroy my home, my dragon, even the pathway for souls to find their way to rest. I tried to delay. I was desperate to work out how to keep you both safe. I had locked the ring away for safekeeping. Something foul must have set it loose.'

'What are you talking about?' Exhausted tears prickle my eyes.

'There is a portal – a doorway – down the well.' He deflates a little as he says it, his spine barely supporting the rest of him. 'A doorway into another world. That world is called the Shadow Way, and it is a world belonging to the dead. It's my job to help the souls of the dead through.'

Could that explain the noises? 'We thought you were hurting them.'

'No,' he says softly. 'Sometimes, they just don't feel ready to go.'

He can actually communicate with the souls of the dead? It all sounds so hard to believe. Except that now I've seen a *dragon*, so maybe it's perfectly believable. It feels like a crooked other world has opened up, right in front of my eyes.

'No one living can pass between this world and the Shadow Way.' He's giving me such a look of sorrow.

'But you said *I* was supposed to go through!' She's in there, somewhere. I can't believe I'm letting him slow me down like this.

'Because you, Shadow-Born child, are not quite living.'

'Um.' I clear my throat a little. 'What?'

Artemis pads across the room, leaps on to the step at the base of the well and rubs herself against my legs, purring. The kindness brings fresh tears to my eyes.

Putch grips the stone rim, urgent words tumbling as though he's been holding them back a long time. 'The day of the last moon-meet, your mother was almost ready to give birth to you. But she and the others were battling to control the corrupt witch, who they planned to banish. Amara was supposed to put a binding spell on her, but it appears there was a struggle, and both that witch and your mother vanished – through the portal, it appears.'

'So I was born here, in this house?'

'No.' He looks at me as though he's trying very hard not to flinch. 'You were never born at all. Your mother went into the Shadow Way – the underworld, where the souls of the dead make their final journey to rest – and we thought she and her unborn child were both lost.'

I stare up at him. *Never born at all.*

'But not long after, my dragon – Grael – raised her head from the well, and across her scales lay draped a scrap of flesh, a creature so close to death that it existed somehow in a gap between realms. A new baby, lungs full of ether from the world of the dead.'

I was born in another world? A world of *the dead*? 'I'm not – really alive?'

You're like my own little shadow.

'Not as such. But somehow, Amara found a way to pass you back through the portal. You shocked the daylights out of everyone when you started breathing the air of our world, though for the first few weeks, you had the uncanny ability to fade into the merest flicker of a being. But you kept returning, growing slightly more solid every time. Your sister helped anchor you here, I believe. She kept chattering to you, day and night. She prodded and poked you until you squalled afresh, your blood pumping life into your cheeks.'

Wonder spreads through me as I picture my tiny sister, motherless, insisting me into her world. Egg made me live.

Now I have to find her and bring her home.

Above us, in the part of the parlour that sees the light of day, the doorbell rings.

It's such a normal, innocent sound, but Putch's face darkens like thunder. 'They're coming.'

'Who?' Fear stabs through me.

'The people who wanted to steal your sister away back to Mouldheels' reformatory, and for you to go through the portal.' His voice grows more urgent. 'The ring is inscribed with a magic curse, designed to drag the wearer through the portal and straight into the hands of the corrupt witch who killed your mother. Her soul dwells in the Shadow Way, still working for the Hunt.'

'So Egg will be dragged to the witch?' The horror of the

words makes my mouth feel burnt and ashy. 'But she'll still be alive?'

'No. *You* would be, because you are native to that place. Your sister will be dead – a soul on her last journey, like all the others in that world.'

A soul. But Egg never earned her soul! She's still Wicked. A surge of panic flares inside me. 'But . . . if the ring is magic, couldn't it keep her alive?'

Above us, someone bangs on the front door.

'Perhaps there is a very slight chance it could,' says Putch. 'Though not for long. And in any case, there's no coming back from the Shadow Way.'

My words slip over one another desperately, like slimy stones. 'Egg's a witch, and she's really good at it.' I wipe the fresh tears that are spilling from my eyes, and stare him straight in the face. 'She'll be able to come back.'

'It's a law of physics, child. Your sister will have no power in the Shadow Way. Unlike you.'

The doorbell rings again. Once, twice, three times, as the ringer's impatience swells.

The undertaker grabs my shoulders. 'They will push you into the well with a binding curse, like the one your sister was wearing. You should go through before they catch you. And if you stand any chance of finding your sister alive, you have to do it before the magic of the ring wears off.'

'What?' I flinch as the sound of smashing glass crashes in

the hallway upstairs. We listen as footsteps move, slowly and deliberately, through the house and down the stairs towards us.

Putch speaks quickly, a sudden storm sweeping over his silvery eyes, like clouds passing across the irises. 'You must cross the lake. Whatever happens, do not fall in. Avoid the ghosts of the Hunt, and their cahoots, and look for the Hagdons.'

Before he can say any more, the door swings open and crashes into the wall.

The golden-haired man steps into the room, wearing his elegant coat, his smile as wide as a cut. 'Ah, Miss Wrythe. How lovely to see you.'

Him, *again*! 'Who are you?'

'There is no need for any of this, Tobias.' Putch steps towards him, but the man sweeps him aside with a violent jab to the ribs. The undertaker falls to his knees.

'Putch!' I scream.

'Just go!' he wheezes.

'Oh, you'll be sorry, Shranken Putch,' says the man called Tobias, lip curled back to show a set of small, perfectly white teeth. 'You know we can find another ally, don't you? We can simply slay your dragon, fill in your well, and cut down all the trees of the Ring.'

Artemis shrieks, skittering across the floor towards the man, all her fur spiked on end. She hisses, ears flattened,

173

teeth long and shining.

'Wonderful to see you, Lady Artemis,' croons Tobias, mockingly. 'I see you've finally got a handle on that temper of yours.' His fingers are curled around a small piece of metal that flashes brightly in the gloom.

'He's got a binding curse!' gasps Putch, still cradling his ribs. 'Hurry, Spel!'

A smile ripens on Tobias's lips. A smile that makes my insides itch.

The well looms, high and stark, seeping a strange sort of sour-smelling calm.

'All you had to do was deliver the right witch. We trusted you, undertaker.' The slash of a grin has faded on the man's face, leaving nothing but dull hatred. 'Never again will you enjoy the luxury of our protection.'

Did he intend to betray us, all this time? I can't keep the shock and the hurt from my face as Putch looks at me helplessly. 'Don't listen to his poison, child. Just hurry!'

As the undertaker and the cat struggle to hold Tobias back, I haul myself up on to the well's stone lip and teeter on the slippery moss growing there. Silvery light shimmers deep down in the water.

Tobias roars towards me, all his elegance lost.

'Spel!' shouts Putch.

Artemis unleashes a bone-piercing screech. Her claws slash Tobias's forearm. He yelps, dropping the shining thing that Putch called a binding curse. The little black cat chases after it, knocking it into a dark corner.

Tobias hops on to the lip of the well and grabs hold of my arm so hard that it feels dislocated. 'Your sister will be lost for all eternity in darkness and a clutching despair, living in the murk, a demonic creature of slime and misery. It will not be undeserved, for a witch.'

A burst of rage, bigger than any feeling I've ever known, rushes up through my body. I kick his shin as hard as I can, and as his face dissolves into a grimace of pain, I twist roughly away from him. Then I jump into the middle of the deep, dark well.

PART THREE:

THE SHADOW WAY

18
Grael

The world is eclipsed by the impossibly loud smash of my body hitting the water; a cold starburst of shock that folds over me, pushing into my nose and mouth.

It feels like I'm going to sink forever. Down, down, down the well. It's so dark. The water is thick with old scales. I stretch out my hands, hoping I might be able to feel for the portal, but the well is so wide that I can't even reach the walls. Panic scrabbles inside me. My lungs spasm in pain. I have to breathe. The pain of it swells and swells. I force myself to hold on.

My thoughts are reeling. How will I know when I've found the portal? And in the back of my mind, a tiny flame of hope flickers – the hope that I'll find Egg somewhere down here, with a pocket of air, and I won't have to go into the Shadow Way.

When I can hardly bear the pain a moment more, something nudges hard underneath my boots and I'm shoved sideways. Instead of sinking further, I bump along a passageway and into a wall of rock. Stars are sparkling behind my eyes, and my lungs are on fire. But when I look up the surface is there, not far above my head. I reach up with the last of my strength and grab hold of the edge of the rock, heaving myself over. As soon as the air touches my face I'm gulping great lungfuls of it. Then I perch, panting, in a cave tucked deep in the bottom of the well.

The water pours off me as I crouch, shivering and staring into the darkness. 'Egg?' I gasp. The air is thin and stinking and it takes me ages to catch my breath. My breath becomes the damp and ragged world, filling the space around my head. 'Hello?' My voice echoes back to me, but no one else answers.

I crane my neck to stare upwards at the craggy stone roof over my head. Here and there, it's punched through with thick, tough-looking roots.

On the opposite wall of the cave there's an oval shape like a mirror, except it's dull and grimy, half covered with a thick crust of scum. It's sort of pulsing with dim light. There are four other ovals, two on either side of the glowing one, but they blend almost completely into the darkness of the rock. Could one of them be the portal?

'Hello?' I call again, feeling stupid. 'I'm looking for my sister, Egg – Meghan – Wrythe. Is anyone here? Have you seen her?'

My feet are on the lip of the cave. Beneath them, something quick and dark spirals through the water. I squirm away from the edge.

Then a giant head rears out of the water, supported by a long scaly neck. Two burning eyes bore into me, set deep in a scaled face, underneath rubbery black eyelids.

The dragon's temples flicker like gills. A gentle purring sound throbs from her scarlet chest. There are wounds on her flesh, maybe from squeezing through the well. Her eyes are liquid-gold with pupils like drops of black paint. They alternately squeeze and relax as the dragon watches me. This must be Grael.

A voice makes the thin air of the cave vibrate. *Did you bring pudding?*

The voice rumbles in my chest. For about ten seconds I'm so startled that I can't remember what pudding even is. I never expected the dragon to *talk*, but if I had, that is about the last thing I'd have expected her to say.

'Um . . .'

The golden eyes squeeze into slits. *Never approach a dragon without pudding! I am especially partial to pink blancmange. The undertaker makes it for me in the shape of a rabbit.* A long black tongue oozes from her mouth, and licks the ends of her sharp, pointed teeth.

'Grael, I – I'm looking for my sister. Have you seen her?'

No pudding? The dragon huffs hot, rancid breath into my face that steams my skin dry. She plunges away from me, back into the pool.

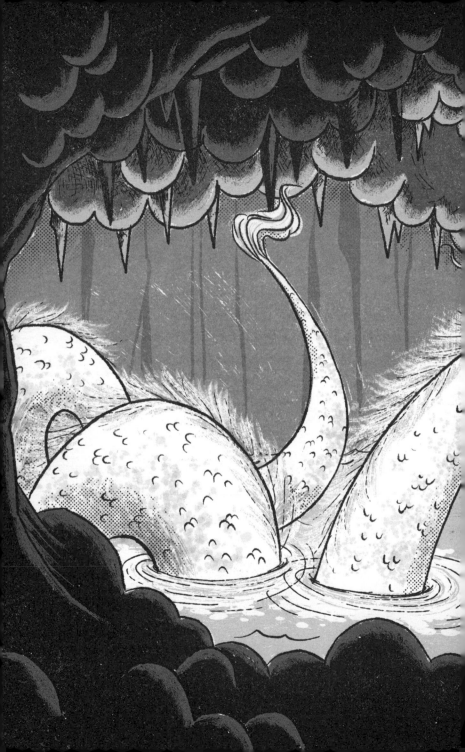

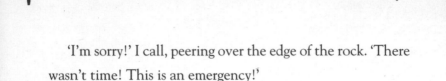

'I'm sorry!' I call, peering over the edge of the rock. 'There wasn't time! This is an emergency!'

The water doesn't stir.

I stare at the flickering oval thing on the wall opposite. It looks like a half-healed scab. Could Egg have gone through there?

I shuffle to the very edge of the shelf and stretch out my arm, trying to reach the mirror, but there's no way I can get to it from here. Should I try swimming across? The only problem is that it's too high above the surface, up on the wall. I'd never reach it from the water, either.

I'm thinking of flinging myself at the mirror from the lip of rock when the water swirls round like a whirlpool, and the dragon rears up again. I yell and scuttle backwards.

Water falls off her in sheets. *So, witch-girl,* she breathes. *You with a wild look about your eyes, like that of a newly captured*

182

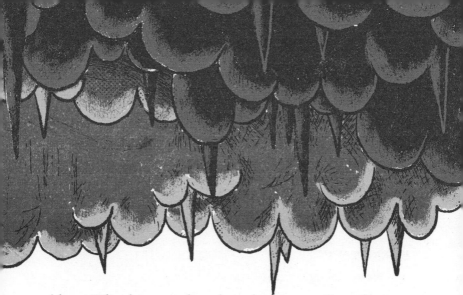

falcon. *What have you brought to honour me, if you have no pudding?*

'N- nothing, great dragon,' I whimper, squeezing myself as far back on the shelf as I can go. 'I'm sorry! But, please – have you seen my sister?'

Nothing? Then she sniffs the air three times, her nostrils wrinkling. *What is this strangeness? You are not quite dead. And yet, you are not quite living.* Suspicion seeps sharply from between her scales.

I wince. 'So I've been told.'

Only once, in all my thousands of sun-turns, have I encountered such a being, she mutters.

She stares, somehow even more intensely, and then she releases a hot, sharp breath through her nostrils. It singes some moss growing on the rock. *You are the Shadow-Born child.* Unexpected wonder sparkles in the dragon's throat.

Your mother begged me to grant you safe passage back through this way, after death. You have grown!

I stare back at her while the water gently shivers, pulsed by the beating of her heart. 'Why would you . . . do that, for us?'

Your mother was the truest companion I'd had for centuries. During every day of her apprenticeship here, she brought me pudding and sat on the edge of my well, stroking my head and whispering stories to me.

'Wow! Really?'

But then the horror of Egg being gone crashes through me again, and again. 'Did my sister go through the portal, just now? Is she alive?'

I glimpsed some kind of wretched creature, which tore through my well and was sucked straight into the portal.

I bury my face in my hands, as a sob of despair rushes up my throat. But . . . 'At least she was alive when she went through,' I snuffle, lifting my head.

She wasn't, corrects the dragon, matter-of-factly. *She was in a frozen state, her heart paused in time.* The cave falls quiet, except for the dripping of water and the great, ragged breathing of the dragon. *Even if you caught up with her, you'd never be able to bring her back to this world*, she says, more gently.

I glare at Grael. Egg *is* alive. Even if her heart was frozen, it can be restarted. 'I'm still going to try,' I assure her, meeting her gaze with as much steadiness as I can muster.

Liquid-gold eyes fix on mine, the pupils lengthening as the dragon drinks me in. *And that, dear Shadow-Born heart, is exactly what I would expect from a daughter of Amara.*

19
Travelling the Other Way

I look at the oval shapes in the rock opposite where I'm sitting, across the pool. The one in the middle is still gently glowing. 'Is that the portal?' I ask.

Grael twists her long neck to regard the wall, before turning back to me. *Hmm. It is already responding to you.*

'What are the others?' I ask, stretching my fingertips towards them.

All those sleeping shapes are portals, but the others have been closed off for many sun-turns. Once they led to Other Ways – Other living Ways, like this one. But only the Shadow Way opens now.

As I shuffle closer to the water, the portal's gentle glow begins to burn more fiercely.

Grael continues. *There is war raging in the Shadow Way. The Way is disrupted and chaotic, because of the wrath of the corrupt witch. You cannot trust every soul you meet. But your magic shall have its true power in that place, so take heart. Have you the witch's timepiece?*

'The watch?' I reach into my pocket and fish out Amara's silver pocket watch, holding it up for Grael to see.

Your shadow-birth means you will survive in worlds where others cannot tread. But to pass through, you must push the hands the Other Way.

I open the clock casing and, taking care not to let Amara's photo fall out, use a fingertip to gently touch the second hand. Just like with the clock in the sitting room, the hand quivers for a moment, before beginning to tick backwards. A burst of dizziness makes my eyes throb. The scabbing on the portal sloughs away.

Then Grael drops her head low. *Step on to me.*

I scoot forward and step on to her great, scaled skull. She rears, and I'm carried into the air, towards the glowing, mirror-like oval in the opposite wall.

'Whoa!' I shriek, clinging hard to the dragon's thick, wet skin.

Somewhere far, far above our heads, I can hear raised voices. What if Tobias comes after me?

Grael waits in front of the portal. I reach out and press it with my fingers. It's cold, damp and spongy. 'Thank you, Grael.'

Take care-pains, witch-ish one, she murmurs.

I push my hands and arms through the squidgy membrane. When I'm up to my neck, I take a huge breath, and crawl head first into the portal.

It's like pressing my face through cold, scaly webbing. My forehead and scalp are forced back, and the pressure peels my eyes wide. There's a twisting feeling, like I'm being spun in a circle, anti-clockwise. I feel as though my brain is being pulled out through one of my ears, and even though I can't catch hold of it, I'm aware of a distant music scattering overhead like metal stars. Images streak through my mind: Egg opening a tin of peaches, Artemis purring underneath my blankets, Shranken Putch quirking his eyebrows up into his hair, Layla telling Isla not to be mean to me.

Mistress Wolsley chanting the Mouldheels' words: *discipline, obedience, atonement*. Shranken Putch painting a different future: *the magic in your blood cannot be undone*.

My hands emerge into cool open air, and the memories fade as I squirm the rest of the way through and fall a few feet on to damp grass. Darkness hugs me like a fur coat. I stand up, head spinning. When I glance back, there's a stone wall behind me, and a faint glow halfway up that must be the other side of the portal.

The next thing I notice is the silence. It is total, numbing and eerie, like standing on the moon. Great clots of mist hang in the air.

Wrapping my arms around myself, I realise I'm buzzing with an unexpected truth. I did it. I actually *did it*. I faced a dragon, alone. I went through the portal to the Shadow Way, and I'm still whatever I was before – a half-living girl. Shadow-Born.

I walk forward, my arms outstretched to try not to fall. 'Egg?' I call.

The darkness is thick. My voice thuds against it, and no one answers. The further I walk, the stranger I feel. It's like being in the space between sleeping and waking. It feels as though something – or someone – knows I am here.

Still I call my sister's name.

And suddenly, I'm blundering into water. *You must get across the lake. Whatever happens, do not fall in.* I yell and flail, making a splash as loud as a thunderclap against the silence. Clutching handfuls of grass, I haul myself out of the shallow water. Then my feet slip from under me, and I fall into a mass of soggy reeds.

One by one, lanterns smudge into life, like stars being sewn on to a black cloak.

I'm sitting on the edge of the lake. The water is full of ghostly, drifting shapes. My stomach flips. The shapes are perfectly round white boats, each hung with a lantern.

Except they're not boats – not quite. Each one is a giant eggshell.

20
The Boy in the Boat

I scramble to my feet. The silent lake, dotted with floating eggshell boats, has to be the most oddly beautiful thing I have ever seen in my life.

While I stare, another boat blooms into life right by the bank of the lake, a few feet from me. It glows chalky-white.

I take a step backwards.

The light from the boat is enough to show a signpost that I must've walked straight past. It points across the lake, which is so wide and dark I can't see the other side. It still feels like being under the well – it's so quiet, without a breath of wind, that it feels like the sky is hiding.

'To the Muddlewood.' My voice is so horribly loud that I wish I could call my words back.

'There is a queue, you know,' mutters a voice.

I spin round. Just behind me and to my right is a stout and round-bellied man, wearing glasses and a loud pink shirt patterned with leaves. Behind him, stretching all the way back and out of sight in the gloom, is a long line of people.

All of them are sort of . . . glowing, around the edges, and through their middles.

I cover my mouth with my hand, to muffle my shriek.

Most of them are glaring at me and tutting. 'You see?' says the man again, impatiently. 'You need to get to the back of the queue.'

'What are you all doing?'

He gives me a look that says *are you really that stupid?* 'We've all died,' he says slowly. 'We're waiting to be collected and taken across the lake.'

'How many of you are there?' I stare down the line again, heart sinking.

'How would I know?' he snaps.

'I'm looking for my sister,' I tell him. 'Have you seen her? She wasn't . . . herself, when she came through here.'

'Not herself?' His mouth quirks up at the edges. 'Don't suppose she was, dear.'

'That's not what I mean.' My voice has withered to a hoarse whisper.

I set off trudging down the line, searching. But every face I pass is overwhelmingly not hers. And anyway, I already know the ring she was wearing means she'll be dragged straight through. But my chest feels crushed. A big part of me hoped I'd just find her on the other side of the portal, and all this would be over with.

'Egg?' I call. The air is so still that it feels like the name hovers just in front of my lips, like I've pushed it into a wad of cotton. No one answers, but they all stare.

They're restless, shuffling and muttering in what sounds like snippets of a hundred different languages. 'When is the next sailor coming?' moans one.

'We've been waiting too long,' says another.

'There's a backlog,' says someone else.

A backlog, in the world of the dead?

I look helplessly along the snaking line of souls. How long will I be waiting? I have to find another way across the lake. Then I notice a man watching me from the line, a little further on. I squint, disbelief spreading through me. It's the man whose body we went to collect, at that tower block. The one who I saw again in the graveyard.

'*Oliver Todd?*'

But when he sees me looking, his face closes like a book, and he turns away.

'Hey,' I call, making my way towards him, but the other souls in the line block my path.

'I just wanted to talk to someone . . .'

An old woman begins to scold me in another language. The souls move closer together, narrowing any gaps in the line. Maybe they think I'm trying to get Oliver Todd to let me go in front of him.

Why doesn't he want to talk to me?

'There's fighting in the skies, dear,' says another woman,

with a kind but weary face. 'They're only allowing the occasional sailor through. Meanwhile, more souls are landing here all the time.' She points behind us, into the distance, and to my amazement I see the shimmering of the undersides of other portals – in the wall I came through; in the trunks of isolated trees; in the grass; seemingly in gaps in the air itself. Souls must be coming here from all over the world!

'The thing is,' I whisper, urgently, 'I'm not supposed to be here, really. I'm just looking for someone, but she's not in the queue.'

'How many times do you think we've heard that?' The woman smiles gently. 'No one thinks they're supposed to die.'

Biting back my frustration, I march away from the queue until I can't hear the muttering of the souls, and sit down with a thump in the grass. As I'm staring out across the lake, with my chin propped in my hands, a sharp pain flares along my thigh. 'Ow!' I glance down, and a brown spike – on closer inspection, a thorn – is sticking out of my trouser pocket. Carefully, I reach inside to pull out the folded piece of paper Egg wrote her list on – the paper with the map sketched on the other side. But as I do, sharp prickles cut into my fingers. I drop the map on to the grass – and my mouth falls open.

The paper has several slim, sharp thorns poking through it. Except it isn't paper, all of a sudden. I lean closer to look. It's a piece of old-looking, slightly yellowed cloth. Taking hold of the edges, I manage to pull the map open. Crumbs of earth fall out. The map isn't a drawing any more. It's stitched with soft threads, and it still shows the Ring, except that the Ring has grown wilder, and denser. There are more trees, and the house has gone. In its place is a lake. The village is still there, but the road has vanished. As I hold the cloth in my hands, a memory surfaces, of the tapestry behind the red curtain, back at Mouldheels'.

How has this change happened?

As I watch, a word begins to stitch itself into the cloth. The threads move in clumsy determination, unpicking now and then, and starting again. As they work, a tingly feeling spreads up and down my arms. M . . . u . . . d . . .

The stitching stops, as suddenly as it started, and the tingling fades. Mud? What does that mean? Grumbling in frustration, I stuff the cloth back in my pocket. The I pull out the watch, enjoying the feel of its smooth casing. Except . . . it isn't quite smooth. There's a tiny rough patch. I flip the watch over and there, etched into its back, is a tiny engraving. OWWW. I wonder what *that* could mean? I take out the photo and stare down at the faces of Amara and Artemis. The sight of the cat carves an aching hollow in my throat. I wish she was here with me now.

Before I can puzzle over everything any longer, a thin, unmistakable sound filters through the gloom and into my ears. It's . . . snoring?

My chin jerks up. It's coming from the eggshell boat

nearest to me. I tuck the photo back inside the watch and stow it in my pocket. Keeping low, I move to the very edge of the lake. I plant my right foot firmly on the grassy bank and stretch out my left leg, leaning to try to see round the edge of the eggshell.

Inside the boat is an empty coffin, lined with silk and padded with pillows.

A boy sits underneath a dangling light, on a low stool next to the coffin. He's wearing a green cloak with the hood pulled up over his head, and he's clutching a long wooden paddle. His head is lolled forward in sleep, so that his chin is almost touching his chest. And a tiny purple animal is curled on his lap, also gently snoozing.

How come last week there were exactly zero dragons in my life, and now I've seen *two*?

Every now and then, the boy jumps in his sleep, muttering, and the dragon grumbles. I watch them for a moment. He's a boy of about my age, and it's the first time I've ever seen one. He's more shocking than a dragon.

What if he can help me cross the lake?

With a quick glance over at the line of souls, I slip down the bank and hop into the boat. It doesn't rock under my weight, and the boy doesn't wake up, so I climb into the coffin, sit down and cross my legs. It's surprisingly comfortable. I clear my throat. My stomach is already boiling with dread, just at the thought of speaking to a boy. Maybe I could row the boat by myself and he won't even wake up?

I reach out for a paddle that's propped against the side nearest to me, and promptly send it sliding over the side and into the water.

Whoops.

'Excuse me?' I whisper.

The dragon jerks awake, snorting sparks out of a long, wrinkled muzzle.

'What is it, Farthing?' The boy's eyes peel open, revealing a brown colour like tree bark wet with rain. He looks at me, dazed. He's small and dark-haired, with a watchful face. There's a lurking laughter around his stubborn mouth. He doesn't *seem* that scary.

'Could you please help me get across the lake so I can find my sister?'

His eyes widen, blooming into sudden focus. He sweeps the little dragon off his lap, and the creature swoops clumsily across the boat to perch on top of the lantern. 'Who are you? What are you doing in my boat?' He grabs another paddle and hops towards me, brandishing it.

'Hey!' I complain, dodging.

His body splinters apart, before pinging back together again. 'Farthing, you were supposed to keep me awake! What if we've missed the signal?'

The dragon makes a chattering noise that sounds like she's protesting her innocence.

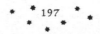

The boy turns back to me. 'What are you still doing here? Get out of my boat! You must go and queue with all the other souls.' He swipes the paddle through the air again, narrowly missing my nose.

I gesture for him to quiet down. 'Shhhh!'

'You seem rather furtive.' The boy peers at me.

'I don't want you to draw any attention to us,' I hiss, through a tight jaw.

'Why not?' he demands, tensing. 'Who are you? What deception do you peddle? Why did you steal into my boat, instead of waiting your turn like all the others?'

His words are making my brain feel tangled. 'Um, I do not peddle any deception! I just need to get across the lake. I need to find my sister. Please, would you take me?'

A look of outrage spreads across his face. 'I must take the next soul in line!'

'This is an emergency,' I plead. 'And could you keep your voice down?'

His eyes narrow with suspicion. 'What emergency? Is it connected to your death?'

I swallow. 'Well, I didn't die. Not exactly. Or . . . at all.'

He shakes his head. 'There may at times be a struggle to accept –'

'No,' I whisper. 'No, I really *didn't* die.'

He levels his paddle at me. 'Now listen carefully. I insist you disembark from this vessel at once, and join the back of the queue. As soon as it is safe for me to make the crossing, I shall be escorting the next person in line, not the self-serving wretch I see before me. Go! Before I summon assistance.'

'No. *You* listen to *me*.' I draw myself up to my full height, ignoring the paddle and staring him straight in the eye. 'I'm not quite dead. But I'm not quite living. I'm Shadow-Born. I was born here, and now I've returned, to find my sister.'

21
The Hagdon's Signal

'There *is* something strange – something different, about you,' the boy whispers. 'You must be maddened. Yes. That would explain such behaviour.'

My heart plunges. He doesn't believe me. But there's no *time* for him not to believe me.

He presses back against the far side of the boat. 'You shall wait your turn, beast.'

'You jagged thorn-patch! What if I were to tell everyone you were asleep on the job?' I put my hands on my hips. 'You'd get in trouble then, wouldn't you? In fact, you're the one all those waiting souls will be most angry with, not me!'

The small purple dragon, Farthing, flaps her wings and chatters angrily at me from her perch on the lantern.

'Oh, be quiet!' I snap. 'You're acting like a goose, and geese aren't even *that* scary.'

Farthing pauses, eyes blazing. Then, very slowly, she turns her back.

The boy's solemn face puckers into a frown. 'You are even

more fiendish than I first perceived.'

'I may have jumped the queue,' I hiss in desperation, 'but it's for a good reason! My sister came through the portal wearing a cursed ring. She has been taken to the corrupt witch, and I need to find her.'

He's watching me as though none of what I'm saying makes an ounce of sense – which is understandable.

I sigh. 'I know how it must look. But honestly. I just need to –'

'Find your sister,' he finishes, wearily. 'I heard you the first ten hundred-or-so times you said it.'

'So you'll help me?'

His jaw hardens. 'You seem to be my passenger, whether I like it or not. And I . . . had sisters, once. A very long time ago.'

Something about the way he says it tells me I shouldn't ask more, plus I don't want to upset him now he's agreed to help me. 'Thank you!'

He sits down with a bump, watching me like he's afraid to look away, while the dragon snoozes from the top of the lantern.

'So can we go?' I ask, failing to keep the impatience from my voice.

'Not yet,' he says, looking at me as though he thinks me extremely rude. 'This journey is no longer safe, and we must wait for the Hagdons' signal.'

'Are you a . . . soul, too?' I breathe.

'I am a Timothy. A sailor between the realms.'

'Oh.'

'And you are a . . .'

'I'm an Elspeth. Wrythe. Assistant to the undertaker of the Ring.'

'That is a good name,' he says, grudgingly. 'Perhaps I had a family name, once.' A faraway look drifts into his eyes, and a moonbeam drops right through him.

I try to keep my face neutral, even while fear curls my toes. Seeing the shimmery shapes at the dead man's flat and the funeral was one thing, but it's quite another to be sitting here talking to a real-life ghost. It is probably extremely Wicked of me. 'Timothy?'

He smiles, becoming more real again. At the same moment, high overhead, an electric-green flare fizzles into the opaque sky. 'That's our signal.' He fumbles around, tutting. 'Where is my other oar?'

I wince. 'I might have . . . knocked it overboard?'

'You knocked my oar *overboard?*'

'Just a tiny bit. Only slightly.' I raise my hands in surrender.

He appears to deflate slightly. 'So I've been threatened, and now this crossing will be thrice as much work for me.'

'I'm really sorry!'

'Just don't touch anything else.' He looks at me pointedly, before dipping his oar into the water, and my stomach lurches as the boat begins to move away from the banks of the lake.

'Lie down in the coffin, then.'

'What? *Why?*'

He gives me a pained look. 'As quickly as you can, please. That is how souls cross the lake. You are moving away from the in-between, now. You must focus on your inner journey, to reach your soul path.'

I open my mouth, but he cuts me off. 'You are utterly, coffin-nail dead, and the sooner you realise it, the more at peace we shall all be!'

There's obviously no point trying to reason with him now, so I resign myself to pretending to go along with things until we're across the lake. '*Fine.*'

The air fills with the sound of the water against the bottom of the eggshell. I'm conscious of how thin the shell is.

I'm settling myself down in the coffin when angry shouts replace the sound of the water. 'One of the boats is setting sail!'

Timothy blinks. 'Well, we have no sail, so I'm not sure that is quite correct.'

I sit up again and peer out to watch as a crowd of souls surges towards the edge of the lake. I remember Putch's warning about not falling into the water. 'Be careful!' I shout, to warn them. 'You mustn't fall in!'

The man in the loud pink shirt points at me. 'You!' He blunders forward and one of his feet plunks into the water, in a way that startles me, given that I'd have expected souls

203

to be much lighter. Maybe it's got something to do with what they believe about themselves – I remember Putch talking about how some weren't ready to accept their own deaths – or maybe things just work differently in the Shadow Way.

'Stop her!' yells someone else.

But I've noticed how others seem much more lethargic, like they're half asleep. They straggle forward with the angrier ones, but seem unaware of what's happening.

As the man flounders in the shallows, a shape glides towards him. I point. 'Get back! There's something in the water!'

He scrambles on to the bank, then turns to watch me resentfully.

'Lie down!' hisses Timothy. Farthing chatters something at me, spitting sparks that look like fireflies.

I sprawl out in the coffin, trying to breathe away my guilt. I know it's not fair on the others, but Egg needs me, *now*. She isn't dead, and I can still bring her home. 'Have you seen my sister come through here? She's about six feet tall, she has dark hair and dark eyes, and brown skin.'

A shadow of sadness passes briefly over his face. 'Well, people come through here constantly, as you've seen, so it'd be hard to remember one girl in particular. I am but one sailor of many, when we can get through the conflict zones.'

'She might have seemed different from the others, though. She's sort of . . . frozen.' I almost say 'by a curse' but bite the words back down. I don't even want to think too hard about what that might look like. 'Did you see anything unusual?'

He puts his head to one side, considering, as he pulls the paddle through the water. 'There *was* an incident out on the lake, shortly before I rowed across. The word is that something stormed over the water, overturning boats, dredging beasts from the depths, working against the natural flow in the Shadow Way. Whatever it was did not need a boat or a sailor. It was torn across the lake as though being pulled by invisible forces.' His expression darkens.

Egg. It *must* have been her. 'So no one here has ever seen

anything like it before?'

Timothy steers his boat through the black water. 'Not to my knowledge.'

I nibble my lip, staring up at the sky. 'That was my sister, you know. You might choose not to believe me, but it *was* her.'

Timothy stays silent, and his doubt stirs a bubbling pan of anger in the depths of my stomach. Let him believe what he likes. I'm going to find out as much as I can about what's going on around here, and make a plan to find Egg. 'What was that green light before, that you said was a signal?' I ask. 'Why do you need one?'

'When the Hagdons win a brief pause in the fighting, there's a clear path for us to bring souls through. Another boat or two should reach the souls shortly – unless there's another attack straight away.'

'What are the Hagdons?'

His face grows thoughtful. 'All I know is what they appear to be – great raggedy birds, with the ability to change into women. Or perhaps they are women, with the ability to change into birds.'

'But that's –' With a sigh of resignation, I let the word 'impossible' die on my lips.

The lake is dark except for the soft glow of Timothy's lantern. I pull the coffin silks around my shoulders, and watch the boy's face. There's something about him that seems ancient, even though he looks my age. His clothes are very old-fashioned, and his speech is much more quaint than anything I've heard before.

'Elspeth, your mother must be fretful now at home, with you and your sister both gone. Why would you inflict such punishment on her?'

I grit my teeth. 'I don't have a mother. She died when I was born.'

'So you never knew her,' he says, abruptly. 'That is sad.'

'So what?' I shrug. 'I never knew *anyone* with a mother.' I hate the creeping sense that he feels sorry for me, even though I barely feel the loss myself.

Timothy guides the boat onwards. 'My sisters and I lost our mother, too. Last year, shortly after I celebrated twelve years.' He flinches. 'I mean, many years ago.'

Despite myself, I soften. 'Did you ever see her –' I stop, realising the hugeness of what I'm asking, and how my question is connected to so many other things I want to ask. Did you ever see her again, in the Shadow Way? Why do you work on these boats, why haven't you found peace?

But my questions are too big and too personal and taste like opening a wound. So I choose an easier one. 'Timothy . . . are you dead? You didn't say yes or no when I asked if you were a soul.'

'Oh yes,' he replies. 'Quite dead. I recall there was a plague.'

'When?'

'I believe the year was 1646.' He looks thoughtful. 'Yes, that must be right, because I had recently celebrated my thirteenth birthday.'

1646! A coldness shivers through my bones. And he really is – was – my age. I stare at him in dismay. 'You died very young. I'm thirteen, too.'

He smiles like I know nothing. 'A common enough occurrence! What was the year, when you passed?'

I cast my eyes down, inspecting the bottom of the boat. He still doesn't believe my story. 'Well, it's 2021 now.'

His image splinters again, and for a moment he buzzes in the boat, just the half-imagined shape of a thing that might be a boy. 'It has been that long?' His voice comes in a whisper, from somewhere far away. 'Unless I ask someone newly passed, I have no way of knowing. Time does not exist in the Shadow Way.'

The little purple dragon zips down from the lamp and chatters angrily in my face, burning my nose with the embers she spits.

'Ouch! I'm sorry! I didn't mean to upset him.' I try to wave her away, but she doesn't budge until the boat bumps against something in the water, and the whole thing begins to turn around, drifting sideways. There's a tapping sound on the underside of the shell.

'Um, Timothy?' I reach out and touch the boy's arm. My

hand passes through him, but slowly, as though he's made of fog. My fingers are coated in a cold, sparkly slime.

He settles into his shape again, turning and blinking at me. 'Yes?'

'Are you okay? Your dragon seems pretty angry.' I eye the little creature warily. 'Also, I think there's something in the water?'

'Oh, Farthing is many things. A scoundrel, a menace, a pest.' He ticks off the attributes on his fingers. 'A dragon is the very least of what she is.' He smiles at the creature, who sweeps across to settle in his lap, glaring at me through narrowed eyes. 'But yes, she is very protective. The things in the water will be the knuckers. In some places the water is choked with them.'

'Knuckers?'

'Don't look so frightened,' he says briskly. 'Knuckers are water dragons, and they have never been interested in hurting people. They've been driven into hiding by this war. Many of them have been hunted for their skins.'

'That's terrible!' I think of Grael, waiting at the bottom of the well for her pudding. Is she in hiding, too?

Just then, pinpricks of cold tiptoe across my skin. The air tightens, growing heavier. I feel like a mask is pressing down over my face. When I stare through the lamplight, there are trees leaning low over the water, with roots coiled around their feet that look like frozen goblins, or grimacing demons. The shadows between their branches begin to thicken and swirl. The sight makes me dizzy. 'What's happening?'

'We're going through an evil place now,' whispers Timothy, tugging his cloak more tightly around him.

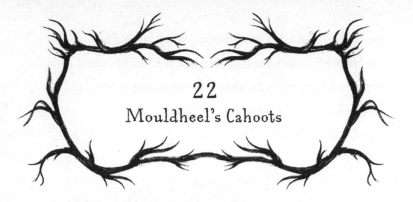

22
Mouldheel's Cahoots

Oh, help. 'What do you mean?'

'The Shadow Way is at war,' replies Timothy, shoulders tense as his oar moves more swiftly through the murk. 'Mistress Mouldheels rules one side, and the Hagdons fight for the other. Mouldheels has watchers – her cahoots – everywhere. Her servants terrorise the Shadow Way, attacking dragons and undertakers, and making souls lose their path home. Those are some of Mouldheels' cahoots, awakening.'

Farthing hovers over the boat, chattering furiously at the burgeoning shadows.

'Hush, beast!' scolds Timothy. 'Do not anger them!'

'Mistress *Mouldheels*?' I feel as though my stomach is dropping away from the rest of me. '*She's* the corrupt witch?'

Timothy shoots me a startled look. 'You have heard tell of her?'

What if this is all some kind of elaborate trick? I need to remember that I don't know this boy, and I can't trust him. Not yet, at least.

'That must be where the curse is taking my sister – to Mistress Mouldheels.' I remember the voices of the Wicked Girls, whispering rumours of what happens when Mistress Mouldheels comes for you. I can't let Egg face her alone.

'A curse?' Timothy glances at me, his eyes like terrified caverns, all traces of light lost.

I'm opening my mouth to reply, but the words turn to ash. The dark air begins to fracture, and then it's smeared with oil-black feathers and glinting with gleaming eyes, blinking open from where there had been nothing – hadn't there? A snuffling sound leaks out of the reeds.

'You need to hide now.' Timothy is barely an outline, and his voice seems to come from a great distance. 'Servants of Mouldheels search the boats, and if they find anything unusual . . .'

'Where are the Hagdons?' I whisper, clutching the sides of the coffin.

The roots of the nearest trees begin to writhe and pull free from the soil, snaking along the banks beside us. Memories squirm in my brain: seeing that thing hit the window of our dorm; being hunted by a shadow.

'Just hide!' Timothy hisses, struggling to pull the boat through the thick, tangled water with only one paddle.

'What about you?'

He peers at me for a moment, seeming surprised that I care. 'They cannot hurt sailors between the realms.'

I cower in the coffin, shrinking back against the silks. It's as though someone has undone a hidden seam in the underworld sky, and now it's swarming with huge, jagged patches of shadow, stretching and snaffling. They suck in the space around them, devouring clumps of roots and reeds, searching with shrewd, probing eyes.

Timothy pauses his rowing to shut the lid on me. I'm alone with the beating of my heart and the rasp of my breathing. A list unrolls in my mind.

The secret life of Spel Wrythe: Timothy, who is a ghost

1. *Is my age, but also ridiculously old*
2. *Can I trust this boy?*
3. *I feel like I can*
4. *But feeling isn't the same as knowing, is it?*
5. *Even though he hasn't been very nice to me, he's easier to talk to than any of the girls from school. Maybe because he's so straightforward? He just talks to me like I'm a real person, and not someone else's shadow.*

The pocket watch digs into my leg. I reach down into my pocket and pull it out. It's too dark in the coffin to see its face.

The boat stops moving. Then it shudders as something thumps aboard.

'Servants of Mouldheels,' says Timothy, in a shaky voice. 'Greetings.'

'*We are border patrol,*' hisses a group of voices, like wind biting through reeds.

I'm suddenly aware that the watch has grown hot in my

hand, and there's a silvery light glowing around my fingers. My breathing quickens.

'*The Lady sees you. She knows all that you do.*'

'I am performing my ancient duty,' quavers Timothy. 'There is no need for you to interfere with the journeys of souls.'

'*Insolent soul! We may not be able to devour you, but we can find your soul path, and destroy it – forever.*'

There's a sound of angry chattering and rapidly beating wings – Farthing, defending her master.

'No, Farthing!' pleads Timothy.

'*There is one soul in particular that we seek,*' seethe voices. '*Help her, and your rewards shall be rich.*'

The very air seems to pause. *He is going to betray me.*

I open the cover of the watch. The silver light streaks through the air as I move my hand. The watch's hands are still, so I wind them again, remembering how Grael told me to push them the Other Way to go through the portal. The cahoots come out of nowhere – out of hidden gaps in the air. What if I can tuck myself away, somehow?

Timothy shouts, and there's a thump, and the sound of struggling.

I take a breath, and channel my intention through my fingers, and touch the second hand. It begins to move backwards. I feel as though I'm tilting, like my brain is being pulled around inside my skull.

The lid of the coffin is thrown open. A shadow fills the air above me, and set within it is a woody, bulbous face, peering down. I fight down the urge to scream. The cahoot's eyes are made from the brown knots in wood, just like that eye in the banister at the Ring. The eyes quest around the coffin silks, doing the seeing for Mistress Mouldheels. Mistress Mouldheels, who has kept me hated all my life. A fleeting thought traces across my brain. What if I let them take me to her? I'm the witch she wants. As I think it, the woody eyes narrow and almost focus on my face. Horror tiptoes along my spine.

No. I clench the watch tighter in my fist. *You will not find me.*

Long, spindly wooden fingers grow out of the shadow. They delve into the coffin, rootling, clutching, pinching. I feel myself pull further back from the world, like an invisible barrier descends between me and everything else. I'm only half here.

Distantly I can hear a voice calling on the wind. The voice of Shranken Putch, whistling up out of the reeds and trickling down through the portal. Across the distance, Grael's gaze burns into mine. *Where are you, daughter of Amara? Are you safe?*

I am in the between-place, replies a little wild voice. A voice from a place as deep and dark as the well. The voice of my certainty, the same one that told me how the Ring was not nowhere, but Elsewhere.

Grael's voice curves with her smile. *Very well. Your Shadow powers are blooming.*

The cahoot's face is inches from mine, and yet, I realise with a chill, *it can't see me.* I don't know where I've disappeared to, but the sounds are slow and stretched, the air is cold and sticky. Dank, and damp.

Finally, the creature slithers away from me. '*Where is the soul you were sent to carry?*' it demands.

Timothy shoots across to me and stares down into the coffin. 'I – do not know, great servant of the Mistress. It must have escaped, somehow. I shall sail back to look for it at once.'

A shriek claws the air. I bite my tongue to keep from whimpering. '*Remember what is at stake for you, sailor! Do not deceive us. You cannot perform this duty for all time. When you are called to seek your path, you may yet find it erased. You may find yourself wandering, lost, for all eternity.*'

The boat shudders again as the cahoots depart.

I release my grip on the watch, and wriggle my fingers and toes. The lantern light touches my eyes. Sounds come, faint but heavy, as though my ears are underwater. Then I feel myself sigh back into the here and now, like a wave washing in with the tide.

Timothy's startled face appears above the coffin. His hair is sticking in all directions and a jagged tear runs through his cloak. 'Well. I have never seen a soul do *that* before.'

'Well, I did try and tell you I'm not one,' I retort, flinching from his tone. *But what if it was a Weird Thing? What if I really did become invisible?*

Timothy gapes at me, little bursts of silver dust sparkling around his head as though I can see his thoughts. Then his expression sours. 'Whatever treachery you're about, we need to hurry – the cahoots are still close by, and even if the Hagdons come to fight, we cannot be certain that they will be able to hold all of them back.' He starts urging the boat faster through the thick, mysterious waters.

Farthing buzzes around the boat, chirping and trilling and chattering at me, a frenzied look in her eyes. 'I can't!' I tell her. 'There's only one oar!'

She turns to fly back to her spot on the lantern, clipping my ear with her wing as she goes. 'Ow! I already feel useless enough, you know!'

I sit in the coffin and bury my face in my hands, while the tiny dragon spits burning embers at me that bite at my skin. I can't really blame her. Timothy was brave when they boarded his boat, and even though he obviously doesn't quite trust me, he didn't betray me either. And I've already put him in danger. 'I think my sister has already reached Mouldheels,' I murmur into my hands.

'Hmm?' grunts Timothy, from the front of the boat. 'How would you know that?'

'They said they wanted one soul in particular. She's already looking for me.'

'Why is Mouldheels looking for you?' Timothy's voice has grown colder.

'I don't know. But it isn't my sister she wants. The cursed ring that pulled my sister across the lake was meant for me.'

Silence, except for the oar pulling through the water and Farthing muttering under her scorched breath.

I stare ahead, into the distance, willing the boat on. Impatience squirms inside me. 'When we reach the Muddlewood, will you help me find the Hagdons?'

'Why?'

'I was told to seek them out. I'm hoping they can help me.'

'The Hagdons dwell deep within the Muddlewood – at least, when they're not fighting,' he tells me, leaning back and forward as he rows. 'I have never stepped into the wood, let alone seen their home, and anyway, it has been said to move around at will.'

'All right, so it's going to be difficult,' I snap. 'But we're talking about my *sister*. I'll do whatever it takes to find her!'

He pauses his rowing long enough to throw me a scowl.

Then I replay his words in my head. 'Why haven't you ever been into the Muddlewood?'

'The wood is where souls find and follow their path home. Once they've found it, they eventually flicker out, like candle flames. I have time to serve as a sailor.'

It feels like such a personal question, but I still can't help asking it. 'Why haven't *you* . . . followed your path home?'

He stares at me, evenly. 'Because I still have not accepted my death.'

His bluntness startles me. I think of the souls at Putch's funeral parlour, struggling and fighting. So desperate to avoid the truth. If he still hasn't come to terms with his death after hundreds of years, what sort of state must he have been in when he first passed through?

Timothy offers me a wry smile. 'Those who cannot let go are approached by the undertakers and offered places as sailors. I believe I am now the eldest, though I appear the youngest.'

He grows distant, as though lost in a dream. I feel exhausted, overwhelmed, and terrified for Egg, so I fall to picking my lips and jumping at the slightest noise from the reedy banks.

'It is said that those who cannot find their soul path will wander the Muddlewood forever,' whispers Timothy, his voice barely lifting above the pulling and sighing of his paddle. 'If you choose to step into that place, you should know you may be lost, and never return.'

'You haven't been listening.' I'm cold to my bones, and his words have only made me colder. 'I *have* no choice.'

As though on cue, the hazy shape of land begins to form up ahead of us. Timothy guides us closer with every oar stroke. The sight of the place we're approaching snatches the breath from my lungs.

It is the edge of a great forest.

23
The Muddlewood

The trees are the deepest green, dense and wild, and look tall enough to graze the moon. Birds cry from within. On the waterline is a dock lined with bobbing eggshell boats. A cluster of them begin to move off, oars dipping and pulling. Beyond the dock, just visible in the shadow of the trees, stands a row of painted wooden huts with star-shaped lanterns in the windows. Smoke puffs from the chimneys. Farthing swoops into the air and starts doing little cartwheels, as though she can't wait to get there.

The secret life of Spel Wrythe: the first forest I've ever seen

1. *I want to explore!*

2. *I can't believe that for once my first reaction wasn't pure fear*

3. *I've never seen a green so rich and deep*

4. *If this is the only way across the lake, then Egg definitely came through here*

5. *The sky looks bruised, as though it's dawn, or dusk, but somehow I feel like it's neither*

Timothy propels the boat closer to the dock. We're near enough now to see people bustling up and down a wooden walkway in the shadow of the looming trees. My breath steams. 'I've never seen a wood before.'

'Never?' Timothy looks baffled. 'How is such a thing possible?'

'I never used to go outside at all.' Oh, *hello*, embarrassment, my old friend.

He looks openly shocked. 'Why not?'

'I wasn't allowed to, most of my life.'

The boy looks at me, his expression a mixture of concern and curiosity, so I take a breath, and I tell him some of my story. How all the Wicked Girls were brought up to believe that our parents were criminals. How it shaped my whole sense of myself, but now it feels like that's all unravelling and I don't know which bits of myself to keep and which bits to let go. How we were summoned to the Ring, where Egg disappeared into the well. But I hold some of the story close. I'm not ready to tell him that we're witches. The word still makes my mouth burn. Plus I have no idea how he'd react.

'They kept all those girls locked up?' Timothy goggles at me, eyes shining. 'But girls are so iron-fierce! If anyone had tried to lock up my sisters, they'd have savaged their faces.'

'Hmm. My sister did try!'

He guides the boat closer to the wooden dock, glancing at me. 'Elspeth, I will do my best to help you get into the

Muddlewood. Once we've docked, we must wait until no one is watching.'

'*Seriously?* You'll help?' I stand up, clumsy in the boat, and throw my arms around his neck. He feels cold and damp and sort of – jittery, like he's made of a lot of little dots buzzing to stick together.

'Yes, of course.' He looks startled. 'Could you not tell my seriousness?' He peels my arms away and holds the boat steady while I climb out and up a ladder fixed to the dockside wall. When I step off on to the dock, my foot sinks through six inches of surprising snow. The funeral parlour of the Ring feels as distant as a star.

There's a chirrup, smooth and joyful-sounding, as the small purple dragon zooms into the air with a *click-click-whirr* of velvety purple wings.

'*Farthing!*' Timothy hisses, glancing around. 'I told you to stay hidden – pets aren't allowed!'

Farthing's colour darkens, and a film of moisture – sweat? – begins to form beads across her leathery skin. Her eyes flicker shut.

Timothy sighs. 'When you can't see *me* I can still see *you*, you know.'

With a great burst of spitting and chattering, she zooms back towards the boat and out of sight.

'Hmm.' Timothy squints at me. 'You did not spend any time preparing for your soul path. You still look suspiciously – alert.'

I glare. 'That's because I'm not actually dead, if you remember.'

A few other sailors are standing around, or fiddling with things in their boats. There's an atmosphere of tension here, like a thin band of elastic that might snap at any moment. I watch as one of them glances up at the towering trees, his expression wary.

'Do not speak to anyone,' instructs Timothy, fiercely. 'If we're questioned, I will say you are in denial.' He beams. 'Which is true!'

'No, it isn't!' I snap.

A fat golden beetle whizzes through the air and lands on the back of his hand.

I wrinkle my nose. 'There's a bug on you!' I reach out to brush it away, but he catches my wrist.

'It's just a firecat.' When he taps the beetle with a forefinger, it stays still on his hand. 'People use them to send messages.' The beetle flits to the helix of his ear and begins to vibrate. *Sailor 54891!* it blares. *Proceed at once to the assigning office.*

'Why is the volume always so high on these contraptions?' He bends to pick another item out of the boat, grabbing a neatly folded dark blue cloak. 'Here, take this, and keep the hood up!'

I put it on, and find that the hood is lined with the most deliciously soft fur. 'Thank you!'

A tall, bearded man bangs out of one of the huts and strides along the dockside, yelling ferocious instructions. 'Sailors!' He's wearing a gleaming black top hat and suit. 'We need a quick turnaround! We do not know how long the Hagdons can hold this peace. But remember – war is no excuse for sloppiness!'

Timothy straightens, the whites of his eyes stark.

'Who's that?' I gasp.

'A thorn in my side,' grumbles Timothy. 'The Head Undertaker.'

'Caskets neat and tidy, silks uncreased and *clean*!' instructs the undertaker. 'I want every last soul logged in the book, with no exceptions. If I find so much as a speck of slime or grot inside these caskets –' Here, he pauses for maximum effect, staring straight at Timothy. 'I will personally ensure you never work another shift again.'

Another firecat loops through the air, settling on Timothy's arm. *Sailor 54891!* it screeches, as it crawls towards his head. *Proceed at once to the assigning office!*

'Sailor!' barks the Head Undertaker. 'Why do you ignore your summoning?'

I stiffen.

'Sir,' says Timothy, in a small voice. 'I have not yet secured my boat.'

The man's shrewd eyes observe the boat and return to Timothy's face. 'Do not delay. Get this soul logged and get back out there before the fighting starts again. We have souls in need of our help.'

I dig my nails into my palms, as nerves begin to surge through me. I need to get going, but I can't talk honestly in front of this undertaker.

'Yes, sir,' says Timothy.

But instead of letting us get on with it, the Head Undertaker claps his hands. 'Come on, step to it!'

As we hurry along, I stare at the huts lining the walkway and the trees beyond them. A thick, powerful silence radiates from the wood, and I notice how even the Head Undertaker keeps to the far side of the walkway, avoiding looking at it. I nudge Timothy. 'How do I get in there?'

Timothy shakes his head at me.

'Why is your soul talking?' demands the Head Undertaker.

'Because I am not –'

Timothy pinches me. 'Sir, she is one of those souls that I believe may be having difficulty accepting the situation.'

'Hmm.' He fixes me with two inscrutable steely grey eyes. 'Another recruit for us, perhaps. Just as well.'

I swallow back a scream. There's no time for any of this! I peel away from them and take a few running steps towards a gap between two huts, but the Head Undertaker sprints after me.

'Whoops! No, you don't, missy.' He grabs my arm and steers me back to the walkway.

Timothy glowers at me, shaking his head.

We approach a larger wooden building near the end of the dock. The Head Undertaker grips my elbow and marches me all the way up the front path and through the double doors.

I feel my eyes bulge in my head. We've entered a hive of frantic activity. Sailors and undertakers bustle around, faces hollowed with worry. In the middle of the room, hanging from the ceiling, is a huge board crackling and pinging and popping every few seconds with messages. They look like notifications of deaths. But so many are coming through that the screen keeps freezing, and loads of voices groan, and then it flickers back on again. 'These alerts are still days behind!' exclaims one sailor, a gloomy-looking woman with folded arms. 'And we're only getting through in ones or twos. This is an unprecedented disaster!'

24
The Assigning Office

06821 – gentleman – 81 – ski-lift tumble – boat 45

08275 – gentleman – 52 – trip down casino stairs – boat 87

68250 – lady – 67 – died in sleep – boat 43

73902 – gentleman – 97 – horse riding – boat 13

09351 – lady – 37 – toothbrush – boat 82

The board makes my eyes feel scrambled, so I tear them away and gaze around the rest of the office. Some parts of the room are thick with firecats. They land on people's necks and crawl up to their ears, and sailors stand around listening to whatever messages they're carrying. It feels like chaos.

'You, wait here.' The Head Undertaker pushes me into a chair. 'And you – with me,' he orders Timothy.

'Don't move!' hisses Timothy, as he's spun away amid the Head Undertaker's constant whirlwind.

I stand up and stare at the board again for a few seconds. Every time a message pops up, a ticket rolls out of a machine nearby, like a little white tongue. I watch as a sailor traipses across the room and tears off the ticket. 'Twenty assignments a shift,' she grumbles wearily. 'And mostly sitting around waiting to be let through a war zone. I'm getting too faded for this.'

She stomps across to a table, where a large book lies open. Then she peels off a sticker from the back of the ticket, and leans down to press it into the book.

I sneak up behind her, peering at the pages. Every sticker shows a name, and the date. Egg might be listed here!

After the sailor sets off back across the room, I make sure no one's watching, and begin to scan the entries.

Each name and number is written by hand in a neat square, and each square is half filled with a ticket sticker – to show the job's been assigned, I suppose. But I can't see any mention of Egg.

Then, on the previous page, I find an entry that looks different from the rest. It's written in a quick, scrawled hand, and stamped at the top with a red stamp.

The writing says:

On-lake emergency registered — boats overturned by violent, ghoulish being. Cahoot attack immediately followed. Emergency flare fired. Senior input received. Post-emergency actions: incident report submitted, debrief completed. No follow-up required; no soul detected. All sailors instructed to exercise high vigilance following these untoward events.

I can feel tears carving a big aching hole in my throat. One drops on to the page, bleeding the ink across the paper. I'm vaguely aware that, across the room, the Head Undertaker is shouting and gesturing.

A shadow spills over the pages of the logbook. 'What's going on here?' asks a voice.

I freeze, then slowly turn and stare into the surprised-looking face of a sailor, who's leaning down to log a sticker in the book. 'Nothing,' I say quickly, stepping away. 'Nothing's going on in the slightest.'

'It's not possible,' he persists, suspicion furrowing the deep lines of his weathered face. He looks from my face to the page, and then grows very still, watching my tear sink into the writing.

Timothy springs to my side and starts dragging me away. 'She's a soul in denial,' he stutters.

'She's crying real tears!' says the sailor.

Around us, the voices and the chaos grow still. Everyone turns to look at me.

'Didn't I tell you not to move?' grumbles Timothy.

We back further away, bumping into another sailor, who is staring at me open-mouthed.

'What have you done, boy?' barks the Head Undertaker.

'Let's go,' says Timothy in a low voice. We walk as fast as we can towards the doors.

'Stop!'

We slip through the doors and turn left, breaking into a run as we head back along the dockside. I risk a look behind. A few sailors have followed us out and now they're hurrying towards us.

We draw near the far end of the dock. To the right is the vast expanse of water that leads to the lake. To the left, just beyond the line of painted wooden huts, the waiting hush of thousands of ancient trees, their tops almost scraping the stars. A mist has rolled in from the lake. Timothy whistles, and Farthing pops up above the waterline, trilling inquisitively.

Boots thud behind us. 'I said, stop!'

'This way!' says Timothy. He turns left and squeezes between the last hut and the edge of the dock. I follow, gripping the wooden railing to keep from sliding into the water.

Timothy hesitates at the threshold to the forest. Deep darkness spreads like a puddle at his feet. Farthing darts overhead, chattering what sounds like a hundred questions. The boy glances back at me. 'No one will follow us in here,' he murmurs, calmly.

'What do you mean, *us*?'

He doesn't answer.

A warning begins to form in my mouth, but he's already moving.

He steps across the line of shadow.

A bolt of fear shoots through my stomach. 'What are you *doing*? You said some souls get lost in there, and never return!'

He doesn't reply, but takes another step, disappearing into the dark.

The footsteps draw closer. 'They went this way!'

I draw a deep breath and follow Timothy. The glittering stars and pale moon are eclipsed above me.

25
Memories

It feels like a heavy velvet curtain has fallen over my eyes. I gasp as Timothy races ahead of me, barely the vague outline of a cloaked figure. When I glance back at the gap where we entered the wood, it already seems to be sealing shut.

'Wait!' I stumble, wrapped in a darkness so thick that I keep tripping over twisted roots. It takes a good ten paces before my vision adjusts to the gloom, and for my feet to get used to all the lumps and bumps in the ground.

Farthing settles on Timothy and hooks her glittery tail possessively around his neck. As he walks, she shoots mean looks at me over his shoulder. I stick out my tongue. Her eyes bulge in outrage.

'Search for a path for us to follow,' calls Timothy, as he ducks and weaves through low-hanging branches. 'Away from the path is said to be the domain of cahoots and familiars, scaly strangulators and vengeful ghosts.'

My mouth turns dry. I have to do this. *He* doesn't. Even though he hasn't exactly been friendly to me, I don't want him to end up wandering lost in this wood forever. 'Timothy – you can still go back, you know. I won't mind.' I force the lie out, because it's more important that he gets back to safety if he wants to.

He slows to a stop. That's when I realise his hands are bunched into fists at his side, and he's shaking with anger. 'No. No – I *can't* go back.' He turns to face me, and his eyes are two wet streaks in his face. 'I have no choice now, either.'

'Why not?' I whisper.

'The Head Undertaker was already vexed with me. Now he is livid. Livid enough to exile me from my post forever.'

'What do you mean?'

'First I sleep through my duty. Then when I finally return, I bring a soul who has not observed the proper preparation. Then –' Timothy shakes his head – 'I am found to have brought something Wicked across the lake, something that can weep living tears in the Shadow Way. What are you? What kind of a mess have you dragged me into?'

I stare at him in wonder. 'You *believe* me.'

He laughs bitterly. 'What use could I find in not believing you now? You may as well tell me you're a three-headed blue-bearded dragon with long swords for teeth. I would believe you then, also.'

I have no idea how to deal with this raw bundle of emotion standing in front of me. 'I'm sorry,' I tell him, because it's all I can say and I really, really am. 'I owe so much to you,

Timothy. I would be in such deep trouble if you hadn't been asleep in your boat.'

'Yes. And yet now, I am the one in such deep trouble.'

He strides away. I trudge after him miserably. Behind me, there's a rustle of leaves and the sound of a twig snapping. I turn, so fast that I yank the muscles in my neck. A tall, winter-stripped tree looms overhead, branches waving though there's barely a breath of wind.

If I felt as though something was watching me before, now I feel like it's breathing on my skin. However snugly I pull my fur-lined cloak against my body, the feeling persists. Jaw set, nerves on a knife-edge, I step forward again across the uneven ground.

Every few hesitant steps, the moon peers down through the trees. I remember being back in the kitchen with Putch and Egg and Artemis. I wish we were all sitting around the table, watching the moon through the window and drinking his hot chocolate. I wish it so much.

But instead I'm getting deeper and deeper into this wild tangle of a forest, with only a ghost and a dragon for company. Either side of us, trees crowd close. Some are straight and tall, with old leaves piled at their feet. Others are thick and gnarled and drooping, their branches plunging earthwards, claw-like, to dig into the ground along with their roots. Those ones have slender green needles instead of leaves. There's a path that runs between them – 'A path! There's a path!'

Timothy tuts. 'I know. I led us on to it.'

'Oh.'

The path mostly runs straight and sure, but sometimes it turns and spirals away in a sudden new direction. Here and there a tree has swept an arm across it, and I walk right into a sharp and startling faceful of twigs and needles.

'Watch out!' calls Timothy, too late. Maybe too late on purpose.

The further we walk, the stranger the sounds become. At first there's nothing except my footsteps crunching through piles of leaves, or thudding softly over mounds of pine needles or half-dried ridges of mud. Timothy's footfalls are silent.

But then, so subtly that I can't remember when I start hearing it, new sounds begin to trickle into my awareness.

Weeping. Shouted words, disconnected from any logic. Muttered fragments of sentences, as separate as ancient bones. A memory floats into my brain, from the night we first heard those noises from the basement at the funeral parlour.

I spot wisps of grey, green, blue or violet. The wisps are in the vague shapes of people. Are they souls?

Every time I hear a voice, I jump and stare away from the path, into the forest to either side of me. Then I pull my cloak tight, take a deep breath and start walking again. I have to keep going. Egg needs me.

The glowing shapes of spirits move between the trees. Long, drifting shapes, in green, violet, blue or silvery colours.

Odd assortments of words and snatches of tears or laughter echo off the tree trunks. The moonlight reveals eyes and faces hidden among folds of bark. I gaze up at one: a distinct, hooded eye, wide open and staring right at the place where my heart leaps in my chest. Maybe it's just the trees that have been watching us.

To the right of the path I pass a house under a tree, with an open front door and a garden full of brightly coloured flowers. Sunflowers and roses and a great, draping lilac bush, visited by bees. At first, as though I'm in a dream, I barely realise how strange it all is. Then a peal of echoing laughter rings around the forest and I flinch, staring around.

'Timothy?' I whisper. 'Could this be where the Hagdons live?'

'No,' says the sailor, scathingly. 'That is someone's memory. Another soul has found their home. In the forest, memories play out like dreams. We must be careful not to get tangled inside them. We must not lose our way.'

I can't stop myself smiling at him.

'What is it?' he asks, frowning.

'Nothing.' But it isn't nothing. He said *our* way.

The glimmering outline of a girl shivers past me, running up a pathway to the house. The hazy shape of a woman in an apron waits for her at the end of the path, and sweeps her into a hug, their laughter joining together.

With a stifled yelp, I take a plunging step forward, swiftly trip over a root, and fall flat on my face in the mud.

'We are watching other people's memories,' says Timothy, solemnly. 'They cannot hurt you.'

But a creeping sense of terror inches across my skin. It feels like I'm lost in someone else's skull. It makes me dizzy. 'I don't like it.'

'You are not supposed to like it. We are not supposed to be here!'

I haul myself to my feet and trudge on another few steps, into the velvet hush of the forest. A spear of moonlight pushes through the trees, showing the eyes in their bark and the white puffball mushrooms clustered at their feet. My eyes are so wide and focused on staring around that I can't even let myself cry, though the tears are shuddering up my throat anyway. 'Timothy, how do we know if we're on the right track?'

'We don't.' When he turns his head, his profile is a pearly, hazy disc, like a dim reflection in a window.

'What if the Hagdons don't want to help me?' I whisper, throat aching.

'What use are all your *what-ifs?*'

'But what if they don't?'

'Then we will have to find someone who *will* help you,' he replies, keeping his gaze fixed on the path ahead. 'But the Hagdons are the only real resistance against Mistress Mouldheels and her servants, so if anyone should want to help you access her fortress and rescue your sister, it should be them.'

He's properly helping me, way beyond getting me into this wood. He hasn't admitted it, but he is. A huge wave of relief rushes through my body. Then I bump hard into a wooden gate, and the moon steps out from behind the clouds long enough for me to see it – the creature, lurking on the ground at the bottom of the gate. It looks like some kind of goblin, made from bulbous tree roots. Except it's not part of any tree. It's got two bulging eyes and a long, low gash of a mouth. I scream, loud enough to send a bird crashing out of a nearby tree. A bird whose outline is rough as a sketch, and whose feathers drip with ink.

26
A Warrant for Our Capture

I wheel away from the cahoot, plunge through the gate and keep running, along a path between the trees. Even as I run I'm aware of how sick and tired I am of feeling scared.

'Spel!' shouts Timothy, his voice carrying on the wind and shivering among the pine needles. 'Stop!'

My right foot twists painfully underneath me. My legs fly out in different directions. Then I hurtle sideways, whacking my face in the middle of a tree.

I lie still, panting, staring up at the sky between the branches. Warm liquid gushes across my face. When I put up my hand to check, the dark gleam of blood shines on my fingers. 'Urgh.' I let my eyelids flutter shut. I'm on my knees and about to scramble away again when Timothy catches up and squats down next to me, staring at my cheek. Farthing is curled around his neck and shoulders, and watches me with a judgmental expression.

'Elspeth, that wasn't a servant of Mouldheels. It was just a tree root.' His mouth twitches as though he's holding back a laugh, and irritation stabs through me.

The little dragon chatters her teeth together while watching me with imperious eyes.

'You can stop judging me right this instant, Farthing!' She spits.

'What about that bird?' I ask.

Timothy shrugs. 'It's gone. I think it may have been someone's memory of a bird.'

I am very tempted to wallow in the mud and my own self-pity. So for a moment, I do.

'You really aren't dead.' Timothy gestures to my bleeding face.

I grin. 'Imagine what the Head Undertaker would say if he could see this!'

Timothy's small, serious face breaks suddenly into a grin. The laughter he'd been holding back sails free, and it's a really nice sound, his laugh. Like sunlight.

I roll on to my side and push myself upright. 'Ouch!'

'What now?'

'There's something stabbing me!' I pat down my trouser leg and find a thorn poking out of my pocket. The map! I have to snap a vine just to be able to unfold it, and when I do, more dried mud crumbles out. The whole thing is even wilder than before, pierced with more thorns and stitched with a lot more trees – so many that the shape of the Ring has been entirely lost. More deliberate stitching has appeared in the cloth, and where before it just said 'Mud', now the name 'Muddlewood' is written clearly in slightly crooked black thread.

'What is that?' asks Timothy, peering over my shoulder.

'A map of where I was living. It was sent to my sister when we were still at school, telling us to go to Sussex. But it's started changing since I came down to the Shadow Way.'

He bends over the map, tracing the stitching with a fingertip. A look of fascination has lit his features.

As I stare down at it, two new words sew themselves delicately into being: Hagdons' Kettle.

Timothy startles. 'Oh!'

Except . . . 'But you said the Hagdons' place moves. So how could it be on a map?'

'I do not know, but . . . what other guide do we have? Perhaps this map is somehow showing us where the Hagdons' abode is at this moment?'

Farthing swirls overhead impatiently.

My eyes meet Timothy's, and we both nod. For better or worse, we're going to follow the map. And that means leaving the path.

We study a small compass symbol in the top corner of the map and then slip cautiously through the treeline. The whole wood is alive and creeping. What I first saw as shimmers or drifting smoke take shape into beautiful, glimmering ghost animals – horses, deer, dogs, foxes.

Now and then our way is blocked by steep crags or fallen logs, and Farthing whizzes away overhead to find a new route for us. Timothy asks her to watch for signs of the Hagdons – chimney smoke, or dropped feathers.

Eventually we come to a weather-bent tree that stands away from the path, with a purplish trunk and branches plunging sideways towards the ground, like an old witch throwing a spell. I put out my hand to lean against it, before pulling back – there's another eye in the bark, watching us.

There's also a sheet of paper pinned to the trunk. As we read its stark message, Timothy catches my arm, and I'm not sure if he's doing it to support me or himself.

Wanted by order of
Mistress Mouldheels,
Lady of the Shadow Way.

One witch and one
treacherous sailor,
both guilty of heinous
crimes against the realm.

Rich reward for their
retrieval.

While we're standing there, the paper turns glassy and reflects our own faces back at us. 'What sorcery is this?' murmurs Timothy, fascination lighting up his face.

Farthing begins to make a sound in her throat, like a growl.

Too late, I pull Timothy back, sharp fright piercing me. But our images bleed slowly into the paper, until a black and white photo of us is fixed beneath the writing. Now everything in the wood will know what we look like. Terror pools, hot and liquid, in my gut. Mistress Mouldheels is going to find us, but we were supposed to find her first.

We run. As we blunder along, Farthing wheeling overhead,

branches lash our faces and roots seem to bump up from the ground where they hadn't been a moment before.

'Timothy, I'm *not* a witch,' I pant.

'What?' he puffs.

'I'm not a witch. Please don't hate me.' I turn to him, an ache carving its way up my throat.

He looks amazed. 'You think I would hate you? I do not hate witches. I hate what witchcraft brings.' He looks away suddenly, and the moonlight falls through him. 'It is a danger to all it touches.' Then he snorts. 'You speak of cursed sisters and you are not quite dead – though walking in the Shadow Way – and yet you claim you are not a witch!' He laughs, not unkindly.

He does have a point.

'I think we should slow down,' he says. 'We're far from that tree now, and we need to check the map again soon.'

So we walk a little way, staring all around us as we go. The trees we pass have thick dark knots on their trunks, and it takes me a while to work out why they're making me feel uneasy.

'Their eyes . . .' I whisper.

Timothy presses close to my side. Where his arm touches mine, a cold, damp feeling seeps through my clothes and on to my skin. 'What?'

'Their eyes are missing.'

Timothy flinches. Every tree we pass has had the eye in its

245

bark gouged out, leaving a deep whorl of scarring. Some are seeping sap like tears, or blood.

Some trees hold worse surprises. We pass one with a bloated toad staked to it, the body pieced with a dozen thorns. Another has a little lump of thorn-pierced muscle hanging from it; a knot of flesh I think might be a heart.

We trail to a stop. I pull out the map, but the light is so gloomy that it's hard to see it. The moon hasn't appeared for a while. Timothy takes the map from me, turning it this way and that to try to catch a slice of moonlight. A growing sense of unease settles over me, as we stand near another dangling heart pierced with thorns.

Then an unpleasant – but familiar – smell tickles into my nostrils. I glance around, trying to place the smell, which is like drains, or blocked gutters, or something slightly sweet rotting in a hidden place. As I bring my gaze back to Timothy and the map, movement flickers in the corner of my eye. I dart my glance back into the thickness of the trees, just in time to see a shimmery shape blend out of sight. It was the outline of a man.

Maybe it's just another soul memory.

Cold all over, I tug on Timothy's sleeve to get us walking again, and won't say a word however much he whispers, 'What's wrong?'

I shake my head, glancing back over my shoulder every few steps.

A great, twisted tree stands in our way, so we edge around

it, searching for a place to squeeze past. But then the moon emerges overhead, illuminating a black shape that begins to writhe inside the bark, squirming and peeling itself out of the wood.

Farthing hisses, spitting embers and ash.

The black shape – a stretchy shadow, contorting itself bigger and smaller as it wriggles – flexes a wing. As its face peels free, it unleashes a scream like a dagger splintering the air into shards. And all in a rush I understand it's another of those things that came to our dorm window at Mouldheels'. That came hunting for us in the corridor the day we left. That was lodged in the throat of the chimney at the funeral parlour, delivering a curse.

'Cahoot!' yells Timothy. 'Run!'

27
The Hagdons' Kettle

Trees blur past; silver streaks with scrubbed-out eyes, reaching for the moon. Now every trunk we pass bears the warrant for our capture. More cahoots join with the first, and an enormous sound of sniffing fills the air.

'What are they doing?' I pant.

'Sniffing out the witch?' replies Timothy, eyes wide with fear. 'Hurry!'

Farthing roars ribbons of fire at the cahoots, and hits a few of them, but it doesn't stop the main bulk of them from wheeling closer and closer.

'Stop looking back!' yelps Timothy. 'Just run!'

But I can't help it. The next time I risk a glance, one of the cahoots has come close enough to suck at the bottom of Timothy's cloak. The fibres begin to split and fray, and his steps slow as the cahoot drags against him.

'No!' I scream, whirling around to face them. They're like a wall of shadow, hissing and snuffling, pressing closer, eyes stretching in sockets of slime. I should be able to do something about this. I should be able to get us out of danger. Otherwise what is the point of powers?

'Elspeth, go! Leave me!' begs Timothy, as one of the cahoots absorbs more of his cloak.

'I won't let them do this to you!' In the tiny pocket of time that surrounds us, my mind races. If I use the watch to turn invisible, I'll be leaving Timothy behind . . .

The cahoots gather into one seething mass and then they're upon us. A hideous sound rises into the wood. A laughter that scrapes all the bones in my spine.

But a deep instinct stirs in me. *These beings are not part of nature. Someone has made them hateful, and turned them on us. But I am destined to be a keeper of the wise ways. Nature will help me.* As my thoughts make me stronger, I'm aware of a restless feeling in my fingers. When I glance down, white-silver light is glowing around my hands.

The cahoots slurp up the rest of Timothy's cloak and –

I leap towards them, screaming at the top of my lungs. 'Get away from him!' I throw my hands into the air – and when I reach back down, I'm carrying bright threads of silver moonlight just like Egg did all that time ago, on our way to the funeral parlour.

I stagger under the pressure of the moonlight in my hands. It swirls against my palms; heavy and cold as liquid crystal. Little beads of it trickle down my arms. I dig my heels into the ground and hurl it at the cahoots with all my strength.

Farthing joins her fire to my moonbeams. As the light touches them, the creatures make a sizzling sound like water in a hot pan, and shrink backwards, bleeding pools of inky shadow into the undergrowth.

Timothy is staring at me and trying to form words, but failing.

'Come on!' I yell. We tear away from the creatures, blundering between the trees. Branches tear at my face. Within moments, the cahoots have recovered their strength and slither after us, spitting angrily, sharpened claws rupturing from their growing bodies.

'I've made it worse!'

'Just keep going!'

We stumble into a hollowed clearing, like a bowl in the forest. The earth is strewn with mushrooms and clusters of bell-shaped flowers.

Farthing chatters overhead, then crashes down through the branches and straight on to Timothy's shoulder, where she cowers, trembling.

The panting of the cahoots fills the path behind us.

Up ahead, a giant black kettle towers into the air, dented and patched, and oozing intermittent bouts of green-tinged smoke. There's a spout at one end, and a handle on the top, and an assortment of skulls, in various shapes and sizes, arranged in a circle around the base. Creatures lean out of trees and jump down on to its lid, hang from its handle, or dangle from its spout. Others scurry in the shadows under its base, yowling.

Timothy, Farthing and I press close together, turning in a circle to keep watch on the path behind, and the path ahead. 'Why is there an enormous kettle in the middle of this wood?' I whisper. 'Why is everything here so weird?'

Before he can reply, the cahoots break free from the trees and enter the clearing. They've grown again, and as we watch, they devour a tree whole, swelling even further. Another eye pops open in their bulk. It squeezes out on a stalk, coming towards us.

'They're going to eat us,' whimpers Timothy. Farthing rears, flexing her purple wings, but her teeth are chattering with fear.

We shuffle backwards, away from the cahoots. I trip over a tree root and land on my back in the wet grass at the base of the kettle, jarring my spine. As I roll on to my knees, everything feels in slow motion. I watch helplessly as the cahoots lunge at Timothy.

I'm crawling towards him when my hand comes down on a big orange mushroom. It breaks, releases a foul stink and a stream of yellow slime.

The kettle begins to rumble and quake. The cahoots seethe, pulling away from Timothy. He and his dragon stand shivering in the grass. I reach for him, calling his name, but my voice is drowned by a thunder of colourful sparks mingled with black feathers shooting out of the top of the kettle.

Timothy pulls me to my feet. We cling to each other as the whole kettle whirls around, showing two squat little feet and ankles underneath, before it settles itself back down.

Then I'm blasted up into the air. The end of the kettle spout rushes closer and closer. I stretch my arms in front of my head, dimly aware of my own screaming. I'm sucked inside, my whole body rattling violently as I'm propelled up, down, left and right inside the twisted tube. It's dark, and cold, and my bones ache from being knocked against the sides. Then, finally, I pop free and fall a few feet on to a wooden floor.

28
Hawthorn Tea and Covenstead Bread

I barely have time to catch my breath before Timothy comes wailing through the spout after me, closely followed by Farthing, who shoots through as a tightly wrapped purple cocoon. She hits the wall on the opposite side of the kettle and unfurls her wings, flapping around and shrieking.

Pushing myself to my feet, I gaze around with my mouth hanging open. This place is far bigger inside than it has any right to be.

A fire burns in a large grate on the opposite wall. Lined along the mantelpiece are foggy crystal balls resting on black velvet cushions. Cat ornaments clutter every available surface, some made of china, others of gemstone, or carved finely from wood.

A real cat is sleeping on a squashy sofa. It pops open an eye to watch Farthing disdainfully. It looks so much like Artemis that my stomach gives a little leap.

'Timothy, do you think the cahoots can get in here?' I ask, staring up at the hole in the ceiling that we dropped through.

He climbs to his feet, cloak hanging in ragged scraps from his shoulders. 'I hope not.'

A series of tiny balls of fur emerge from the skirting board and proceed across the floor. Some are grey, some are ginger, others are black, and all appear to be . . . singing. Their voices are tiny and high-pitched, but I can just about understand their words.

You are safe, they can't get in, you are safe, so would you like a cup of tea?

I feel a smile fill up my whole face.

'What devilry is this?' Timothy presses himself against the far wall, as Farthing stares at the little creatures with a look of disgust.

'How can you say that?' I grin. 'Whatever they are, they're so busy and positive!'

Would you like a cup of tea? they repeat, slightly louder.

Just then, the air grows tense. I feel a prickle on the back of my neck. The kettle sways on its feet. We crouch in a corner and watch as, one by one, three bundles are spat through the spout into the room; bundles made of squawks and greasy feathers. Great, raggedy birds that, one by one, dump themselves down on the floor. They're all black-dressed, tangle-haired and muddy-booted.

'I heard a something,' says one, bending to pull up a striped stocking. Her hair is feathers but the rest of her has changed back into the shape of a woman. 'There must be a spy a-lurking.'

'I heard a nothing,' says another, her fingers still talons and wings sprouting from her shoulders, all hunched and slickened with filth. 'Oh, curse our stolen eyes!'

Eyes . . . the eyes in the trees?

'Well, I heard a mingling of a nothing and a something, but you don't catch me getting my haunches all riled up over it,' says the third: broom-handle thin, with silver eyes like plates of weather. 'We should be refuelling our spirits, ready for the next assault. Not lingering in this corrupted part of the wood.' She spits a glob of something on to the ground. A glob that looks like a mess of fur and bones.

Farthing gives a faint little groan, ears pinned back against her skull.

Suddenly, three pairs of eyes focus intently on us.

'Told you, sisters, spake it so, did I not?' rasps the one with the feathers for hair. 'Spies in our midst, and the clews are merrily serving them!' She clicks her fingers, and a broom appears in her hand. She sweeps the tiny balls of fur back under the skirting board.

'Are you the Hagdons?' I breathe, straightening up and stepping forward.

'Truth be known,' says the one with talons where fingers should be.

'Truth be told!' chorus the other two.

'And what are you?' asks Feathers. Three barely human faces squint at me. 'Stray soul or Mouldheels' minion, we cannot allow you to trespass here.'

'She hasn't done anything wrong,' declares Timothy, stepping to my side.

'We are guardians of the Shadow Way, therefore we shall judge the wrong-or-rightness. And *you* are?'

'A sailor,' says Timothy boldly, standing straighter. 'I depend on your fighting to be able to bring souls across the lake. Thank you, for everything you do in the Shadow Way.'

Feathers-for-hair looks surprised, then proud. But she studies me, and her expression falters. 'Wait, sisters.' She points a crooked finger. 'She walks our muddled paths, yet – listen. Her lungs and heart are breathe-beating. How?'

'Why?' caws Talons.

'Why so special, so different?' rasps Weather Eyes.

'She is alive!' shrieks Feathers.

'Who is she?' they screech together, the *she* ringing off the walls.

'I'm Spel Wrythe,' I answer quickly, glancing at the spout opening in the ceiling. 'Please help us – we're being hunted!'

'You're the ones on that warrant that has appeared throughout the wood,' says the Hagdon with talons. 'The warrant issued by Mouldheels.'

'Sit down, sit down,' says Feathers, eyeing our weary faces.

We're shooed towards the sofa so fast that I end up sitting on the cat's tail, earning myself a jarring screech and a reproachful look.

'Jagged thing, all thorny-wild,' scolds Weather Eyes.

The three Hagdons stand facing us, while Farthing hunches on the mantelpiece, emitting a constant low growl.

'Silly little beast,' chides Feathers, chuckling.

'I need your help,' I beg them. 'Mistress Mouldheels has my sister. I have to find her and get her to safety.'

'First things first,' says Talons. 'You should explain yourself. As *my* sister said, you are not like the others here. You appear to be somewhat alive.'

Feathers wags a finger in her sister's face. 'It is impolite to make demands of your guests without first inviting them to sample the infusions.' She claps her gnarled hands. 'Clews!' She winks at us conspiratorially. 'Never do the housework yourself. Isn't it irksome?'

The jolly little balls of fur proceed again from under the skirting board, trilling happily.

'What are they?' asks Timothy with suspicion.

'Clews?' says Talons, with distaste. 'So-called little helpers.'

'But what –'

'They're formed from dropped cat hairs. One of my sister's experiments gone awry.'

'Awry?' Feathers looks scandalised. 'I don't see you complaining any time you want something done!'

'We have no time for this,' says Weather Eyes. 'We cannot stay stranded here now that we have lost this part of the wood.'

'I agree,' I say, standing up again. 'I need to keep going.'

Timothy looks horrified. 'I did think this might be Mouldheels' territory, with the missing eyes and the thorn-piercings scattered around. Then, when the cahoots attacked . . .'

All three Hagdons look pained. 'Mouldheels' servants scratched out the eyes of the trees, stealing our far-sight in the wood,' says Feathers. 'But there is a fault with our kettle, meaning we cannot flee until the repair is done.'

The clews reach the middle of the floor and then begin to form a sort of tower – one jumping on top of the other until they're all assembled and singing at the tops of their voices. The cat looks at them in irritation.

Once they're in the tower formation, they stagger over to us. *Sit down, please.*

'It is quickest just to do as they say,' admits Feathers.

Swallowing a growl of frustration, I sit.

Hawthorn tea, or hot chocolate? they intone, voices louder now they're joined together.

'Um, hot chocolate, please?' I stammer.

Timothy chooses hawthorn tea, all the while watching the clews like they're about to rush at him with knives. Mugs of hot liquid materialise in our hands, the same moment that the clews disappear – in a cloudburst of hairs and dust that makes me splutter. Now I can see why Talons said the experiment had gone awry. Stray cat hairs float on the surface of my hot chocolate.

One of the Hagdons snaps their fingers, and more clews scurry out of the seams of the sofa, the cracks in the wall, and the patches of mould near the spout. This time, they produce trays of food. There are tiny pale green eggs, and delicate mushrooms, sliced neatly in half and fried golden. There are glossy green leaves, still steaming from the pan, and round radishes, red as flushed cheeks. Butter gleams under and over everything, in oily yellow splashes. And there are cakes, too.

'Covenstead bread, pumpkin muffins and pumpkin pudding!' declares Talons.

The cat jumps down from the sofa and twines around Feathers' ankles, almost tripping her over. 'Bog-cluttering frog spittle!' she yelps, steadying herself.

I taste the hot chocolate. It's thicker than normal, with an earthy taste. It's only when I take one of the muffins that I realise how my hunger isn't even hunger any more – it's a creature all of its own, digging out the flesh of my stomach with clawed hands.

The Hagdons watch me closely while I eat and drink. I've devoured almost everything before it occurs to me that no one else is eating. My chewing slows, and I look up at them awkwardly. 'I know I'm being hunted, but I do have a right to be here, you know,' I say, in the strongest voice I can muster. 'I mean, I'm not exactly dead, but I was born here, in the Shadow Way. So I'm not entirely alive, either.'

'Elspeth.' Weather Eyes steps closer. 'That is what your mother named you. It's really you? You've returned, after all this time?'

29
Amara's Book of Shadows

'You knew my mother?'

'We met her when she came through here. We were with her when she gave birth.'

They tell us their true names. The Hagdon with feathers for hair is called Moonwort, and the one with talons is Pearl. The third, with the strange silver eyes, is called Yarrow.

'Who are you?' I ask them, forcing back my true question. *What are you?*

They smile ruefully at each other. 'The last bastions of guardianship and protection for this Way,' says Yarrow.

'Specifically,' says Pearl, with a wink, 'we are calcified witch souls.'

'Witches?' whispers Timothy.

'Oh yes,' says Pearl.

'We are so ancient that we have acquired some of the abilities usually out of witches' reach,' says Moonwort. 'Abilities known only to other organisms, usually. Hagdons have always been part of the Shadow Way, but there used to be a few more of us.'

'And what, pray tell, are you doing back in the land of your birth?' asks Yarrow.

My story spills quickly from my lips. I watch them grow set and grim as they listen.

'Will you help me? Please?'

'We must act quickly,' says Yarrow. 'If Mistress Mouldheels is hunting you, the ghost of the Witchfinder General won't be far away. Their cahoots will have sniffed you out and spread the message far and wide – in the Muddlewood, and beyond.'

Gratitude soars in me, because we don't have to go any further alone, but Timothy's face turns streaky and splinters into fragments that buzz around his shoulders. 'The Witchfinder General?' When he resolves again, his face is taut with terror. 'But he can't still be hunting here, in death?'

Yarrow nods, grimly. 'I'm afraid he is. And he has passed his title on to every male heir in his lineage. There has always been an active Witchfinder General, though over time the role has become a secretive one.'

'If Mistress Mouldheels has issued a warrant for your capture, it would seem that she's realised she's got the wrong sister,' says Moonwort.

'But in that case, what will she do to Egg?' I try to keep my voice steady.

I feel a cool pressure on my wrist. When I look up, Timothy is smiling at me gently. 'We'll find her, Spel. Take heart.'

Moonwort's eyes sparkle. 'I've been saving something for you,' she says, pulling a wooden chest out of a cupboard behind a circle of crystal balls. 'Something that might help, and is yours by birthright.' She rubs away the clotted dust with her hand, takes a key from her pocket and unlocks the chest.

She hands me a small, fat book with a dark blue cover.

'What is this?'

'Your mother's Book of Shadows,' she whispers. 'She wanted you to have it, but she must have lost it in the wood. We found it after you'd already gone through into the living Way.'

A faded gold border gleams quietly around the edge. Otherwise, the cover is blank. 'She wanted *me* to have it?' I put my nose to the top of it and sniff – it has a warm, almost spicy old scent, and the pages are uneven, some poking out higher than the others.

'Yes.' Moonwort smiles.

She *did* leave something for me! I open the cover to read:

Amara's Book of Shadows.
Work thy magic for the good of all.
If it harm none, do what you will.

The next page is a chaotic contents list, with lots of crossings out, arrows and ink smudges, but some of the entries are clear: *potions, plant medicines, scrying, wands, crystals.*

I leaf through the book. It's densely written, full of different coloured inks, pressed leaves and flowers, brown tea stains, faint pencil sketches, diagrams, and cuttings glued in from magazines. There are several drawings of Grael, and lists of her favourite puddings. There's even a sketch of Artemis, labelled *'the undertaker's wake cat'*. The sight makes my eyes brim with tears.

There are lists of funeral proceedings and rituals for the time between a death and a burial. The wake dirge – the song for the dead that Shranken Putch mentioned, such a long time ago – is written out on a page bordered with pressed flowers. A flutter of unexpected excitement tangles in my stomach.

I can't *wait* for Egg to see this.

Farthing hovers curiously over my shoulder, and I glance up at her, grinning. I point out a drawing of Grael. 'This dragon is a knucker, back where I came from!'

Her wings spark against each other, and she drifts closer, before finally settling on my shoulder to look at the book. My breath catches. Her smooth belly and paws are warm and solid, and my ear tickles with her contented breathing. I hardly dare move in case she flies off again.

'What *is* a Book of Shadows?' I ask.

'It's a bit like a witch's diary,' says Timothy, in a strained voice. He's looking at the book as though it's a poisonous snake. When our eyes meet, his are stark and fearful.

'Yes.' Moonwort gestures at the book. 'As you'll see, it is a record of all sorts of things from your mother's magical life:

notes, dreams, spells. The book will tell you.'

'But . . . I don't think it can be for me, in that case. I'm not a witch. My sister is the one with powers.' I close the book and put it down.

'Elspeth,' says Pearl gently. 'You are a witch. You are destined to be a very powerful witch indeed.'

'You are the rarest kind.' Moonwort bounces on the balls of her booted feet. 'A spirit witch. And the most powerful of the spirit witches, for you were born in the Shadow Way.'

Unexpected anger bursts inside me. 'I might be a witch, but I'm also a soulless Wicked Girl. So how can anything I do "harm none", or be "for the good of all"?'

'The Hunt has been telling these lies,' says Timothy, with a strange calmness.

Pearl glances at him in surprise. 'The boy is right. They blamed the witches for every misfortune. They made reformatory schools for the children of witches because they wanted to drain your powers for themselves.'

Gently, I pick the book up.

A boom like a thunderclap breaks overhead and all around us. The kettle shakes on its feet. Farthing's claws scrape the skin between my neck and shoulder as she swoops up and away towards the ceiling.

'Attack!' yells Yarrow, silver eyes flashing. 'Get the younglings to safety. We fight!'

30
The Library of Spells

Pearl ushers us towards a door in the corner of the room. When I twist to look back, Moonwort is growing a heavy cloak of feathers that erupts from her collar bones. The cloak is already tattered and bleeding where chunks have been torn out. Are these three really the main resistance against Mistress Mouldheels and her servants? How much longer can they go on fighting like this, while the backlog of souls grows longer and longer?

'Where are we going?' asks Timothy, while Farthing trembles around his neck.

'The Library of Spells,' says Pearl, jaw set. 'You should be safe there.' I don't like the sound of *should*. 'Through here, quickly!'

Behind us come the sounds of battle – thuds and scrapes and the fizzing of an explosion.

Pearl holds the door open for us and we slip inside. Then she pulls the door shut.

I stare around the room. The ceiling is dug high into the

middle of the kettle, and lit by hanging glass orbs filled with drifting sparks. Farthing zooms up to inspect one of them, bumping her snout on the glass and clouding it with steam.

Timothy flickers between visibility and invisibility with the rhythm of a heartbeat. I've come to suspect that means he's extra anxious.

On shelves stretching all around the circular space are brown glass bottles. Each one is labelled. There are rich green liquids, with mud smeared across the labels, and blood-deep purple potions, glinting with twists of gold. In the middle of the floor is a large wooden workbench, complete with a stool to sit on.

Another explosion sets the kettle rocking, and I reach out for Timothy at the same moment he reaches for me. Farthing shrieks, clinging on to one of the hanging lanterns with her tail.

Determination settles over me. The quiet, wild voice swells in my bones; the voice I have never quite managed to silence. *This is my undoing. This is my untaming.* I set Amara's Book of Shadows down on the workbench. That's when I notice that the cover isn't blank after all. Something has been carved into it, but it's hard to make out. I tilt the book in the light and small letters show up in the leather.

Once
We
Were
Witches

When I run a finger across the etched words, tingles spread through my body. OWWW. That's what the engraving means on the pocket watch. Amara was leaving clues about who we are.

'That book is a dangerous thing,' says Timothy, eyeing it warily. 'It would incriminate you if they found it on your person.'

I shoot him a dubious look. 'Who I *am* is incriminating.'

The truth expands into the space around and between us. I can't avoid this truth that continues to haunt me. My mother was a witch. My sister is a witch. I was sent to a school dedicated to cleansing the witch from my veins.

'I am a witch.'

His shoulders stiffen, and his profile thins until I can see the walls through his skin. 'Witch. So many times in my life I heard that word whispered and spat and shouted.'

How is it I already feel like I've known this boy my whole life?

He turns to me. 'We have much in common, Elspeth Wrythe.'

My throat tightens with tears.

'My sisters were the daughters of a witch too. As I was the son.' As his words touch the air, a rich, damp smell of earth rises to fill my nose. Wetness tips down his cheeks like rain down the bark of a tree. Timothy stares at his hands. 'The Witchfinder General rode into Knuckerhole village, before dawn, one day. I had just risen to fetch the morning loaf. I heard the hoofbeats

268

before the baker's oven was lit. They took seven women from our village alone. One of them was my mother. He dragged her from her bed with his own hands.'

'What happened to her?'

He looks at me with a sadness that distorts the likeness he's been clinging to: the shape of a boy that he won't abandon. 'She was killed. Burned in the village square, with the other women taken by the Hunt. They made us watch.'

An image flashes into my mind. Young faces, hundreds of years ago, bathed in smoke and ash, ears clogged with the screams of their mothers and sisters. I pull him towards me, my fingers sinking into the cold, sticky not-flesh of his arm, and let him cry into my shoulder. The tears are only memories, which flow as little black shadows from his eyes into the air.

'The care of my sisters fell to me after mother died,' he sobs. 'But then I sickened. My death was their abandonment.'

'It's not your fault you got sick!'

'And now I learn that the Hunt locked you away all your life, and never allowed you outside.' He pulls away from me and stares me straight in the eye. 'I was supposed to meet you, and help you on your way. I know it. I failed my sisters. I will not fail you.'

'Thank yo—'

A wrenching, tearing sound rends the air. I cover my ears

269

with my hands. It sounds like something is cutting into the side of the kettle. 'What if the Hagdons can't hold them off?' I say.

Timothy looks grim. 'You should consult the book, and we'll see if there's anything useful here. We have to hurry.'

I climb on to the stool and turn to the book. When I open it, the urgency of Amara's writing almost jumps off the page to meet me.

I am a witch. They tried to tame me, but they did not succeed. If anyone finds this book and tries to punish me for my own nature, let it be known that being sensitive is no crime, and that is what it means to be a witch. Attuning to the secret rhythms of life, the mysteries of the unseen. Knowing the spirits living within every creature, rock, tree, river or plant.

My eyes are gulping, and until now I never knew I was so hungry for truth.

While I pursue my apprenticeship I am also learning as much as I can of witchcraft and witch heritage. It feels like a justice issue as much as my own interest. I've learned how potent the craft once was. How the fire witches could make flame from their own fingertips, and read the future in the fire, while the air witches worked hand in hand with the wind, stirring up great gusts or listening to the voices carried on it. As for water

witches, no sea or river flowed immune to the twitching of their fingers, and rain fell or stopped according to their preference. Earth witches were the ones with the most affinity to the trees and plants of the world; where they stepped, roots followed, and flowers bloomed in their wake. The spirit witches were the rarest: their element is the fifth one, and if it be for the good of all, they could summon plants from winter sleep, and call forth storms from calmness.

I leaf through the book, searching among pages of scrawled handwriting. Finally, I find a page with a heading underlined in glittery, purple ink.

Basic Spellcraft

As I read, the words begin to lift and dance off the page. They form two spirals that take the shape of two miniature girls. They're about as tall as my index finger and made of silvery light.

'Hi!' says one. 'I'm Amara. And this is my best friend, Gretel!'

The second tiny figure does an elegant twirl above the page. 'I'm gonna be the most powerful witch, ever!'

Amara nudges her. 'No, you're not!'

'Anyway,' says Gretel. 'We're here – in secret, shhh! – to tell you everything you need to know about learning your first spells, aren't we, Amara?'

'We sure are, Gretel!'

They turn to each other and do a high-five.

Timothy stares agog at the page. 'What are these creatures?'

'They're just images,' I breathe, eyes fixed on the two girls. 'It seems like some sort of . . . recording? One of them is my mum when she was about our age.'

'To start with, keep your choices simple,' says Amara. 'Find three ingredients per spell, and mix a little of each in a cauldron – see below for the dosages.'

'Always add a mind-diamond at the end of each spell to bind it!' says Gretel.

'Oh yeah,' says Amara, laughing. 'I always forget about them. Anyway. Burn candles in all four corners and the centre of your workspace. Light a bundle of sage, to cleanse the space and create your circle. If you have crafted your wand, you can use it to channel your intention.'

At the end of the paragraph, the two girls begin to unravel, and the silvery threads disintegrate back into words that sink into the page.

'That was an impressive enchantment,' says Timothy.

'I've seen the other girl somewhere before,' I tell him. But however hard I wrack my brain, I can't quite place her. Still, it's great to have found out that my mum had a best friend. It looks like they had a lot of fun together. Speaking of friendship . . .

The secret life of Spel Wrythe: I think I have my first real friend

1. His name is Timothy

2. He is a ghost

3. I'm not sure how our friendship is going to work

4. But I don't care right now

5. He just seems to really like me, and it's nothing to do with my sister

I let my eyes scan the page, searching for spells that might be helpful – something to break the curse on Egg, and something to help the Hagdons fight the cahoots, or failing that, get us out of here.

I find a spell to break a curse quickly, and mark the page while I keep looking for another. There are no mentions of cahoots or familiars, though there are a lot of smudged words that are impossible for me to read. Swallowing a growl of frustration, I keep searching. Finally, there's something that sounds like it might help us, though it's hard to tell if it's specific enough: a spell to cast a light on the darkness. I ponder it, chewing my lip.

The cahoots seem to blend straight out of the shadows, swallowing everything in their path. The moonlight I managed to grab seemed to hurt them. If they're constructed from patches of darkness, a shining light might make them recoil?

Only one way to find out.

31
Spellcraft

I spin around the room, up and down the stairs, gathering ingredients. Farthing goes with me, curled around my neck and peering at everything, chirping questioningly, and I enjoy the warmth of her growing trust. I walk past the glass bottles, glancing high and low, reading as many labels as I can at random because it's all just so . . . *wild.*

The breath of a dragon
The deep croak living in a cat's miaow
A robin's frost-song
The quiet strength of mountains
Salt spray from the sea at dusk
Wet sand that has felt the impression of toes
An ache for distant places
The warmth of sunlight on fur
A look exchanged between raindrops
The stillness of snow
Rain-smell

Thunder-grumble
Spiderweb dew
The feeling of looking out over snowy rooftops
Wind in the trees
Library hush
The solidness of a horse
Things the rain washed away
Book-smell . . .

'How?' I whisper suddenly to Timothy. Another explosion outside makes the bottles chatter on the shelves like loose teeth. 'How did they capture all these things?'

'They are fragments of soul memories, collected from the Muddlewood where they snagged in branches, or flew on the wind,' calls a voice.

I peer down from the ladder I'm standing on. 'Moonwort!'

'We haven't much time, child.' She looks at everything I've gathered on the bench so far, and smiles. 'You have used your time wisely. Now please also collect betony and vervain, from the herbal supply closet, and then two things from the memory wall, storm-smell and homesickness: the storm lends electric power against the curse, and homesickness helps the cursed remember themselves.'

The spell ingredients are arranged in alphabetical order, and I have to climb up a spiral staircase fixed in one corner to find S. I rush along the upper gallery, which is also stocked full of mysterious brown bottles. Some of them glow, others vibrate slightly. One has a tiny curl of smoke escaping over its lip. I can feel the power sneaking past the cork. It's labelled *Storm-smell*. I carefully lift it down and return to the lower level, setting the brown bottles on the workbench.

'Almost there,' says Moonwort. 'You should find another ingredient that you associate with your sister. And perhaps one to keep her alive after the curse is lifted?'

I snatch a breath. 'You really think she will be alive? That I can bring her home?'

Sadness touches her eyes. 'I can have no way of knowing that, child. But we must act as though that outcome has already happened. That is part of witchcraft too, you know – visualising what you want to make manifest.'

I nod at her, trying to steady my nerves. 'Okay. So what should I use?'

'Blood, preferably. She will need life to transfuse her, after an ordeal like hers.'

'Blood?' I wrinkle my nose. 'Whose blood?'

Moonwort smiles. 'Don't worry — we have a small amount of dragon blood taken only after a dragon had perished. It was not obtained by cruelty.'

So I search a little longer, until my eyes fix on a bottle full of something called *The ability of stars to widen eyes*. I snatch up the bottle, brushing dust from the glass. Egg has the same ability as those stars. Then I fetch down a bottle of dragon's blood from a shelf next to the herbs.

On a ledge overhanging the bench is a container holding a few jars of something shining like a lantern. I read the small looping lettering on the label. *Mind-diamonds*. I almost forgot that Gretel mentioned those! The only thing is, each jar of mind-diamonds is a different colour, and I have no idea which ones I need. When I leaf through the book, I find a page that explains how the diamonds are *Tiny brilliant sparks*, like flashes of inspiration. The colours are white, blue, red and green. I choose blue, because the book tells me that is the colour of distant travel, yearning and midnight skies. Skies hold stars, and my sister is the very brightest.

Moonwort helps me pack everything into the pockets of my cloak and trousers. Then she places a calloused hand on my arm. 'Go. Quickly!'

I look up, and smother a scream.

The bulging eyes of a cahoot have pushed through a crack in the kettle's enamel. They squirm around wetly. The cahoot strains against the seam. Then it stills, eyes throbbing, watching me. '*Elspeth Wrythe!*' it rasps, with a hideous urgency that plucks at my skin. I cover my mouth with my hand. We edge away, ease the door open, and slide through into the heart of the kettle as the cahoot drops into the library like a splatter of ink.

We promptly crash into Pearl and Yarrow. Yarrow presses a finger to her lips, as Pearl slips past us and locks the library door. An enraged screech punches our ears.

'We fly,' whispers Moonwort. 'We must escape this place, and then we will take you as close as we can to Mouldheels. I will include you in the spell. Do not fight it.'

One by one, each Hagdon jumps up and down three times, shaking out their arms and legs, which change swiftly into great black wings and scaled yellow feet. It's as though turning into birds is their version of putting on their coats to go out. Then they begin muttering, under breath reeking of fish and muddy worms.

I'm flung up, into the air. I can barely bite back a shriek as I'm thrown head over heels, the room spinning around me.

The room grows bigger and bigger. I feel very sick. The Hagdons' spell is shaping me like clay – I'm being squeezed, moulded, nipped. Shrunk.

One of the Hagdons pulls open a pocket in her side, just as though she really is wearing a coat. It's a deep dark cave, rushing to swallow us up. Pedalling my arms and legs, I shoot headlong inside it, followed by Timothy and Farthing. The light is blotted out as the Hagdon lets the pocket fall shut.

Then the only sound is my own heart, thumping loud enough to wake the dead.

32
Wolfwyrm and the Scaly Strangulators

Inside the Hagdon's pocket, it's so snug and stuffy that I can barely breathe. The three of us huddle in the bottom of the pocket. 'What is happening?' I whisper.

Timothy starts to speak but the ground shakes beneath us and then we're being thrown up and down with the Hagdon's steps. Farthing whimpers. Another few moments pass, and then – with a horrible lurch – my stomach turns over as the Hagdon leaps into the air and rattles through all the twists and turns of the kettle's spout.

But instead of the impact of landing in the clearing, all I feel is a strange, sickening sense of rising higher and higher in the air. Grabbing fistfuls of feathers in my hands, I walk myself up the wall of the pocket and poke my head into the open.

'Spel!' shouts Timothy. 'Get away from the edge!'

'We're flying,' I call down to him, unable to suppress the laugh that gurgles from my mouth. The strength of the wind – interrupted only by the steady drum of the Hagdon's wings

– feels like it could slice my head off my shoulders. Its bite makes my eyes stream. Wiping them with my sleeve, I stare down at a landscape blanketed in green. The forest stretches in all directions, beyond the limit of what I can see. In the distant north, there's a hazy outline of mountains, so tall that the stars gather around their pinnacles.

Sticking my elbows over the edge of the pocket, I hunker down with my chin cushioned in the feathers, and the wind stops feeling so ferocious. Timothy joins me, and Farthing nuzzles her way in between us. I stroke her head.

'The Muddlewood,' whispers Timothy. 'It's so beautiful from up here!'

'It is a bit, isn't it?' Clouds and treetops rush by, the mountains slowly looming closer. I think of the spell ingredients I'm carrying, and decide that the next chance I get, I'll try to work the magic I need to help my sister. A strange calm settles over me.

But then the sky ahead is blotted by a long shape writhing towards us, like a ribbon of crimson silk. Smoke billows from the front of the shape, tainting the air with ash. One of the Hagdons begins to croak out a warning, but in an awful darting movement, it's upon us.

And I see that it's a dragon. Fifty times bigger than Farthing, and even bigger than Grael and the lake knuckers. This dragon is a deep blood-red, with shimmering, veined wings, and long claws protruding like daggers.

'Wolfwyrm!' scream the Hagdons. 'Mouldheels' servant!'

It throws back its head and lets out a bone-shattering bellow. The Hagdons scatter. I can't hold back my scream as we wheel around in the air. 'Hold on tightly!' yells Timothy.

The Hagdon tucks into a dive. 'Timothy!' I shout, as we hurtle earthwards.

Farthing plucks at the hood of my cloak – but when the Hagdon suddenly halts and begins to turn, she and Timothy are hurled past me, out into the open air.

Time seems to freeze as the little dragon spirals away through the sky, and I lock eyes with Timothy as he falls. 'Don't look for me – find Egg, please find her and help her stay alive!' I scream. My last word is butchered by the fierceness of the wind. Then he's gone, drifting alone until Farthing zooms to his side.

Before the Hagdon can plunge towards the shelter of the treeline, a set of curved claws lashes towards her. The claws fan out, as though in slow motion. I can't tear my gaze away as they slice through the Hagdon's body, just underneath the wing with the pocket in, inches from the seam where I'm watching. The Hagdon screeches, a wrenching sound of agony, and I realise I'm screaming with her.

And then I'm freewheeling towards the forest, a lone, severed wing spiralling like a windborne seed. As the trees loom closer, I duck back inside the pocket and brace myself, with my head tucked between my knees. But I glide down

quite gently, landing with a rustle in a pile of dead leaves.

I scramble out of the pocket and stand, swaying with dizziness. My throat feels cut by all my screaming. Blood oozes from the Hagdon's severed wing, staining the leaves. I bend double and throw up.

When I look back at the wing, it's slowly buzzing, and growing paler, and quivering. It looks like it's blurring into another shape – into an arm. I feel the vomit rise in me again, but when a great blood-clanging screech fills the air, I turn away and run. When I look up, two spear-billed birds are piercing the sky, battling with the dragon. Conjoined fury paints the sky storm-black.

I'm aware that, as I run, I grow. Up. And up. And up. When I finally stop to rest for a moment, the trees are smaller than they were, and I can see past their trunks. I stagger, placing a palm on to one to keep from falling. I'm my usual size again.

Please, let Timothy be on his way to Egg. If I don't make it, someone has to. Someone has to be with her, someone who cares. I wish he was with me still, though. And faithful Farthing, however much she likes to grumble. I only just found my first real friends. I don't want to lose them already.

My eyes are sore and gritty with exhaustion, but I start moving again. My legs are so tired I can barely lift each one to take another step. I also have no idea where I'm going. Pausing to lean against a tree, I pull the thorny map out of my pocket and hold it open between my hands. It's muddier and wilder than ever, but more details have been stitched into the fabric, too. The Hagdons' kettle is there, complete with the damage inflicted by the cahoots. In fact – when I look very closely – I can actually see tiny dots of shadow swirling through the trees near the clearing.

Is the map showing me the Shadow Way, in this very moment?

I turn the fabric slightly in my hands, and suddenly the perspective shifts. Between my thumbs a slender chalk path, like a ribbon of white silk, unfurls between the trees. A tiny figure stands in the centre of the map, and when I move, so does the figure.

It's showing me where I am! I search the embroidered landscape for any clues as to where Mouldheels might be keeping my sister. Near the top of the cloth, partly obscured, is a large building, set behind huge gates. There are a few other buildings scattered around, but that one's the biggest and most important-looking. Would Mouldheels be there? Or would she be lying low? I don't have anything else to go on yet, so I keep the map folded in my hand and set off down the path, terror nipping at my heels.

I come to a part of the Muddlewood where ghoulish, tattered shapes hang from the trees, drifting in the stillness. When I go closer to look, my heart bolts into my mouth and sets my teeth throbbing. The tattered shapes are green scarves, snagged in the trees.

Mouldheels' school scarves.

I blink, take another step closer. Why would I think that? They're probably just scraps of moss, or . . . I lift my hand, but my fingers tremble in the air. They *are* Mouldheels' scarves. I recognise the weave of the cloth, the way two sides are thinner where they're been tied obediently under chins. But how – *why* – are these here? I want to check they're real, but

I can't bring myself to touch them.

I feel like the trees are closing in on me. When I turn in a circle, my eyes scan the undergrowth and the branches and the dark spaces in between, watching for eyes or movement or shadows with unnatural intent. But although I've got that same feeling of being watched, nothing actually stirs.

So I hurry on, head down, every muscle and nerve strained to attention.

Little bright blobs of light distract me from my sadness, and the endless trudging. They flicker around the trees and dance into my path, so golden against the growing dark that they seem to drink the shadows. They must be fireflies. I put out my hand to touch one – and snatch it back, wincing. There's a small burn mark on my skin. I stare again at the dancing lights, and back at my palm. These aren't fireflies – they're sparks.

All of a sudden, I'm aware of a slithering sound, overlaid with a faint, wind-like whispering. But the air is still, and the trees are creaking even though there is no wind to move them. I crane back my head and cast my eyes from tree to tree.

Creatures stare back at me through blazing eyes. Smoke steams from their long, pointed snouts. The smoke is peppered with sparks. All around me, dragons are snaking through the trees.

With shaking hands, I unfold the map again. Fright

spikes into my mouth. All across the cloth is one small word, stitched again and again.

Run.

Run.

Run!

My feet slip on dead leaves as I race away. But the further I run, the more dragons I see. The map didn't tell me which way to go. What if I'm lost here, forever? There's a rich smell of earth in my nose, and the bluster of a restless wind on my face. I tug my beanie lower over my ears, waiting for my eyes to adjust. My boots are up to the ankle in thick mud. The air is so clean and cold that it burns my lungs. Every tree's face has been gouged like the ones near the kettle.

Panic stabs my belly. The dragons' sparks dazzle my eyes. The damp of endless twilight means that my clothes can't keep out the chill.

My feet begin to sink into wet, marshy ground. At first I can pull my boots out and find drier patches of mud or grass. But soon I'm up to my shins, and can't find a way out. My frantic activity draws the attention of a dragon, which leans its head towards me, teeth glimmering in the spark light.

I'm sinking. As soon as I realise it, it starts to happen much more quickly. I put my hands in the mud, trying to drag myself out, scrabbling and paddling, but the movement only seems to make it worse. And it's not so much mud now, as water.

My stomach spasms hotly into my mouth as the dragon climbs down from the tree, on short little muscled legs, breathing eagerly in my direction.

The muddy water is up to my thighs and I'm still sinking deeper. The dragon's eyes are locked on to mine with an intensity I can't bear.

It hums to itself while it slinks closer, licking its lips.

It reaches a clawed hand up to my cloak, one of its talons snicking a tear in the cloth as easily as if it were made of butter.

I slip, struggling and flailing, covered in mud. 'Get away!' I scream. 'Please, *please*, just get away from me!' The grasping mud is up to my waist. Egg's face flashes in my mind. Missing her hurts like a chunk torn from my body. *I'm sorry. I'm so sorry.*

Timothy's face replaces Egg's. Maybe he'll find her. I cling to that thought like a lifeline. But I've lost my sister and my first real friend. The pain is like a physical spasm, locking on to me, making me grit my teeth so tight that the muscles in my neck feel like they're going to snap.

A drumming sound disturbs the path, away to my right. Soon a scrap of light pierces the darkness of the wood. The scream lodges in my throat as the trees part before a huge black contraption that's hurtling towards me. A lantern swings wildly from a pole at the front. It's a carriage drawn by two enormous ghostly horses, steam billowing from their

287

nostrils, their hooves thundering across the ground.

Just as the carriage reaches me, the cloaked driver lashes a whip at the dragon, sending it hissing backwards. Fast as a lightning lick, the whip snaps out at the dragon again, making it roar. The whispering and slithering of the other dragons grows louder, and the sparks in the air thicken.

'Get back!' yells the driver. 'Back, or there'll be no more puddings for the entire scaly strangulator clan!' The rope flicks, cracking against the dragon's shoulder. It begins to stumble further backwards.

Puddings? Did absolutely *everyone* know about dragons and puddings, except for me?

'Now, you, quick!' The whip is dangled in front of me, and I cling on to it. 'Don't struggle, else you'll sink deeper!'

I'm hauled out slowly, the pressure of the mud easing away from my legs and middle, until I'm finally standing on the edge of the marsh. Electric, horrible energy races around my body, and I stand there and shake, panting for breath. I put out my arms to balance, then wipe the mud from my mouth. I'm so dizzy that black spots cloud my vision and I can't even see the person who saved me.

A door in the side of the carriage clunks open. 'Come along, then,' says a different voice. 'My place isn't far. You're probably in shock, poor thing.'

33
The Lady of Barrow House

A slim, gloved hand extends towards me. I take hold of it and climb up the short row of steps into the carriage.

The interior is warm and plush, with cushioned seats of jewel-green velvet. Soft lamplight fills the compartment, illuminating the features of the woman who saved me. Her eyes are a clear sky-blue, and focused steadily on my face. She's shimmering like all the souls do, but her shimmer is like silver sparkles. She's slender and long-limbed, sheathed in a long dress of black and coffee-coloured silk, which is covered in a pattern of interlocking snakes. Her gloves are oyster-grey silk, and rubies wink in the auburn tumble of her hair. On top of all that, she smells like strawberries and honey.

I become quickly and horribly aware of my muddy, smelly clothes. I'm so dazzled that all I can do is open and close my mouth a few times.

She pulls a blue-feathered fan from her pocket, using it to stir the air before her face. A long black tassel hangs from the handle. What with the clothes, and her perfume, and the intent way she's staring, a wave of anxiety crashes over me. I've never been near someone so elegant in all my life.

'I am the Lady of Barrow House,' she says gently, watching me with concern in her round eyes. 'And you may call me Lady Barrow. What's your name?'

She's having to talk to me as though I'm two years old. Shame floods my body. Through watery eyes, I force myself to look at her and take a breath. 'I'm Spel. Wrythe. What . . . what were those things?'

'Scaly strangulators? They are a dragon clan, living wrapped around the poor trees, hugging the life out of them. I'm sure they were relishing the thought of hugging the life out of a blood-and-bone girl! You are very fortunate, Spel Wrythe.' She gives me a long look, her clear eyes staring calmly into mine before flitting over my face with an expression I can't name. 'Now, then. I'm in rather a hurry. Would you mind if we set off?' She raps on the smooth black carriage ceiling with her knuckles. 'Onwards, driver!'

'Lady Barrow, are you a soul?' I blurt.

She raises two perfect brows. 'Well, now. You *are* well informed. As it happens, everyone in the Shadow Way is a soul.'

'But not everyone has found their path, and gone to their rest?'

She smiles patiently. 'Exactly.'

'So are you a *lost* soul?' As soon as I've asked the question,

I feel hideously embarrassed. 'I mean, I know someone who is a bit like that – lost, I mean.' I think of Timothy. Please let him be okay.

'Oh,' says Lady Barrow, glancing out at the blur of trees rushing past the carriage window. 'It's all rather a complex matter, really. But some days, I still keep a lookout for someone who *I* lost.' She turns back to me, and her eyes are so bright they almost burn my skin. 'A very long time ago.' Then she peels off her gloves to rummage in her leather bag. 'Would you care for a toffee?'

'Yes, please.' The mention of toffee reminds me of Putch's baking. Then the thought of him makes me feel too small and too far away from everyone I care about. In fact, it's getting harder to properly remember things about the living world. Like how the sun and the rain feel. Maybe *I'm* the lost soul.

Lady Barrow's nails shine with black polish as she passes me a sweet. For a moment I could swear I glimpse my own reflection in her thumbnail. She catches me looking, and smiles.

Allowing myself to rest back in the cushioned seat, I unwrap the foil and put the toffee on to my tongue. It's buttery and smooth, and laced with hard pieces of sugar that pop against the roof of my mouth.

'Nice, aren't they?' She folds her hands in her lap. 'How are you feeling after your ordeal?'

'A bit shaken up.'

'Let's get you dry and warm, and fed.'

Her words leave me rattled by a sudden panic. It's like the warmth and luxury of the carriage have lulled me into forgetting what I'm trying to do. I pat down my pockets, feeling a trickle of relief that the book, the watch and the little potion bottles are all still there.

Lady Barrow watches with a bemused expression. 'Is something wrong?'

'No, it's just . . . thank you so much for your kindness, but I can't stop. I'm looking for my sister, and it's really urgent that I find her.'

She stares down at me, as though encouraging me to go on, and I feel as though I could tell this person anything. It feels like any secret I could give to her would be kept safe.

I clean the last lumps of toffee off my teeth with my tongue. 'Have you heard of Mistress Mouldheels?'

'Of course.' She shudders delicately. 'I'd have thought everyone in the Shadow Way has heard of her.'

'I think she's holding my sister prisoner. And I have to find her before she dies. You see, because of a curse, she came through here alive.'

The lady watches me with a fascinated expression. 'Oh my! I am very glad our paths crossed. Young girls shouldn't really be out wandering these paths, alone. Anyone might have found you.' Her eyes shine, almost wet. 'Thank goodness it was me.' The carriage lurches around a bend. 'I will help you find her, Spel. Although it will be very dangerous.'

'Thank you,' I tell her earnestly, gripping the carriage seat. 'Thank you so much!' It's such a relief that someone is just believing me without any questions, and offering to help straight away.

Lady Barrow smiles, pulling the silk gloves back over her delicate hands.

The carriage slows. When I look out of the window again, we've left the cover of the trees and passed into the middle of a small clearing. The twilight of the Shadow Way spills pale over the bare winter trees, and the carriage wheels scrunch over a blanket of snow.

The Lady unfurls the black curtains at the windows, obscuring the view. 'That's better,' she says, smiling at me. 'You can let yourself have a little sleep, if you need it?'

But before the curtain fell, I'm sure I glimpsed the face of someone, peering from behind a tree. I don't know if I'm imagining things, but for a moment, I could have sworn they were wearing a green headscarf.

34
The House on Barrow Hill

A squeal scythes the air. I tense, sitting forward in my seat. The Lady covers my hands with her gloved ones. I hadn't known I'd made mine into fists until then.

'Don't worry, Elspeth,' she says gently. 'My guards were just opening the gates to my house. Ridiculous old iron monstrosities. They need oiling.'

All my held breath comes rushing out in a gale. I try to force myself to relax.

We're pinned to the backs of the seats as the carriage inches painfully up a slope that's almost vertical. I can hear the sound of the whip lashing the poor horses, and keep hoping that we're almost there.

The carriage levels out, and then stops again. Soon the sound of the wheels is replaced by the crunching of the driver's feet on the ground outside. The Lady said she'd help me find Mouldheels. Does she mean now? It *has* to be now.

There's a flurry of cursing as the driver clambers around on the roof, retrieving luggage. 'Don't mind him,' Lady Barrow assures me. 'His language is colourful and his driving a little reckless, but he does make me chuckle, he really does.' She tosses her hair, then studies her reflection in a small, round mirror that she pulls from her bag.

The driver pulls the door open on Lady Barrow's side. 'Ma'am.'

She steps down from the carriage and throws a multicoloured cloak of sequins over her shoulders. I scurry after her, climbing down the carriage steps and jumping to the ground. She turns to me, lifting her hood over her hair. 'Come along,' she says, before striding towards a sweep of steps leading up to a huge house.

The house is several storeys high, and imperious in the way it looks down past the great iron gates and over the hill to the smaller buildings far below. A single light shines in one of many windows – too many to count. It's more like a mansion, really.

The stone is dark and there's a brooding atmosphere rolling off the place, almost as though it has its own will. As I stand there staring, a memory flickers into life, somewhere in the back of my brain. I've been here before.

My breath catches in my throat. The building looks exactly like Mistress Mouldheels' School for Wicked Girls. The realisation is like being hit in the chest.

Lady Barrow pauses on the steps leading to the large front door. 'Come on, little Spel!'

295

The way she calls me 'little Spel' gives me a pang of guilt and sadness. It reminds me so much of Egg.

I stand staring for a moment, before hurrying after the Lady.

'Excuse me, Lady Barrow?' I call out. 'I really can't stay. I have to find my sister.' I chew the rest of my thoughts down deep, so they can't get out. *I really can't go into that place*.

A firecat lands on her ear. She holds a finger up. 'Sorry, I have to take this.' She continues, blood-red satin ankle boots clicking decisively up the stone steps. 'Come on, Elspeth!'

Elspeth. That's the second time she's called me that. But didn't I only introduce myself as Spel?

Behind me, another shriek rips the air. The gates. They must have closed. I'm trapped here. Goosebumps flare along my arms. A voice deep down inside me speaks, urgent and low. *No one who cares about me knows that I'm here.*

I try to tell myself not to be stupid, hurrying up the steps after the Lady. Just before I follow her through the front door, I peer inside, half braced to run.

But then relief swoops through my body. The entrance hall is ornate and graced with a high ceiling, soft light blotting the shadows. It's not the same as the school here.

I step inside.

A servant in an apron hurries up to take our coats, scrutinising mine with an expression of severe distaste. 'Boots,' she instructs me, before I can take another step.

Obligingly, I pull my wellies off and hand them to the maid, who holds them at arm's length. If I were Egg I'd be giving her the W sign for *whatever* right about now.

Another servant approaches us with a tray. 'Hot towels and refreshments?' he asks.

'Oh yes, we have had a trying journey, haven't we?' says Lady Barrow, flashing a warm smile at me.

I fold my arms. 'No, thank you.'

'None of that nonsense, miss,' the servant says brusquely. 'If you're a guest of the Mistress, you must be a clean guest.'

Mistress . . . the word sends a tremor of fear rippling along my spine. I feel my body tense, and nervous sweat begin to gather on my palms.

I sense the Lady stiffen. 'Lady will do,' she says, with a sternness that jars with her image.

The servant offers me a flannel cloth that's been heated and wrapped into a perfect roll. I pick it up, trying to smile, but the servant's eyes are fixed too intently on my face. It feels weird. Like they know something about me. After quickly washing my hands, I take a glass of something fizzy and pink.

'Pink lemonade,' says Lady Barrow, with a wink. 'Very refreshing!'

I take a sip, and it's obviously delicious, but my stomach is clenched so tight I can barely keep it down. *I have to get out of here. I shouldn't have followed her in.* 'I really need to keep going,' I tell her, working hard to keep my face calm and blank. 'Can you help me find my sister?'

She sweeps an arm around my shoulders. 'Come with me.' We walk up the stairs, which are a spiral, curled in the house's heart, just like the ones at Mouldheels' School. The reassurance of the entance hall begins to dissolve, a sick feeling growing in its place. The banister is wooden and here and there are dark, eye-like knots. I move rigidly, and I can't help looking back over my shoulder at the front door.

'I will explain all, I promise you,' murmurs the Lady, peeling off her gloves.

Old-fashioned portraits hang on the walls, and great glittering crystal lights – the Lady calls them chandeliers – shiver as we pass beneath them. A brilliant gold firecat lands on her ear, and she murmurs serenely into it – *Yes, no, don't be ridiculous, that would be lovely* – before it flies off again.

I look up through the spiral. There are a lot of floors in the house, but the room she shows me to is only on the second floor. 'We'll take our breakfast here, and then I'll organise a bath and change of clothes,' she promises. Her black-painted fingernails apply the smallest amount of pressure to my shoulder. But it's enough to make me look up into her face, startled. Her clear eyes are like a blue winter's sky, brittle and desolate.

I force myself to smile, trying to look grateful. 'Thank you, Lady Barrow.'

'Such a solemn little thing.' She watches me closely, as though I am a creature for study. 'You know, you may call me by my first name. Call me Gretel.'

'*Gretel?*' Hearing the name again so soon is like a jolt of electricity. 'My mother knew someone called Gretel. They were best friends.'

'Really?' She puts her head on one side. 'How interesting. You know, it's not even a very common name!'

The breakfast should be dazzling. Glasses of freshly squeezed berry juice, fat white bread rolls spread with butter and honey. Fluffy poached eggs and slices of tender pink fish and steaming cups of coffee. Pastries – dough twisted into plaits, and studded with thick lumps of chocolate. Photographs watch us from a magnificent wooden bureau – Gretel smiles out from each one, while she shakes hands with important-looking people, or uses large scissors to cut ribbons. One of them is a school photo – one of those ones with the whole school outside on the grass, arranged in rows.

'You've barely touched the food,' she says, quietly.

And the strange thing is that she hasn't, either, and yet items have been disappearing. Smudging out into nothing, even though neither of us have moved.

'I wish I *could* eat,' I try to explain. 'But I'm too worried about my . . .' I let my voice trail off. Her attention is heavy, over-alert, and suddenly I don't want to say another word about Egg. Instead, I lean forward and pick up a mug of coffee, hiding behind its brim.

'I don't understand how either of you are here,' Gretel says sadly. Then a slow smile eases her lips into a curve. 'But I am *oh* so happy that you are.'

My fingers tighten on the mug. I hold myself very, very still.

Another gleaming firecat lands on her ear. 'Mmm, yes. Yes, of course. Fine!' She brushes the gold beetle away irritably. 'I must just pop and see to something urgent, but do feel free to make yourself at home.' Tension strains at the edges of her mouth. 'Spel, is something the matter?'

300

I grew up under threats, and I can sense one now. So I brighten my face and get ready to lie. 'No, everything here is wonderful!' My words are dull and false even to me, but Gretel doesn't seem to notice.

Another firecat circles in the air, dropping towards her ear. 'I know!' she snaps, swatting at the device. It falls out of the air and lands with a little thump on the carpet. She rings a silver bell, and a servant peels himself out of the shadows at her elbow. I had no idea anyone was there.

Before I can blink, he's cleared away the food and faded into the background of the room again. Except that I never saw him pick anything up, but I know he *did* do it. I shake my head, squinting into the corners of the richly decorated space. Why is it that reality feels so . . . *manipulated*, here?

Gretel rises, and holds out a hand for me.

I don't take it. Instead I pull myself stiffly to my feet, and watch her nervously. Something hard presses into the sole of my foot. I glance down – it's the firecat, crawling along the carpet, faintly buzzing.

Gretel smiles and starts towards the door. I bend and scoop the firecat into my palm, then straighten quickly. Gretel pauses, gripping the doorframe. Her black nails gleam. Small pale shapes are reflected inside them. I squint. They almost look like tiny faces. 'Oh, that's what I wanted to say.' She turns back to me and clicks her fingers. '*Never* try to leave this house.' She stares into my eyes, with an undisguised coldness that seeps through my skin and into my bones. 'There have been reports of something – a creature, a *serpent*, of some sort – terrorising the countryside. Awful business, honestly. I would so hate for you to be caught up in any horrors when you could be safely tucked up waiting for me.'

'But I do need to –'

'I'm sure it'd be better to wait for me and then fashion a plan together, don't you?'

'Yes, of course.' I force the meek words between my teeth, while my skin itches.

She puts a cold finger beneath my chin, forcing me to look at her. 'Promise me you won't worry. I have lots of contacts that we can use to find your sister. It is much better to go about these things strategically. Don't you think?'

When I nod enthusiastically, she laughs. But I know lies. I was raised on a whole heap of them.

'If you look in the wardrobe in the bedroom down the hall, you'll find something clean to put on. I'd like to see you wearing it when I return.' She whirls a silk scarf around her neck. 'Now I must dash. I will see you later, little Spel.' And in a cloud of drama and luxuriant elegance, she's gone.

Suddenly, I'm alone in this great, solid old house – though never quite alone. I can feel the eyes of the servants peering out at me from the shadows, and from behind almost-closed doors.

35
Parallels

The firecat looks broken. I turn it over in my fingers, examining the way one of the wings is crumpled and the buzzing comes intermittently, like a badly tuned radio. I drop it into my pocket and sag against the chair. *Layla, Mariam, Jameela, Isla. Chloe, Emily, Leah. Charlotte, Annabel, Bethany. Harri, Lorna, Soraya.* The hallways of the school snake, tilting, through my mind.

I'd half expect to walk into one of these rooms and find Mariam, sitting on her bunk, unwinding her long thick plait and studying the duty roster.

'*Elspeth, you're in the laundries tomorrow,*' *she instructs, looking through her list.* '*Isla, you're on kitchen duties –*'

Isla buries her face in her pillow, red hair splashed bright across the white. '*I'll stink after that,*' *comes her muffled whine.*

'*Jameela, let me see . . .*' *continues Mariam,* '*yes, you're laying the fires and cleaning the chimneys, Layla's on bathrooms, and Meghan –*'

'*Yes?*' *enquires my sister, sweetly.*

'Dusting and polishing.'

'Oh, goodie.' Egg unties her headscarf and shakes out her glossy black hair, before jumping on to the edge of my bunk and vaulting from there into the one directly above. 'What about you?' She always asks it, because Mariam hates being brought back down to our level.

'Weeding.' She glares. 'Not that it's any of your business.'

What happened to them?

I'm heading to the door when Gretel's school photo catches my eye again. I have a flashback to when Egg and I were in Mistress Wolsley's office, looking at the photos there.

Because in this photo, in the middle row, there are two girls, leaning their heads together as though they're in on a secret. One is fair-skinned, with light hair and piercing eyes. The other is – Amara Penhaligon. Our mother.

My gaze flicks back to the girl beside her. I half recognised her when I saw the magical recording of her in the Book of Shadows, and now I know where I've seen her before. This is a copy of the photo in Mistress Wolsley's office.

Gretel *is* Amara's best friend! So why is she being so creepy and what is she doing here? And if she's dead, why hasn't she found her soul path?

I shake my head to clear the questions that are clinging like cobwebs. Never *mind* that stuff now – Egg's all that matters. I run to the door, steel my nerves and slip through. But I've barely put a toe on the staircase when a servant pops out from behind a marble pillar, gently shimmering. 'Anything I can do for you, Miss?'

'Oh!' I startle, twisting my neck painfully to look at her. 'N-no, I'm fine. Thank you.'

'May I ask what it is you plan to do, while Mistress Gretel is on business?'

Again, the word Mistress sends a squiggle of fear rooting through my insides. 'Oh, I don't know, really. I thought I might have a nap.' Before she can say anything else, I start backing towards the dining room, smiling at her in as reassuring a way as I can muster.

She points down the hallway, but her eyes never leave my face. 'You'll be wanting the guestroom, then?' She turns less visible, then gives herself a little shake and appears more solidly again. A ball of shimmering slime falls down her cheek, like a tear. She wipes her face, absently.

I shudder. Part of me wants to ask her why she hasn't found her soul path. But a bigger part of me just wants to get away from her empty stare. 'Yes, thank you!' I hurry away and shut the door to the bedroom. Then I stand with my back to the door, mind whirring. Gretel doesn't want me to leave the house. But what can I do if the servants don't even want me to leave the room?

A memory of Egg flickers to life in my mind.

'That world out there,' says Egg, jerking her thumb towards the barred window. 'I want to know all about it – more than the

guff that was in that stupid mag. I want to live. By all the power of those stars out there – I will get out!' She turns her beautiful face towards the blackness outside the window, sewn with thousands of bright pinpricks of light.

'*Dramatic,' stage-whispers Jameela, rolling her eyes.*

If my sister could attempt to escape our high-security school in a meat cart, then surely I can work out a way to leave this room. Then I remember. I feel for the pocket watch. Maybe I could get out of here by making myself invisible.

Behind me, footsteps approach the bedroom door. I squirm away, braced to run, but then there's a metal scrape as someone turns a key in the lock.

Cold tingles spread across me. I try the handle – I'm locked in.

Someone is breathing against the door.

Horror wriggles across my skin. 'Who's there?'

'Be a good girl, now,' says a voice. 'Do as Mistress Gretel says, and get changed. If you don't fight her, all will be well.'

That gives me an idea. What if I make Gretel *think* I'm going along with whatever she's got planned? Remembering what she said before she left, I step across to the wardrobe and pull it open. Then I back away, staring, as bile rises through my throat. A white lace gown hangs there, complete with satin slippers and a white bonnet, like a moon.

36
The Other Hall

It's a ceremony gown. I reach out and touch the fabric. It's real. How is this happening? Where am I? My brain whirrs, and another piece of the puzzle drops into place. Those times when the servants called Gretel 'Mistress', and now this . . .

What if Egg is somewhere in this house? What if this is Mistress Mouldheels' house, and Gretel is also a Mistress here?

Even though it makes me feel sick, I pull the gown from the hanger and dress as though I'm going to my ceremony. The stiff white bonnet sits heavy on my head, straining my neck. How did the Mistresses wear these things every single day?

The dress is roomy enough for me to keep my clothes on underneath, so I transfer the watch and the small brown potion bottles into the front pockets, and slide the Book of Shadows and the map into a back pocket. Then I roll up the bottoms of my trousers so that they don't show beneath the hem.

I cross to the window and look out at the view down the hill towards the dense tangle of the Muddlewood. The taunting voice of golden-haired Tobias, back in the basement at the funeral parlour, trickles through my mind.

Your sister will be lost for all eternity in darkness and a clutching despair, living in the murk, a demonic creature of slime and misery. It will not be undeserved, for a witch.

'No,' I spit, through clenched teeth. 'There must be something I can do! There must!'

A crackling sound comes from the pocket of my cloak. The firecat. I lift the little golden beetle on to the windowsill. I thought it was broken, but now the crumpled wing has smoothed itself out. On impulse, even though I've no idea how the things work, I put my face close to the beetle.

'Message to Timothy, sailor between the realms. Spel trapped at Barrow House. Need help. Come quick!'

I crack open the window just enough to let the firecat crawl out and take to the air, where it hovers for a moment before streaking away down the hill, and out of sight.

Then the only thing to do is make magic. Or give it a try, at least.

With no clue how long I have until Gretel returns, I pull all the ingredients I have out of my pockets, plus the Book of Shadows, and spread them out on the bed. There's a page in the book with a list of essential tools, which includes a pot called a cauldron. Casting around for anything that might be useful, I spot a little bowl on the bedside table that's full of scented dried petals. I dump the petals out and add the bowl to my kit.

First, to brew a spell to lift a curse. No big deal. Except I *so wish* the Hagdons had had time to teach me at least one or two basics of witchcraft.

I sit cross-legged on the bed. To start the spell, I take an incantation that Amara has written out and bordered with stars, and speak it as solemnly as I can, remembering what Moonwort said about visualising what you want to happen.

> *By the stars and the moon,*
> *By earth and flame and sun,*
> *By river flow and winds that blow,*
> *As I strike this bell,*
> *The spell's begun.*

Instead of striking a bell, I flick my fingernail on the iron bedstead. As soon as I've done it, I feel an electricity in my bones. The silvery light I saw before is glowing around my fingers.

Next I put the herbs in my 'cauldron' and add three drops of each of the potions I brought from the Library of Spells, finishing off with a mind-diamond. Then I take a deep breath, focus all my intention on the liquid, and wind my finger above the bowl. The silver light flows out of the tip of

my finger, and the potion moves all by itself, mixing.

Just as well, since I don't even have a spoon.

Gripping the book in one hand, I whisper the magical words with as much strength and power as I can summon, more silver light streaming from my fingertip into the bowl. 'By the power of the moon and sun, the earth and stars, this spell is done. May it work for the good of all, bringing light to those it touches, so mote it be, and blessed be.' As I say the words and watch the mixture churning, I imagine Egg drinking it and the curse leaving her body, until she's herself again.

There's a faint pop and spluttering sound, and then a metallic smell floats off the mixture, and little puddles of dragon's blood bubble on the surface. The liquid bubbles, then it boils down to a thicker syrup, and turns into a deep clay colour, threaded with strands of gold. Following the book's instructions, I pour it into one of the now empty bottles.

Gently, I turn the glass bottle in my fingers. 'Please help my sister,' I whisper, lips salty with tears I didn't know had spilled. '*Please*.'

There's a tap on the window. When I look up, my heart soars. Timothy and Farthing are both hovering outside, noses pressed to the glass.

I wrench open the window. The firecat worked!

They tumble into the room. Farthing whirrs around my head, then settles around my neck, tongue rasping against my skin. 'I missed you, too!' I tell her, rubbing her head.

Timothy hugs me quickly, which is strange because it's more like a feeling of being in thick fog than a real hug. 'What are you wearing?'

'The ceremonial gown. It's how we Wicked Girls receive our souls.' I lift an eyebrow, aware of how ridiculous it all sounds now.

'What?'

I sigh. 'It's a long story.'

He searches the room, checking the walls and inside the wardrobes.

'What are you doing?' I hiss.

'Checking for firecats.' When he's satisfied, he turns back to me. 'The Hagdons sent me to search for you while they battled. Farthing led me here after we passed the quagmire where the strangulators dwell. I think she picked up your scent there. This house – it's a place of maleficent power. I think it's connected to the Hunt.'

I grip the back of a chair. My hands meet the brightly coloured cloak Gretel was wearing earlier. All at once, I realise how heavy it is, and how cool to the touch – like dead skin. The sequins are sewn together, but one has come loose. when I push my fingernail underneath it, it lifts up. Underneath is a scaly surface. A sick feeling turns my stomach hot.

Timothy's head splinters apart and buzzes like an angry black cloud above his shoulders, before reforming again. 'Dragon skin,' he says.

I let go of the cloak, my fingers feeling burnt. 'I know you're right about this place. And here's the other thing that's strange about it – it's a twin of the school where I grew up. The one I told you about, where we were all kept away from the rest of the world.'

'All those hundreds of girls,' he whispers, staring around as though one might materialise at any moment.

'This is Mouldheels' house.' The certainty is spreading

through me as I speak. 'You know it's still not too late for you to get out of all this, don't you?' My voice catches. 'You're still free. You and Farthing could just find your way back to the docks, and beg for your job back. Or . . . you could find your soul path.'

Timothy takes my hands and looks into my face. Farthing stares up at me from her place around his shoulders. 'It wasn't until I met you that I allowed myself to understand how long I had been lost. It was time, Elspeth. I never could protect my mother or my sisters. I was powerless against the Hunt. But now I want to help you. It's time for me to fight.'

I swallow, then rush on, afraid my tears will steal the words from my lips. 'I've never had friends of my own before, you know.'

He grins, and Farthing's face lights up as brightly as if a lantern has been lit from the inside. She yowls out a pure little trilling sound. Then she stands on Timothy's shoulder and expands her wings wide, pressing her snout against my cheek.

All my life, I thought I was just empty, except for badness. A vessel with a rotten core. But if Timothy and Farthing are my friends, maybe that can't be true.

The moment is shattered by the sound of voices below us, in the entrance hall. Footsteps click away from the hall, moving underneath us. I move towards the door and listen closely. 'Timothy,' I whisper. 'I need to search for my sister here. But I'm locked in. I think you're going to have to try to find the key.'

He nods. Then he turns very faint, and as I watch, he blends through the door and disappears. Farthing buzzes around the room, spitting sparks that fall and singe the floorboards.

It feels like forever until Timothy pushes the door open from the other side. 'Quick!'

We slip out of the room. On impulse I lead us in the opposite direction from the main staircase, hoping this really is a mirror image of Mouldheels' School. Sure enough, we find a set of smaller stairs hidden at the back, in the dark. Moments later, a servant emerges from the other end of the hallway, and proceeds quickly towards the bedroom. They're already checking up on me again.

We move silently down the back stairs. Just as well that the Mistresses taught silent movement as well as needlework and good housekeeping. They always said that Wicked Girls should be seen and not heard.

We reach the entrance hall and hide in the shadows underneath the stairs, peering along the hallway. I strain my ears, and there it is – Gretel's voice, murmuring in the distance. 'The servants are going to follow us,' I warn Timothy, and he nods. Farthing tightens her tail on his neck, mewling faintly.

'This way!' I whisper, leading Timothy along the corridor

towards Gretel's voice. On our left we find a set of double wooden doors, exactly like the doors to the assembly hall at Mouldheels' School. For a moment I feel as though the weight of all the water in the well is pressing down on my spine, and Grael's eyes burn inside my mind. Everything is upside down. Everything has its Other, in the Shadow Way. We push the doors open and step silently into the cold, dimly lit hall.

Slugs jewel the walls, their slime sparkling like frost. Rows of benches line the hall, and at the other end, just beyond the water basin, hangs the red curtain.

The benches are filled with shimmering souls. Most are men in old-fashioned clothing. Three chairs are positioned at the front of the hall, just like at Mouldheels' School. Gretel sits in the central chair, with *Oliver Todd* in the chair to her left and a severe-looking man in a wide-brimmed hat to her right.

'It's him.' I feel a slight pressure at my side as Timothy grabs my arm.

'Who?'

He's staring hard at the man in the hat. 'The Witchfinder General, who took my mother away,' he whispers.

37
The Weaver

Timothy brims with an earnest hate that I can't stand to see scrawled across him. Then he sags against me, buzzing with a grief and anger that send a blizzard of arrowed shapes storming around his head. I hold on to him, fear rising in my throat. We keep to the shadows. I can't let them see the boy and his dragon.

Gretel clicks her fingers, and almost imperceptibly, the red curtain is moved aside by servants hidden in the shadows.

Something large and dark is fixed to the back wall. A tapestry, identical to the one at the school. A high-pitched sound rings around the room, like a saw blunting itself back and forth across stone.

At the foot of the tapestry is an old woman at a spinning wheel. A Mistress's bonnet is sitting askew on her head, and a thin line of spit trails from her mouth like slug slime. A pair of long, tapered needles are in her lap, with threads running off them. She's been weaving the tapestry.

'Let's get out of here,' whispers Timothy, splintering and

then reassembling himself.

I shake my head. 'Timothy, I can't. I needed to find this. This place isn't just like Mouldheels' School – it *is* Mouldheels' School.' Realising it is like having a bucket of freezing water tipped over my head. Beads of ice trickle down my neck, chilling me to the core. 'You should go,' I urge him. '*Please.*'

'I won't leave you.' He reaches up for Farthing, crying and grappling to uncoil the little dragon's claws from his cloak. 'Farthing, it is not safe for you here! You must go and hide.'

But she burrows closer to him, twining her tail firmly around his neck, cat-like amber eyes shining. She won't leave him, either. We're in this together.

'We grow in strength, day by day,' announces the Witchfinder General, staring round at the sea of shimmering faces. 'But we will not return to our former glory until the Lady can be reintegrated to the living world. For that, we need the girl. The witch not of this world, and not of the living world.'

'The wrong sister came to me at first, but I have the right one now.' Gretel's voice ripples through the room. 'Join me in honouring Huntsman Oliver Todd in helping lead her to our door.'

I stifle a gasp. The man whose body we went to collect is a member of the *Hunt*?

Oliver Todd looks around the hall proudly as the ghosts applaud him. 'My thanks to you, great Mistress Mouldheels, in continuing the legacy of witch control, keeping the pestilence of witchcraft at bay.'

I stiffen. Timothy presses close by my side.

Gretel *is* Mistress Mouldheels.

'As some of you know, a programme is in place, at reformatory schools all over the world,' says the Witchfinder General. 'Witch children's freedoms of body, mind and spirit are suppressed, preventing accidental discovery of power, while allowing precious energies to accumulate. At the time of ceremony, these powers are drained, and captured for our own use. We simultaneously cleanse the evil from these children, while claiming the power for our own. This power ought always to be in the hands of the rational elite, for what could witches ever justify its use for?' he scoffs. 'They should be thankful. By doing this, we are saving their souls.'

The old woman at the spinning wheel jolts, beginning to work the wheel again. It clanks and clatters, and she mutters under her breath, filmy eyes flickering.

I once thought myself empty, believing that if I gained my soul I'd have a future, and keep the Unwicked safe from my evil. But the truth is, these people – the Hunt – made us believe we were bad, so they could steal our lives from us and make themselves stronger. The horror of it washes over me in waves.

'As present-day Witchfinder General, my brother Tobias has been leading the programme in the living world,' says

Gretel. 'He was instrumental in ensuring my plans for the Wrythe sisters were carried out after we were temporarily thwarted by Mistress Turner – whom we discovered to be a long-term undercover witch at the school.' Gretel's face contorts with an expression of disgust. 'Turner tried to hide the sisters from us, but did not succeed for long. My cahoots dealt with her.'

I grip the wall for support. There's still a Witchfinder General! And it's Tobias? I remember the struggle just before I jumped into the well, and the way he called Artemis by name. The little black cat seemed to really hate him, too. How did she know him?

My thoughts are broken by a surge of gratitude for Mistress Turner. She must have risked so much to try to help us. And what if she's been really hurt, or worse? I clench my hands into fists. I have to defeat these people. There's too much at stake. Too many people have suffered because of the Hunt's greed.

'The time has come for another ceremony, to cleanse the wickedness from a witch's bones.' Gretel – Mistress Mouldheels – looks up, and then beckons to me, a bright smile on her face. 'Elspeth, it's all right. Come forward, please – we've all been waiting for you.'

I feel like a spider trapped under a glass. Of course she knew I was here. Of course she did.

Every head in the hall turns to face me. Every face is filled with a greedy hate. A word swells and rings around the hall,

forming on the lips of everyone present, before being spat into the air. *Witch. Witch. Witch!*

'Not again,' whimpers Timothy, flickering in and out of sight like a butterfly's beating wing.

I take a step forward, the lamplight trickling slowly over my satin-covered toes.

'What are you doing?' Timothy hisses.

I don't look at him. 'Stay out of sight,' I murmur. 'I have

to do this. Trust me.'

The memory of Cece's ceremony day surfaces as I step towards the front of the hall. The truth of what she was really facing throbs in my blood. How dare they do this to us? The drag of the gown and the weight of the bonnet make walking much slower than usual.

'Soul, instil this child with your purity,' chant the ghosts. 'Soul, find your home here, fill this child with your light. In exchange a sacred thread shall be woven, in the fabric of life. It is spoken.'

'It is known,' I call out, pushing the words past the anger clutching me.

Then the tapestry takes over all my senses. I'm struck by a fresh lightning bolt of horror, as the realisation of what the high-pitched sawing sound is wriggles across my skin.

It's coming from the tapestry. The scene it shows is the same as in the living world: a winter forest. Peering from behind the trees are the tiny faces of girls, wearing Mouldheels' headscarves. The only thing missing is the cloaked woman, with the tumble of long red-gold hair . . . Gretel.

Disembodied voices brush past my ears, sometimes burrowing in. I hunch my shoulders. The voices sound like the echoes of Wicked Girls, atoning for their sins. Unlike the tapestry at the school, this one is twitching with unmistakable signs of life. But worst of all, it is *screaming*.

38
Wicked Girls in Needlework

Spots of mould are scattered across the tapestry like scars. There's a flicker of movement, far to the right. A squirming of threads. A square of cloth has been ripped away, and the area is resewing itself. It looks as though the healing has not come without pain. A crust of blood and yellowy fluid is stuck around the edge of the missing square.

The ghosts of the Hunt hiss as I pass. I pause in front of the three chairs at the front. When Oliver Todd gives me a cold smile, I lift my finger, and point straight at him.

He scuttles sideways out of his chair, and backs away down the edge of the hall. 'Get her gone!' he shrieks.

I laugh at him. 'You really think I've got that much power?'

The old Witchfinder General smacks the floor with a cane. 'Not for much longer,' he barks.

'How many people have you murdered in your lifetime, and helped to murder after your death?' I ask him, lifting my chin. Thinking of those I love, and those Timothy loves, has lent me more courage than I've ever tasted before. I'm more angry than afraid.

'Insolent creature!' he bellows, disgust etched across his ghostly face.

Gretel watches me, then rises from her chair. 'Come, child.' She presses her hand into the small of my back, and though I try to move away, she holds me steady as she guides me close to the tapestry.

Her eyes glisten. 'My sweet brother has never given up on me. At least someone in our family wants to repair the harm done by sending me to that school. What kind of witch-hunting family, on finding a witch in their number, sends the child to a reformatory?' She reaches over, and pulls at a loose thread of the tapestry, making it scream louder. 'I could have learned everything I needed from them. They didn't have to banish me!'

I turn to stare at her. 'You could have used your powers for good, instead of getting involved in all this.'

She cocks her head. 'But I am not just a witch. I am also a Hunter. How about that for a concoction?'

'Where is my sister?' I whisper, through a paper-dry mouth.

Gretel's eyes are glazed and distant. 'Your mother and I had such plans, at one time. We were going to find a place to live together, and reclaim the years stolen by that place. But Amara was a purist.' Gretel's eyes grow wide and dark, like those of a hunting creature. 'Completely wedded to what she called justice, and peace. She wouldn't join me in lending my

324

power to the Hunt. So she left me no choice.'

'Why would you lend yours?' I demand, anger flaring in me. 'The Hunt must be so much more powerful with a witch among them.'

'Infinitely more.' She looks down at me, unmistakable pride glowing in her eyes. 'My family tried to shame me for my powers. That is why I was cast out. But now I am second only to the Witchfinder General in the Hunt. I have taken that shame and thrown it back in their faces. And in working with them, my own power grows. I wanted to share that with Amara. I could have kept her safe.' Her face tightens for a moment, and her eyes soften with a thing that looks almost like sadness. Then she smiles again, and shrugs. 'It was not to be.'

'But they want to kill the witches! And you're a witch! It doesn't make sense.'

'Calm, Elspeth. Goodness, you do look so much like her when you're cross.' She folds her arms, and turns to face me properly. 'Do not forget, I am only part witch. The other half of me is Hunter. Perhaps you underestimate the significance of this. I descend from the *first* witch-hunters. I had to prove to my family that I wanted to purge the witch from myself. How could I ever have remained friends with a witch like your mother?'

I gaze up at her. 'What happened to her?'

A cloud of sorrow passes across her face. 'She was sent to

325

force a binding spell on me. Instead, she confessed everything about the witches' plans to try to stop me, and she begged me to reconsider my membership of the Hunt. She must still have believed there was good in my heart. She loved me, but she loved the witch-cause more. I loved her, but – I loved my family's approval more, I suppose.'

'You killed her!'

'We struggled,' corrects Gretel, coldly.

'She didn't love the witch-cause more!' I yell, remembering seeing the magical recording of the two of them in Amara's Book of Shadows. 'She wanted to stop all this madness!'

Gretel's jaw tightens, and she grabs my wrist in a vice-like grip. 'You realise we have revolutionised our approach since the hunts first began? In the old days, they killed the witches without realising their potential. Now we fully *appreciate* their power – which is something gained by having a half-witch involved.'

And suddenly, I understand. They wanted to stop us having feelings. The Weird Things were a way for us to subconsciously experience the magic that was being denied in us. There was power in our joy, so they banned talking and laughing and made us believe we were bad. They have been draining our powers all this time, not giving us our souls.

But since leaving the school, I've learned something about using my powers. Egg and I are not going without a fight. A bundle of threads twitches inside the tapestry.

My eyes follow the movement.

There – a small figure with dark hair and great, dark eyes. Eyes that my heart immediately whispers belong to my sister.

Her name swells in my mouth and spills over my lips; the loudest sound I've ever made in my life. The threads have stopped moving, and I call louder, until my throat bruises. And then there's a thud against the other side of the tapestry, so heavy and loud it sends me sprawling on to my back on the marble floor.

Spel, Spel, SPEL! The tapestry spits out a gale of howling tears. *Run!*

Horror splits my lips into a grimace that feels as though it'll split my skull into the bargain.

Gretel places her hand in the small of my back. 'Don't you *adore* my creation?' she purrs, by my ear.

I shove her away from me, hard. Then I pull the threads at my sister's feet. Dirty old snow falls out, on to the floor. But Egg is still stuck inside. When I reach out to touch the tapestry, I can feel it sucking at my fingertips, pulling me under its enchantment.

'Spel!' screams Timothy, somewhere behind me. 'Stop! That's what she wants you to do!'

His voice breaks my concentration. The words of the Witchfinder General slip through my mind. *We need the girl. The witch not of this world, and not of the living world.* What if I'm about to make Gretel even more powerful?

'The boy has a dragon!' declares the Witchfinder General. 'Heresy! Seize him!'

'Timothy!' I scream. But I can't help him. The tapestry lifts me up off the floor, and I'm pulled inside, tendrils of frayed cloth brushing my skin.

39
Hunted

I stumble in a snowdrift as high as my shins. When I put out my hands to find balance, freezing wind bites deep into my skin. The wind howls like a beast, hurling slivers of ice. The darkness is thick and almost total.

I take a clumsy step, hauling my feet out of the snow, only for them to sink again. A question forms in my brain and on my tongue, but I push it away. As I stagger forward, painfully slow, with icy water spreading up my legs, my eyes begin to adjust. In gaps between the violence of the wind, I understand – I'm in a clearing, surrounded by trees. Beyond is a big, square shape. A building, staring down over the scene.

Muffled shouts and laughter and sobbing are carried on the wind.

The question rises louder in me, joined by others, increasingly urgent. I stop, wrapping my arms around myself. *Where am I? How did I get here?*

Who am I?

I start moving again, though I have no idea what the point

is, or where I'm going. I do it to stay alive, because I know a cold like this can kill me if I let it.

Somewhere in the distance, dogs begin to bark. Then they start to howl, and the sound moves closer. I turn around, and try going in the other direction, but the wind is ever fiercer, so I turn back again. Then something whistles past my ear, and drops into the snow.

I struggle across to the thin shape, stark against the white. I reach down, touching its lifeless form – and then straighten, shock sending my heart into a frenzy of drumming. It's an arrow.

I may not remember who I am, but I know I'm being hunted.

I hoist the heavy dress I'm wearing up in my fists, and set off at the best impression I can make of a run. I'm out of breath fast, having to lift my knees high with each step just to clear the snow. Howls echo all around, the sound like the edge of a knife tracing up my spine.

'Wait!' shouts a voice, half eaten by the wind.

I spin, skirts drenched and dragging, then duck as another arrow parts the air, thumping into a tree ahead.

'Please!' begs the voice again. A pool of orange light spreads across the snow, and a woman steps through it towards me, oval face full of concern. A fur-lined cloak is pulled around her shoulders, and her eyes are a clear blue, touching my face with pity. A tumble of auburn hair graces her shoulders, the gold picked out by the light of her lantern.

'You shouldn't be out here on a night like this,' she calls. 'Are you lost?' Her black velvet cloak is fastened with thorns dipped in gold.

'I – I don't know,' I answer, barely able to speak above the force of the ravening wind. A sudden sob boils over my lips, loud and ragged and desperate.

'Oh, child,' says the woman, catching up to me and taking my hands in hers. 'You must be a long way from home. Shall we find you somewhere safe and warm, to eat and rest?'

'No, I don't . . . I don't think that's what I need to do.' I cast around, searching for something I've forgotten I'm searching for. My brain feels full of a thick fog, cloying in the corners of my skull. I mustn't forget, I mustn't . . . But I have.

'Come,' she says, tucking a spool of silken hair into her hood. Her nails flash, black and shiny in the lantern light. 'You must be exhausted. It's time to stop fighting, now. It's time to let go, to let yourself rest.'

As I stare into her eyes, I feel my muscles softening. But when she moves her hand away from her hood, I catch a glimpse of my own reflection in her nails. Something about it feels like someone tugging on my arm, trying to get my attention.

'What's wrong?' Her lips twitch into the ghost of a smile, and amusement trickles into her eyes.

This is some sort of game. But I haven't a clue how to play it.

The woman's smile falters as I take a step away from her. Something heavy shifts in my pocket, under the layers of lace and satin in which I'm sheathed. I slip my hand inside and find a lump of smooth metal. When I enclose it in my fist, it beats like a little heart.

Memories stir in the back of my brain. A girl wearing a green headscarf, covering a thick bob of shiny black hair. The same girl grinning down at me, waving her fingers to make paperclips swim in the air. A grumpy old man, mixing a pan of hot chocolate on a stove in a cramped kitchen somewhere.

I look back up into the face of the woman in the snow. Her mouth is carved open into a toothy smile, but there's no warmth in her eyes.

Just outside the circle of lamplight, a figure with a tear-stained face appears. They're wearing a green headscarf. But I can't quite make out their features.

Then the woman lifts something I hadn't seen into her arms, and levels it at me. It's a weapon, with an arrow wedged against its string.

The figure behind her takes a faltering step closer, mouth puckering into a silent scream. It's a girl with gentle brown eyes. Her name slides into my mouth. '*Henri?*'

She vanishes.

'Who are you talking to, dear?' asks the Hunter. And I remember who I am, and where I've come from.

Gretel. Mistress Mouldheels. She's hunting me, out here

in the snow, inside a tapestry in the world of the dead, miles from anyone I've ever known. And I think she might have stolen the soul of a girl who could have been my friend.

'Would you like to play?' A smile spreads across Gretel's face.

I scream, and turn, and Mistress Mouldheels shrieks with laughter, releasing an arrow. My soaked satin slippers catch in a pile of snow and I fall, whacking my chin on the impacted ice as the arrow brushes over me, tearing open my bonnet. The wind rakes at my bald head, trying to rip chunks from my scalp.

Mistress Mouldheels roars, fumbling to fit another arrow into her crossbow. 'There is nowhere to hide!' The gloat sits fat on her tongue.

I stagger away, keeping low, my heartbeat and breath rushing in my ears. 'Egg!' I scream.

Overhead, a bird screeches. Ahead of me, it drops lower and lower in the sky. Then it lands, heavy, turning into the shape of a woman with a shock of filthy feathers instead of hair. It's one of the Hagdons.

Moonwort.

'How did you find me?' I call.

'You have forged friendships stronger than steel, child.'

Timothy and Farthing! They must have called for the Hagdons.

'Hagdon!' bellows Mouldheels, advancing steadily behind me.

'Child, run!' squawks Moonwort.

'You hold no true power here. This is the domain of the witch and the Hunter. You are ancient; calcified. You will turn to dust in this place.'

'Not before this child is delivered to safety!' Moonwort retorts.

Mouldheels bites out a greedy snarl and charges at Moonwort. Her lantern swings, the metal squealing, and the scene is lit up like a fever dream – a perversely animated sea of twitching threads, writhing with stolen magic. Through a shimmering membrane to my left are a press of faces, watching hungrily. The ghosts of the Hunt and the Witchfinder General think they know how this is going to play out. But they don't know me or my sister.

Beyond the battle between the Mistress and the Hagdon stands a bundle of hissing, twisting, struggling flesh. 'Egg?' Whatever strength she found when she told me to run has vanished. Now she's barely human. I glance at Mouldheels, who's glowing with power. Moonwort hurls a spell at her, and the power dims for an instant.

When I turn back to Egg, her muscles have relaxed and she's swaying on the spot. But when Mouldheels recovers herself and fights back against Moonwort, Egg's face twists again, and she starts growling.

I rush at the thing that's almost my sister, knocking her into the snow, and wrench the spell bottle from my pocket.

Egg is a crumpled heap of tattered clothes and sodden hair and exhaustion. But she's still just about a girl with a thick bob of black hair, and a wide red mouth. She's curled into a ball, and her skin looks thin, like all her inner workings are almost growing through it. 'It's time to wake up, Egg!' Even though she tries to bite me, I smooth the hair from her face. Silvery light swirls at the ends of my fingers, and when it touches her she grows calmer.

I take the potion from my pocket and drop three purple drops on to her lips. Then I take hold of her limp hand and wiggle the binding ring from her finger.

'Spel!' warns Moonwort. 'I can't hold her off!'

Mistress Mouldheels staggers towards me, screeching. She grabs my shoulder and wrenches me away from my sister. But then a charge of figures burst through the torn stitching, led by the Head Undertaker from the docks and joined by Pearl and Yarrow. Timothy must have raised the alarm all throughout the Muddlewood, and done it well enough to convince the Head Undertaker to abandon his duties and help us. Pride glows in my chest.

The undertaker knocks Gretel away from me.

Egg spasms, back curling and arching against the floor so violently that I'm afraid her spine will snap. Stinking green vomit flows from her mouth. Every muscle in her body is rigid and corded, and her eyes are pinned open, with the irises flung back in her head. I kneel beside her, almost choking on my tears, which turn to silver and sew themselves into the ground.

When Egg's eyes flicker open, it takes them a while to focus on me. 'Spel.' Her voice is a sore husk. I made it just in time. She's not dead. Relief rushes over me. The dragon's blood worked, but I don't know how long we have.

Chuckling wheedles into my ears. Gretel advances towards us, eyes wild and ravenous. 'Ah, the Wrythe sisters,' she says delicately, examining her black-painted fingernails. 'How your mother *screamed*.'

'How could you hurt your own best friend?' I yell at her, trying and failing to stop my tears.

In answer, her hands craft cahoots from the darkness: squirming shadows coiling up like smoke from her nails, before flexing oily wings and taking to the air. They flank her, pulling the edges of this woven world towards themselves, making me feel sick to my bones.

'Fly!' she purrs, in a voice like poured cream. 'Fly, my bad seeds!' The cahoots dart hungrily towards us.

'Stay back!' I raise my hands and throw a protective circle around us, the same silver light blooming from my fingertips. The cahoots push against its edge, spitting and crooning desperately.

'Mistress Mouldheels!' shrieks Egg.

Gretel raises her arms to point at us. 'You should be more grateful, children.' She grins, hair beginning to lift up to stand on end. 'All girls ooze sin. And a home was made for you, in my name. A place where the world – baying for witch-blood – could not get at you, and you could fulfil a higher destiny.'

'She is not Mistress Mouldheels!' shouts Moonwort, limping towards us.

Gretel jerks her head towards the Hagdon, snarling. 'Be quiet, witch!'

'What do you mean?' I ask, sheltering my sister against my side.

'Gretel is one of the chief masterminds of the Hunt,' clarifies Moonwort, staring shrewdly into Gretel's hate-filled face. 'But the title Mistress Mouldheels is a title stolen, just like the powers stolen from young witches.'

'Stolen?' I gasp, letting in a dagger of cold.

'My sisters and I discovered the truth after seeing the weaver at the spinning wheel.' The Hagdon draws a crystal ball from somewhere in the depths of her feathery cloak and taps it with a finger. Images begin to swirl. 'Your mother banished Gretel to the tapestry, but she was not able to bind her here. Gretel eventually received enough witch power from the Hunt to be able to free herself from the weaving. Then she found the soul of the real Mistress Mouldheels and enslaved her. Mistress Mouldheels is now being used as the weaver of the tapestry.'

40
Creatures They Say We Should Fear

'Mistress Mouldheels was good and wise,' says Moonwort, smiling fondly. 'A great many years ago, her original school was set up to help train young witches.' The crystal shows a scene from inside Mouldheels' school, the faces all looking happy and bright. But then the crystal darkens. 'Eventually, the Hunt took control of the school, turning it into a place for reform, to exploit the shame they seeded.'

Egg's grip tightens around me. She mutters a very bad word.

I remember the old woman slumped over the spinning wheel, at the foot of the tapestry, the black bonnet askew on her head. I barely paid any attention to her, but she was the key. *She* was the real Mouldheels. 'We have to free Mistress Mouldheels!'

Gretel barks a hard, vicious laugh. 'She'll never be freed. None of you have the power to defeat me!'

A flame for Amara burns brightly in my heart. 'I am the most powerful witch for a generation, and the only one ever born in the Shadow Way,' I call out, visualising a bright light around myself. 'You know I have the power to defeat you. That's what you're afraid of!' The binding ring is still in my palm. As I speak, the symbols etched inside the ring begin to glow. And I know I have to finish the work of my mother.

Gretel unleashes a shriek, eyes grown huge in her head. 'No, no, you can't, you wouldn't dare!'

'Go on, Spel,' says Egg, flashing me the ghost of one of her glittering smiles.

I grab Gretel's hand, pushing the binding ring on to her finger. She wrestles with it, but the Head Undertaker and the Hagdons rush to help me hold her.

I open the Book of Shadows and leaf through it with cold-numbed fingers, searching for the spell I need. Then I begin chanting. 'I bind you, Gretel! I bind you to this woven place, never again to roam free and wreak harm on the innocent.'

With a blissful sigh, the faces in her black nails seep out like wisps. Gretel stares at her nails and then back at us, growling like a dog. But she's already weakened.

I summon as much power as I can imagine into my hands, and hold them over Gretel. My light pours on to her, revealing the cold hatred in her eyes. 'I bind you for the good of all, with this ring, and Shadow-Born magic. So mote it be!'

'So mote it be!' chimes Egg, hoarsely.

Gretel screams, a hideous sound that wrenches at the air and pulls at the threads of the world.

The Head Undertaker lets go of Gretel and stumbles away from her as roots push upwards through the snow, wrapping around her ankles. The Hagdons steer me and Egg towards the tear in the cloth. When I glance back, Gretel is being bundled inside a cocoon of thread-roots. She curses and struggles, reaching out clawed hands for me. But then her arms are bound, and the loathing in her eyes is enough to snatch my breath.

'Come away, now,' says Moonwort, and I join the others as we climb back out of the tapestry, into the Other hall.

'Elspeth Wrythe!' Gretel's scream chases after us, but then her voice is smothered by the binding.

Another battle rages here, between the ghosts of the Hunt and a gaggle of Shadow Way undertakers who must have come from the docks to help.

Egg shrinks back from the chaos, looking brutally exhausted. 'Spel,' she whispers, pointing.

The old woman weaver has begun to turn her wheel, spinning new threads into the tapestry. When we approach, her filmy eyes linger on mine. 'Elspeth Wrythe.' Her voice probes the half-light like a blind worm.

'Yes, Mistress Mouldheels, ' I croak.

'Is that who I am? The name sounds familiar.' Her gnarled hands grow still, and the thread slackens. 'And you are the Shadow-Born girl, daughter of the friend to dragons. Destined to be such a powerful witch. I have failed you, as I failed your mother.'

Slowly, like a trickle of water through a time-worn rock, light is returning to her eyes and peeling back the film.

'No.' I kneel at her feet. 'None of it was your fault.' I look at the spinning wheel, and glance over my shoulder at the tapestry – and the place where a scrap of cloth is missing. Then I pull the map out of my pocket and show it to her. 'Mistress Mouldheels – were you talking to me through this? Did you weave the words that appeared, and the warnings?'

She gasps, leaning forward. 'It feels like a dream,' she murmurs. 'But do you know, I think perhaps I did? Tapestry magic is a strange art, young Elspeth. That piece you hold is still magically connected to the whole.'

We flinch as the Witchfinder General bellows a curse and the Hagdons flurry around him in bird form, great wingtips battering his head. The other ghosts flee from the undertakers. 'You cannot avoid your soul path,' cries one.

'Spel!' Timothy rushes towards me. 'This is our chance. Hurry!'

I help Mistress Mouldheels to her feet, and together with Egg, Timothy and Farthing, we hobble towards the doors.

The corridors are eerily silent. Following my memories of the school, we wind our way towards the front door. The others wait behind me while I inch it open, checking carefully for signs of cahoots. 'It's okay!' I whisper, ushering them outside.

We break into a run, just as the servants spill out on to the stone steps behind us. 'Stop, or we will send the barrug crawling!' they intone, together.

'You don't have to do this any more!' I shout. 'Your Mistress is gone!'

They stare blankly.

Mistress Mouldheels rests her shimmering hand on my arm. 'You cannot help the poor souls, Elspeth. Gretel forced them to forget their soul paths. They are lost.'

Anger and sadness swell in my throat. I feel a vow forming in my bones. That as both a witch and an undertaker's assistant, I will always do everything I can to help souls find peace.

At the bottom of the path, the gate is locked. A pack of dogs begin to bark. 'What's the barrug?' I whisper.

'The serpent that has been terrorising the Muddlewood,' says Timothy, grimly.

'We need to hurry,' says Egg, face ashen.

There's a creaking sound behind us. I turn to look, as the others begin helping Mistress Mouldheels over the gate. A long black shape, belly hanging low, claws scritching along the ground towards us. Slime sloughs from underneath it. It's Gretel's carriage, the one I travelled in with her. Before my eyes, it's turning into a beast.

I swallow, hard. Then I fling myself on to the gate and haul myself upwards. Behind me, I hear Egg climbing. Then

I jump to the ground, followed by Egg and Timothy. We're running as soon as our feet touch the ground.

But as we move, I become aware of a whispering voice.

Timothy's face is full of fear, and his eyes shine as though licked by a demon. 'The barrug,' he whispers, dragging me along by the elbow so fast that my feet are barely touching the ground. Farthing flurries around Egg and Mistress Mouldheels, urging them on. Thankfully, Egg's old determination is lighting up her face, and the ghostly old woman is far more nimble than I'd expected.

Soon the creature that was the carriage is loping a short distance behind us, becoming more solid the more palpable our fear grows. I can feel my own fright blossoming like a spot of blood on linen. The barrug turns its head from side to side, moaning long and low. A mouth is carved into its face, open like a knife-slash. This is the serpent Gretel was warning me about. And it's still in thrall to her, even though she's bound.

If it traps me, maybe Gretel will be freed. And beyond my own life, that would spell horrors untold for each and every world. After everything our mother and the witches and their allies fought for, I can't let the Hunt win. I *won't*.

With every lope, the barrug thumps more heavily on the earth. When I glance back, the deathly dark hillside is growing slick with the barrug's juices.

'We'll never get home!' wails Egg.

I grit my teeth. 'Oh yes, we will!'

I sense her twist to stare at me. 'What's happened to you, Spel?'

All I do is grin, into the thick darkness. And I wonder what *has* happened to me. It isn't just about magic and powers. I feel like I know who I am, now.

The barrug – though I can't bear to look for more than a

few seconds – is a monstrous beast, wearing its skeleton on the outside of its body. A hideous, flapping tongue protrudes from its gash of a mouth, like a slab of rotting meat.

When I feel a stab of fear, the feeling is dragged from me by a force coming from the barrug. And when I turn to look, the barrug grows, livid eyes fixed to my head. When I try to run faster, I can hear it panting. I'm so out of breath I feel sick. The barrug bounds closer and bristles over us.

Time slows. I glance sideways at Egg, at her face stretched wild with fright. The barrug grows and grows, now as big as a bus, then – in a blink – as tall as a house.

And I begin to let myself slow down. A plan forms in my mind. I cannot let myself be afraid any more. I just can't.

Egg and Timothy scream at me to run, and Farthing pulls and pulls at my gown, trying to drag me along. But I turn calmly away from them towards the snarling creature. I'm gulping to catch my breath, clutching the stitch in my side. But I'm not running any more. As I gaze up at the barrug, I think of how far I've come, and how sick I am of being scared. So I choose not to be.

The barrug twitches, then shrinks, the tiniest bit.

'I am not afraid!' I feel the truth of my words as powerfully as a cast spell. The relief of not being scared almost makes me stumble. And the braver I feel, the smaller the creature shrinks.

Mistress Mouldheels joins me. 'What else, child?'

'I've spent most of my life afraid,' I say steadily. 'And I'm learning that I'm not afraid of the same things as most people. You see, I've been in training. Surviving each day has made me strong. Because I believe there is another way of seeing all you demons and monsters and nightmares. And I'm tired of being afraid.'

Egg and Timothy step closer, until they're standing with us against the barrug. Farthing settles on my shoulders, looping her tail around my neck and nuzzling close.

'I am a witch!' I shout, at the top of my voice. 'And I am proud!'

Farthing chatters her teeth in a way that makes me think she approves.

'Oh, Spel,' says Egg, clutching my arm. 'You said it. I'm so glad you're happy about it now.'

Together, we face down the barrug. We say kind things about ourselves and each other, and the barrug shrinks, smaller and smaller, until it's the size of a thimble.

41
The Things We Lift
Out of the Darkness

I walk towards my sister. Egg grins, but then winces at a hidden pain somewhere. I wonder how long we have before the dragon's blood wears off. She grabs hold of me and we hug for as long as I can bear before the worry takes hold again.

Farthing presses her muzzle between our faces, her long black tongue tasting the dried tears on our cheeks. I push her snout away, laughing. 'Come on. We have to go.'

As we trudge through the Muddlewood, I realise I don't have to wear this annoying bonnet any more so I yank it off and hurl it into the undergrowth. I pull my beanie out of my pocket and put it on. While we walk I manage to wriggle out of the dress too, relieved I had kept my top and trousers on underneath. Mistress Mouldheels has many questions, and her expression is rapt as I try my best to explain how we're here and what happened at our school.

But Egg grows silent and watchful, and her feet turn heavy and slow. She gets distracted. My mind races. I decide to give her a few more drops of the spell, praying that the dragon's blood will keep her alive long enough to beg Grael to let us through the portal. Farthing flaps away from me and over to my sister, flying alongside her and uttering little trills of concern.

Quietly, I ask Mistress Mouldheels if she knows what happened to the other so-called Wicked Girls.

She looks at me sadly. 'I'm afraid this came too late for many of them. Their powers – and with them, their souls – were stolen forever by Gretel and the Hunt. But we can form an alliance, supported by the undertakers above and below, to ensure no such corruption befalls us again.' Her face brightens. 'Take heart – you saved many of your school friends from a similar fate, by binding Gretel. As to how many, I am afraid you must enquire in the living world.'

'And . . . what about Amara, my mother?'

Egg's head turns at the sound of the name.

Mistress Mouldheels smiles. 'I was not enslaved by Gretel until after your mother died,' she says. 'So I was able to meet her and explain that my name had been corrupted up at that school. But, as everyone must at some time, she died, my dear. She found her soul path, and one day you will be able to meet her. But that day is a long way off.'

Egg and I exchange a watery smile.

'For now it's enough to know that she wasn't a murderer, and that none of us is really wicked,' says Egg, and I nod in agreement.

For the first time, I'm so grateful neither my sister nor I made it to ceremony. We would have been drained of our powers, our souls, everything that made us who we are.

When we reach the centre of the Muddlewood, the kettle looms into view. The Hagdons swoop low, hovering overhead. 'We have left the undertakers to deal with the last of the ghosts of the Hunt,' caws Pearl, triumphant. 'They are running scared.'

'You still have far to go,' screeches Yarrow.

'May we help you?' asks Moonwort, eyes glittering.

I tell the others not to be afraid, and the Hagdons begin their muttered spell, moulding us into shapes small enough to fit into their feathered pockets. Once we're safely inside and flying, I let a lingering fear slowly rise to the brim of me, mixing with my exhaustion. What will we find, back at the funeral parlour? What did the modern Witchfinder General – Tobias, Gretel's brother – do to Shranken Putch after I left?

But there isn't time to worry too much about it now, because soon the Hagdons are landing. I push out of the pocket, staggering slightly because I still feel like I'm flying. The others join me, and the Hagdons garble a strange word that makes us grow straight back to our usual sizes.

'Urgh,' says Egg. 'I can't say *that* made me feel any better.'

We're standing on the banks of the lake, where I first glimpsed Timothy in his eggshell. And I'm just thinking how far we've come from when he yelled at me to get out of his boat, when he catches hold of my fingers. His smile falters, though it still sparkles in his eyes. 'Spel.' His hand is solid, like a living boy's.

Something about his seriousness makes me feel panicky. 'What? We have to hurry up!'

'I know.' He squeezes my hand. 'But I can't come with you.'

As I look into his eyes, there's a strange loosening inside me, like my stomach is falling away and won't ever stop. 'What do you mean?'

'You need to go home, and I can't leave the Shadow Way.' He grows fainter, and a small black shadow seeps from his eye into the air. But then he forces a smile and his hand tightens on mine again.

'But I've only just found you!' I burst out, like a stupid child.

He blinks, then smiles again, but it looks like a huge effort. 'I am dead. I would not be able to pass back through, like you can.'

'No, wait, listen,' I say, babbling to keep the truth away. 'You can stay with me.' A wave of tears rolls up through me, and I feel my mouth turn down at the edges. 'There has to be a way.'

'Don't cry, Spel. You don't need me any more.' He places his hand on my shoulder, and he still feels like a real boy, of flesh and blood. 'You already have so many people in your life, here and waiting for you at home.'

'But none of them are you,' I gasp, certain my lung is punctured. 'I will always need you.'

He smiles gently. 'You may want to be with me, but you do not *need* me. You know it's true.'

'All right, but . . . I'm the strongest witch in a generation.' I lift my chin, looking him hard in the eyes, daring him to challenge me. 'And I know a dragon in charge of the portal, and I've decided I'm going to be an undertaker one day. If I want to bring you through with me, I will.'

He shakes his head. 'No, Elspeth. Even you cannot defeat death entirely.'

And that's when the real tears come, and I bend in half as though someone's taken a hook and gutted me.

'You have helped me make peace with my past,' he says, golden light spilling out of him and radiating all around. 'I am ready to find my own soul path, now. I am ready to join my mother, and my sisters. I am ready to let go of my life. That means I also must let go of yours.'

And even though it hurts more than anything that's ever hurt before, I know that him finding his soul path is more important than staying with me.

He folds his warm arms around my shoulders, burying his face in my neck. 'I'm ready, Spel. I wandered lost for so long a time, wishing to avenge my mother, wracked with guilt for abandoning my sisters. Perhaps you will never fully understand how much you have helped me. Now I am ready to cross over, and be at peace. I finally remember my family name.'

'What is it?' I ask, made sullen by my fear of losing him, mainly asking the question to make this moment last longer.

He smiles, gently. 'Morgan. I am Timothy Morgan.' He takes my hand. 'I only remembered myself because of you.'

'And I only found myself because of you,' I whisper, throat aching.

I let him pull me into another hug. 'I will never forget you,' he murmurs. 'And one day, a very long time from now, you can come and find traces of me again, in the Muddlewood.

Look for my memories. Some of them will include you.'

He gently pushes me away and points across the lake. 'I must go.'

'What about Farthing?'

'I can't really explain how I know, but . . . she has always been part of me. We shall find our path together.'

The little dragon pushes her wet muzzle underneath my palm. I scoop her into my arms and snuggle her under my chin, and she whines softly as my tears fall on to her head. Finally, she lifts up and out of my arms, returning to Timothy.

Moonwort, Pearl and Yarrow slowly approach us. 'When you are ready, perhaps we could help?' says Pearl. 'One of us could carry you across the lake, while the others help the waiting souls?'

But Timothy shakes his head. 'I sense I must wait in line, with the others. I am sure the boats will be here soon, now that the fighting has stopped.'

'Very well,' says Yarrow, with a nod. 'We will inform the sailors that it is safe to make the crossing, in case the undertakers have not yet returned from the fight.'

One by one, they shift into their bird shapes and take flight, cawing to one another.

'Go, Elspeth Wrythe,' says Timothy. 'Live a good life. Be happy.'

All the sullenness falls off me. Terror at losing him rips my heart, tearing it to pieces. I dart forward and grab his hand.

'I'll never forget you, either!'

He gives me a wide, bright smile. 'I know.' And a truth hangs between us, pure and strong and joyful. We found each other against ridiculous odds, and made a friendship that can never be broken.

Eventually, Egg prises me away. Timothy's hand slips out of mine. He turns and walks across the grass, Farthing staring back at me from around his shoulders.

'Find your path safely!' I shout, too loud and clumsy with heartbreak. 'Please don't lose your way!'

He spins to walk backwards, smiling at me. 'Now that Gretel is bound, I won't!' he calls back.

Farthing takes to the air and turns happy cartwheels in the air above her boy, who gazes at me with a strong, contented smile. A shaft of light falls through them both, and for a moment I can hardly tell they're there. Timothy and Farthing are going home. So am I.

We call back and forth to each other until his voice grows too faint to hear. And then I walk towards the portal with my sister and Mistress Mouldheels. The heaviness in my heart swelling all the way to fill my mouth, growing more painful with every step.

'You love him,' says Egg, amazed.

I do not correct her.

42
Goodbye, Mouldheels

Egg grows worryingly silent, and when I take her hand, her skin is clammy. 'Not much further,' I whisper to her, pulling the watch from my pocket.

We part with Mistress Mouldheels quickly, because I'm too worried about Egg to linger. The old woman squeezes both my hands in her softly wrinkled ones, calloused from working the threads of the tapestry. 'Well done, Elspeth. Gretel was imprisoned in the tapestry, with only the souls of Wicked Girls to feed her. But when she summoned your sister here, she was able to get out. If she had swapped you for your sister, she could have moved freely again, through any of the Other Ways. You have served our people well, and all the beings of the earth. You have saved us from a terrible destiny.'

I feel light-headed in the glow of such praise. 'Thank you,' I say, simply. 'I'll always be glad we found out the truth about you.'

She nods. 'And now you may tell your undertaker friend that this Way shall be safe once more. With no one to weave the tapestry, it will serve only to keep Gretel bound.'

I nudge the second hand backwards on the pocket watch, and time begins to shift the Other Way. And on the wall in front of us, the portal begins to shine.

I climb up the wall, finding footholds in missing chunks of brick. Then, with my legs inside the sticky membrane of the portal and the rest of me still outside, I lean down and help Egg climb in after me.

When we're through, we fall into the well water and struggle up, panting and thrashing. We haul ourselves out on to the rocky ledge, and Egg curls on her side, her breathing shallow.

'Grael?' I call, the echo amplifying my desperation.

Grael appears almost instantly.

I see you have prevailed, she mutters, eyes like lamps. *Which is rather a lot to achieve for so small a person. But still, when you have a chance, would you be able to bring pudding?*

'You have definitely earned the best pudding in the world,' I tell her gratefully, relief at seeing her spreading through me like a warm pool.

Never again will I underestimate a woman from your line, she says.

Even in her sorry state, Egg splutters out a laugh.

We climb on to Grael's back, and she's about to carry us through the water and all the way to the top of the well when a clacking sound fills my ears. I twist back to look, and find that the four other portals, long closed, are blinking open like a set of damp eyelids.

Goodness, exclaims the dragon. *What have you done now, Shadow Child?*

When we struggle out of the basement in our water-bloated clothes, we find the parlour changed. It's early morning, and neither Shranken Putch nor Artemis are anywhere to be found, but *Mistress Turner*, of all people, sits in the kitchen face ashen and pensive. When she sees us straggle into the kitchen, she jumps up with a surprisingly youthful yell, spilling her mug of tea all over the table.

Then the stairs thunder with running footsteps. We turn to see Layla, Mariam, Isla and Jameela all racing towards us, dressed in the silliest combinations of dead people's clothes, disbelieving grins lighting up their faces. Our whole dorm!

'They wanted to be here in case you made it back,' explains Mistress Turner. 'I couldn't convince them to wait anywhere else.'

I open and close my mouth a few times. 'How did you –'

We're engulfed in a giant hug – even Isla seems pleased to see us – and I'm almost deafened by all the chattering and questions and incredulous screeches bouncing around the walls, mixed together with plenty of tears.

The girls follow us while we change into dry clothes, and then we all return to the kitchen and Mistress Turner sets about making a continuous round of tea and toast for everyone.

But while I'm as hungry as a pack of wolves, content to slather myself in butter and jam, Egg only manages a few bites before almost falling asleep at the table.

'That's enough for now,' says Mistress Turner firmly. 'You need to rest.'

I put Egg to bed in our attic room. Layla decides to stay and watch over her. The others go back to the kitchen, helping Mistress Turner prepare a lunch 'fit for a homecoming', in Mariam's words.

But where in the Ways is Shranken Putch? What did the Hunt do to him after I went into the Shadow Way?

I know he's got some explaining to do, but I also know he tried his best to keep us hidden here. He must have been terrified too, of angering the Hunt so much that they'd destroy this place, and hurt Grael. I'm relieved to see that everything except him is still here, but what if Tobias comes back?

'Where is the undertaker?' I ask Mistress Turner, later when I can finally get a moment with her alone. 'Never thought I'd say it, but I've missed that old gloomer. Lots.'

'I'm not sure,' Mistress Turner tells me sadly. 'But I'm making it my mission to try and find out.'

'How did you escape that cahoot?' I ask her, wonder carving my eyes wide.

'I really didn't think I would, for a moment there.' Her

look grows dark and distant. 'It started to drink the magic straight out of my body. But I managed to summon a surge of power to stun it, and over the course of a day I fought it off in fits and starts. I wanted to do it in such a way as to avoid being detected by Gretel. I suppose by now you might have guessed that I was a witch-spy, hidden in your midst?'

'We heard.' I grin. 'And the girls? What happened to them?'

'The Hunt used stolen magic to put an enchantment over them. They were entranced. The plan was to locate the Shadow-Born witch and drain their soul through the tapestry to liberate Gretel. Of course, I had put the strongest, most intricate protection spell I could muster on the door to the crypt. But when the cahoot – Gretel's servant – sorted through them and realised you were not there, the Hunt were furious.'

I think back to Gretel's nails, and the way she crafted cahoots out of the air, and I shudder. Were the cahoots Gretel's eyes in the living world?

'So how come the school was empty when we got out of the crypt, apart from the entranced girls?'

She gives me a small, slightly smug smile. 'Well, I suppose you could say I invented a wild goose chase. When it became clear the right witch was missing – at that point only I knew that you were the witch they wanted – the Mistresses completed a full count and discovered you and Meghan weren't there. I had to make a plan quickly. I rushed in, claiming to have seen the two of you escaping, and reminded the others how dangerous Meghan was. Since all the other girls were already under control, the Mistresses, Tobias – the Witchfinder General – and the cahoot left with me to search for you. Later, I hid and then made my way back to the school, aware that you had been locked up far too long. But in the time I was away, you received those instructions telling you to come here – how?'

I chew my lip, remembering the letter and the key coming down the chimney. 'There was another entrance to the crypt – the fireplace. I'm guessing you didn't put a protection spell on the chimney?'

She rubs her forehead wearily. 'Of course. What a fledgling mistake.' Then her face grows thoughtful. 'Gretel must have decided to send you that summoning after learning of your supposed disappearance, from her cahoot. She may well have pushed another of the creatures through the tapestry to do her bidding. However, what a shock it must have been to find you were in fact still locked deep within the school!'

I nod. 'But then the cahoot found us in the hallway with you, just before we left, and almost drained my soul instead. You saved us, Mistress Turner. Thank you.'

'Bleurgh, please don't call me that!' She smiles weakly. 'Call me Annie. But Spel – what happened after you came here?'

I open my mouth to try to tell her, but everything that's happened is an exhausting swirl of pictures in my head that I need time to sort. 'Can we talk about it another time?'

'Certainly.' She beams at me. 'I must say, I am looking forward to hearing that part of your adventure.'

Then a new, much more everyday thought occurs to me. 'Where is everyone sleeping? Can they all fit here?'

Annie laughs. 'You'd be amazed at all the nooks and crannies in this place. Plus it helps that I volunteered to take the sofa.'

At that moment, Artemis finally comes trilling out from behind the back of a heater. Her ear is torn and a chunk of fur is missing from her side, but otherwise she seems fine.

'You took your time!' I bend to stroke her, and she nuzzles my hand. 'At least one of you was home to meet us. What happened to you?'

She sits up tall and looks me straight in the eye. A shine ripples along the moon on her collar. Then she winks.

43
Respect for the Dead

Egg sleeps for three days and nights. We take it in turns to watch over her, and when it's my turn, and also when it isn't, I weep for my friend Timothy.

When Egg finally emerges, hair mussed and cheeks tear-stained, she's skinny as a rake and she's been clawing at her skin with her fingernails. 'I can still feel the curse sticking to me,' she says, voice wavering.

Layla sweeps her into a hug. Mistress Turner tries to cure all ills with tea. I choose pudding.

We stand in the kitchen together, squabbling and laughing and trying to find enough ingredients to bake a decent pudding for Grael.

Luckily, Shranken Putch is so used to making puddings for dragons that we find plenty of things to use – eggs, milk, jam, flour, some blueberries and some butter. We end up crafting a kind of swiss roll, with a jam and custard filling.

After we've brought pudding to Grael, and eaten another one just for us, I sit on my bed and look at all the odd and precious things I've collected on my journey – the half-empty spell bottles, our mother's pocket watch and her Book of Shadows. The map has turned back into an ordinary – but exceptionally dog-eared – scrap of paper. That I should own such things startles me fully awake, so that the world's colours look unnaturally bright. How far I must have come, from that place called Mouldheels' School. I shiver. The old green headscarf from my uniform is still wrapped around my wrist. I touch it.

'Just to make certain it's real,' I whisper to Artemis.

Her whiskers twitch curiously.

'Because that way, I'll know *I* am.'

'You know that already,' says Egg, grinning the widest she has in a while.

She's right. I'm not invisible any more. Not unless I choose to be. 'Will you come for a walk with me?' I ask. 'Just the two of us?'

She nods, looking puzzled.

The sun is bright and a few early spring flowers have gathered at the feet of the trees. We make our way across the root bridge and down into Knuckerhole village. In the little square in the centre, we stop near the village sign that says how this is 'Home of the 1645 Sussex witch trials'. I hold Egg's hand and tell her the real story of the trials, and what happened to Timothy's mother.

The tears fall freely down my cheeks, and I don't move

363

to wipe them away. His face floats before my eyes, and it's *staggering* to me that I'm standing on the same spot where he once stood, hundreds of years ago. He would have lived somewhere very near here, with his family. He was forced to watch his mother burn very close to where we are now.

Egg squeezes my hand and listens very closely while I speak. 'What a brilliant person to have met and become friends with, Spel,' she tells me. 'And what a friendship. After everything he went through before he died, he faced witchcraft again all

because of his trust in you. That will be with you forever, you know. That's a special magic all its own.'

I smile at her gratefully.

We stay for an hour to pay our respects to the murdered witches, ignoring the strange looks the villagers and tourists give us. Then my sister and I stare into each other's eyes and make a vow, like the one I made to myself after we defeated the barrug.

We will learn all we can about witchcraft, for the rest of our days. And we will protect anyone who needs us. We'll always do everything in our power not to let the Hunt hurt another soul.

Me, Egg and Layla stay up late, three witches and a black cat all squished together on the two narrow beds. The others are all sleeping elsewhere in the parlour. We drink hot chocolate in the moonlight spilling into our attic room, while Artemis snoozes on my pillow. Egg leafs through the Book of Shadows, but she's too weak to look at it properly. She still gets headaches that make her sick. 'I can't wait to be able to use this,' she says, excitedly.

'Tell me more about Mum.' I thought I'd lost every last tear in my head, but more come just at saying the word 'Mum'. The brutality against witches has been so violent, and so hateful. Most were women, and helpers or healers at that. I have to bring our mother to life in the air between us, at least.

Layla smiles. 'I'd like to hear about her, too.'

Egg sniffs, wiping her nose on the back of her hand. 'Can I tell you guys the things I've made myself believe I remember? I was only two when she died.'

'Yeah, course!' says Layla. 'That's fair.'

I nod. 'Yes, please.'

'Where to start? She sang all the time – anything, just old songs and stupid kids' songs and jingles from the radio. She had all this long dark hair, tangled masses of it. Her eyes and mouth always looked ready to laugh.'

'Like you,' says Layla.

Egg grins at her. 'I remember clouds of incense, and crystal balls. If magic has found you, you should let it in, especially if it makes you anything like Mum. She was brilliant, Spel. And so are you.'

'Why didn't you tell me anything before?'

'This is going to sound really stupid, but . . . it just hurt too much, you know? The unfairness of it all.'

'It doesn't sound stupid at all. Why do you think I never asked?'

We all sit in silence for a while. I let my mind wander. Inside me is a restless thing, a sense of the huge unfairness we experienced from birth, and the violence justified by the beliefs held against us. I look over at Egg's finely made profile, and Layla's open-hearted smile.

'We never were Wicked Girls, not one of us,' I say. 'That was just a story, told to excuse what they did.'

Egg nods, eyes growing distant as though she's trying to process the scale of it all, like I am. Then she focuses on me again, and her face shows a flicker of the old her, the one I have missed so fiercely: a mixture of mischief and determination. 'But now we make a new story.'

Artemis stands and stretches, releasing a croaky yowl that makes us laugh. 'Yes,' I say, stroking the cat between her shoulder blades. 'Now we tell our own story. We fought for the freedom to tell it.'

Layla leans up on to her knees, and takes both of our hands. 'And you won!' she yells, beaming.

The night grows old. At some point, Artemis must have left the room, because now there's just a cat-shaped dent in my pillow. Funny how cats can move like that, unseen when they choose to be. While Egg and Layla doze, I pull Mum's Book of Shadows out from under my pillow, and trace the pattern tooled into the cover. I open the book and leaf towards the middle, where the blank pages are waiting for me.

In a moment of inspiration, I pull a pencil out of the cupboard between our beds and press the lead to the page.

The secret life of Spel Wrythe, lists, spells and stories.

I stare at what I've written for a long time, dreaming of all the ways I might be able to help the world and all the things

I might fill these pages with. But I can't rest. I close the door to our room quietly, all the while half expecting Shranken Putch to emerge, grumbling, from some darkened doorway or other. I'm sad when he doesn't.

The moon is fat enough that as soon as I step outside, I see Artemis in the grass, staring past the parlour towards the Ring. Her fur is blacked deeper by the settling ink of night.

'There is something afoot,' I murmur. 'Isn't there?' As we gaze into the sky; still a dark blue even though the Ring has faded into a blot of gloom, a grey, tattered cloud scuds across the cumulus-white banks that dominate the air like swan queens. And across the top of the clouds zips a tiny, arrowed diamond. A craft of some sort. An untoward mechanism, intent upon some distant point and entirely alien to this Way.

The vigil trees and the ripening moon look on, unfazed.

But my skin – like my heart – blazes with fire. What was that thing? Could it have escaped from the Other Ways? The streaking diamond disappears from sight.

Slowly, the cat turns to face me. Both our heads are damp with dew. A slip of bright gold, wings whirring, zooms towards my face, making me stumble. A beetle. It's a *firecat*. The device lands on my neck and crawls slowly up to the helix of my ear.

The portals to the Other Ways have awoken, says the little cat, with a curl of mischief in her throat. *You know that you alone can cross into any of them and back again, don't you?*

'Artemis? Is that . . . you?'

Of course!

That put me in my place. 'How did you get hold of a firecat?' I stammer. My heart is thrashing against my ribs so hard that I can't keep my voice steady. I knew she was much more aware of everything that's happened than she should be, but this? 'Don't you play games with me,' I add, trying to trick her into thinking that I'm calm.

Games? The cat's ears flick as though the word is a fly. *There will be no time for games, Elspeth Wrythe. The Ring is in want of an undertaker. So there can be no adventures in the Other Ways until Shranken Putch returns. Your story as an assistant undertaker must resume.*

My skin twitches as the golden beetle lifts off my skin and away into the deepening night. The little cat turns tail, disappearing between the trees.

'Artemis, you have so much explaining to do!' I scold.

From the depths of the Ring comes a small, insolent miaow.

As well as writing magical books for children Sarah Driver is also a qualified nurse and midwife. She is a graduate of the Bath Spa Writing for Young People MA, during which she won the Most Promising Writer prize. She is the author of the critically-acclaimed fantasy adventure trilogy, The Huntress. When she's not writing, she can be found walking by the sea, reading or researching a story. She has learned that even horrifying bouts of sea-sickness make excellent research material.

Fabi Santiago is the author and illustrator of Tiger in a Tutu, which was shortlisted for the Waterstones Children's Book Prize. After studying art and design in São Paulo, Fabi graduated with an MA in Children's Book Illustration at the Cambridge School of Art. Fabi's illustrations are full of movement and bold limited colours, and her medium of choice is screen-printing. She lives in London and has three cats, Daisy, Bear and Pepper.

ONCE WE WERE WITCHES

2

Join Spel and Egg for a new other-worldly
adventure, featuring covens, familiars,
stolen magic, concealed curses and ghosts
demanding ice-cream.

Will they find the exiled witches to help the
resistance fight against the Hunt?

Coming soon

Acknowledgements

Thank you to super-agent extraordinaire Jodie Hodges, for having such an expert eye and spotting the sparkle of this project when it was still barely imagined. Your skill is a wonder to behold.

To the seemingly tireless and endlessly supportive editing genius Liz Bankes: a thousand thanks for everything you have done to make this book the best it could possibly be. I'm so looking forward to having proper meetings again, with snacks!

To Ali Dougal for championing this book from the beginning and being such a conduit of magic and wonder.

Fabi Santiago – working with you has been so exciting, and I'm in love with each and every one of your illustrations.

To Laura Bird, Olivia Adams and team for all your amazing design work. It's been great working with you again on this.

To David, for your support, encouragement and invaluable critique. Also for playing the 'let's read out bits of each other's manuscripts in silly voices' game with me during a storm in a barn as a global pandemic approached.

Thank you to my friends and family, for all your love and support.

To the Ashmolean Museum, Oxford, for your inspirational exhibition 'Spellbound: Magic, Ritual and Witchcraft'. My visit was a highlight of the research process.

Finally, to all the readers showing continued support by writing to me about The Huntress or asking when I have another book out: every time I hear that you have enjoyed one of my stories I know I must be somewhere on the right track. I really hope you enjoy this one.

Once We Were Witches is a book about finding your voice, and learning that you matter. Learning who you are, what you care about and how to fight for it. My time of telling and shaping and re-shaping this story has drawn to a close. Now it's the readers' turn with the tale.

A sea-churning, beast-chattering, dream-dancing, whale-riding, terrodyl-flying, world-saving adventure series.